I0744718

Malicious LOVE

BOOK NINE OF THE SYDNEY LEGAL SERIES

CHRIS TAYLOR

© 2019 LCT Productions Pty Ltd

© 2019 by LCT Productions Pty Ltd

(All Rights Reserved)

Without limiting the rights under copyright(s) reserved below, no part of this publication may be reproduced, stored in or introduced into a retrieval system, or transmitted, in any form, or by any means (electronic, mechanical, photocopying, recording, or otherwise) without the prior permission of the copyright owner.

LCT Productions Pty Ltd
18364 Kamilaroi Highway, Narrabri NSW 2390

ISBN. 978-1-925119-62-6 (Paperback)

Malicious Love is a work of fiction. Names, characters, places, brands, media and incidents either are the product of the author's imagination or are used fictitiously. Any resemblance to actual persons, living or dead, events, or locales, is entirely coincidental.

Published in the United States of America.

Books by Chris Taylor

THE MUNRO FAMILY SERIES

The Profiler
The Investigator
The Predator
The Betrayal
The Deception
The Negotiator
The Christmas Vigil
The Ransom
The Defendant
The Shooting
The Maker
(Available in Audio)

THE SYDNEY HARBOUR HOSPITAL SERIES

The Perfect Husband
The Body Thief
The Baby Snatchers
The Final Bullet
The Debt Collector
The Lab Test
The Stolen Identity
The Cliff-top Killer
The Likeable Fraudster

THE SYDNEY LEGAL SERIES

An Accidental Murderer
At the Hand of Her Father
A Woman Scorned
Lies and Deception
Ordinary Evil
The Ties That Bind
The Perfect Crime
A Toxic Inheritance
Malicious Love

THIS IS WHERE IT ENDS SERIES

Jessie's story
Ryan's story

Holly's story
Sarah's story
Veronica's story

THE CRAIGDON FAMILY SERIES
Callum
Joel
Isabella
Nicholas
Sophia
Flynn
Noah
Logan
Elizabeth

THE BARRINGTON FAMILY SERIES
Broken Lives
Broken Promises
Broken Bonds
Broken Spirits
Broken Vows
Broken Minds
Broken Dreams
Broken Hearts
Broken Homes

Get a FREE book when you sign up for Chris Taylor's
newsletter at: www.christaylorauthor.com.au

Love Audiobooks? Check out Chris Taylor Books on audio
on Audible.com, Amazon.com and Apple Books.

Join Chris Taylor's Facebook reader group/fan page and be
among the first to receive news of book releases, read and
review books prior to release and other amazing offers. Join
Now at: www.facebook.com/groups/1758023621144744/

Find out more about all of Chris Taylor's books, by visiting her
website at: www.christaylorauthor.com.au/about/books

DEDICATION

*This book is dedicated to Detective Superintendent
Michael Kilfoyle (ret) for his continued enthusiasm, advice,
encouragement and support and his scintillating conversations
about books, policing, life and everything in between.*

*And as always, to my husband, Linden.
My best friend, my soul mate. I love you to the moon and back.*

Acknowledgments

As usual, no book comes into being without a lot of help and support by my friends and family. A world of thanks must go to my wonderful editor, Pat Thomas. Thank you for everything that you do to make my stories even more amazing than I could ever dare to dream. To former Detective Superintendent Michael Kilfoyle, thank you for lending my story credibility. Any mistakes are wholly my own.

To Damon Freeman, Alisha Moore and all of the staff at damonza.com, thank you for yet another fantastic book cover. To my sister, Nicole Guihot and to my friend, Ally Thomson, thank you for your excellent editorial comments, proof reading skills and suggestions. I hope you like the final result.

To Amy Atwell and her dedicated staff at Author E.M.S. who are so much more than book formatters. Amy, once again, thank you for your magic.

To the fantastic writer organizations such as Romance Writers of Australia, Romance Writers of

America and Romance Writers of New Zealand for all the help, support and encouragement they offer new and aspiring writers, including me.

To my readers, thank you for your support and love for my stories. Your encouragement and enjoyment make this journey all worthwhile.

And lastly, to my friends and family, especially my husband and children. Thank you for putting up with late dinners and even later conversations as I've emerged day after day from the sometimes scary but always enthralling world I've created on my computer.

PROLOGUE

Joey Fielder's breath came fast. His shoulders ached from the weight of his backpack and he had blisters on both heels. His mom had warned him about bushwalking in his new sneakers, but he'd refused to listen. At the time, he'd been too excited at the thought of exploring with his best friend, Carver Lewis.

He and Carver had been friends since pre-school. Now at the age of twelve, there wasn't anything they didn't know about each other. They spent all their free time together and now it was the beginning of summer break. Christmas was just around the corner. They had six glorious weeks before they had to return to school and they were determined to make the most of it.

Today, Carver had suggested they explore the walking tracks around West Head, a popular part of the Ku-ring-gai Chase National Park, north of Sydney. He'd sweetened the deal by mentioning to Joey that there were caves in that part of the park.

"Caves?" Joey had asked, his attention now fully on his friend.

"Yeah. Plenty of 'em. There might even be glow worms."

Joey had instantly become keen. He loved everything there was about caves. His mom chided him over it, but he didn't care. There was something fascinating about them. Crawling around in the dark, musty spaces made him feel like he was an explorer from another time. Or Indiana Jones. He'd anticipate that at any moment he could discover a lost treasure, hidden for centuries. He'd be famous. And rich.

But they'd been walking for more than two hours and his feet were sore. Carver was getting further and further ahead.

"Hey! Wait up!" he called.

Carver turned momentarily. "Come on, slowpoke. We haven't got all day"

"How much further is the cave?" Joey panted, tugging his T-shirt down to cover his protruding belly. He wished he was fit, like Carver.

"Not far. Come on. Keep going. It'll be worth it. I promise." Carver shot him a wide grin and then turned away, his athletic body and nimble grace making the rough track look easy.

Joey swallowed a sigh and concentrated on putting one foot in front of the other. He couldn't wait to get to the cave so they could take a break. He just hoped the pain was worth it, like Carver had assured him.

"There it is!"

Carver's yelp of excitement spurred Joey on. Ignoring the discomfort in his shoulders and the pain in his heels, he picked up his pace and tackled the steep incline that apparently led to the mouth of the cave. Carver stood at the top, peering down at something. Joey hurried the final few steps, his breath coming fast.

"Where is it?" he panted.

"There!"

Carver pointed toward a clump of rocks mostly concealed behind tall grass. Joey frowned.

"I don't see anything." He didn't bother to hide his disappointment.

"It's just there," Carver replied, a hint of impatience in his voice. "Beyond those rocks. See that dark patch? That's the opening."

Joey squinted against the mid-morning sunshine and looked again. When at last, he saw it, he was filled with a surge of excitement.

"I see it! You're right! It's the mouth of a cave!"

Carver grinned. "See? I told you, didn't I?"

Joey nodded. Carver said he had found the cave a few weeks earlier. He'd come to school full of excitement about his discovery. Joey had been busy with end of term stuff and hadn't been able to come there—until now.

He let out a *whoop* of excitement.

"Let's go!" he yelled and took off at a run, his blisters and aching shoulders forgotten.

Carver laughed. "Hey! Wait for me!"

The two boys ran toward the cave entrance. Tugging out flashlights from their backpacks, they made their way inside. The cave's opening was wide enough for them to walk through side by side. It was dank and dark and scary enough to set Joey's heart thumping. He looked across at his friend in the dimness and smiled. Carver's eyes reflected his excitement.

In silence, they made their way further into the cave. The pitch blackness was broken only by the thin beams from their flashlights. Joey put his hand against one wall. The stone was cold and damp and rough. Then soft in the places where moss grew, tickling his fingers.

"Do you think anyone lived here?" Carver whispered. "Like, a million years ago?"

Joey shrugged. "Maybe. It's not real big, but big enough, I guess. Maybe Neanderthal?"

Carver chuckled and Joey grinned. He was being silly, but it felt good. The cave opened up into a kind of room. It was at least two arms' span across. If he stood on his tiptoes, his fingertips could almost graze the roof. He switched off his flashlight and looked around, hoping for a glimpse of glowworms.

"Hey! Get over here! I found something!"

The excitement in Carver's voice interrupted Joey's search. Switching his flashlight back on, he hurried over to where his friend kneeled on the ground. Carver was digging at the loose earth with his fingers.

Joey dropped to the ground beside him. "What is it?"

"I don't know. It feels like some kind of blanket."

Joey ran his flashlight over the area. There was definitely some kind of raised area on the ground.

Carver kept digging and finally pulled on the edge of what looked like a piece of carpet.

Joey kept the light steady. Each tug Carver gave revealed more of the rug. It was like it had been rolled up and left there. It had been there a long time by the look of it.

"Oh, my God!"

Carver's cry was filled with alarm. Joey stared down. Bones the color of chalk gleamed in the dimness. Ribs, arm bones, a skull...

"Shit!"

The curse word fell from Joey's lips as he scrambled backwards. He was glad his mom wasn't there. She'd ground him if she'd heard. Twelve-year-old boys were not supposed to curse.

"What the hell is it?" he asked, his heart still thumping.

Carver looked as scared as he felt. "It looks like a skeleton."

Joey nodded grimly, keeping his distance. "Yeah, that's what I thought, too."

"Who do you think it is?" Carver whispered, his eyes wide in the dimness.

"I don't know. But whoever it is has been here a long time."

CHAPTER 1

Mallory Patterson tucked an errant strand of hair behind her ears and spooned more cereal into her mouth. The morning paper was spread out before her. The ten minutes or so she got to read it before she left for work were some of the most enjoyable minutes of her day and she looked forward to it every morning. Her father sat opposite, scrutinizing the *Financial Review*.

"How's work?" he asked, chewing on his usual morning fare of vegemite and toast.

Mallory shrugged. "The same."

"Are you in court today?"

"No. Just a full day of client appointments. How about you?"

"I'm in the final stages of negotiating a billion-dollar property deal. We hope to sign the contracts before the end of the week."

John Patterson was a senior partner at Sydney Legal, the most prestigious law firm in town. Unlike his daughter, he chose to pursue a career as a commercial lawyer. Mallory had chosen family law. It didn't hold the same prestige that a bigwig commercial property lawyer held, especially a commercial lawyer as highly regarded as her father, but she enjoyed working with people who were desperate for a solution to what was often an exceptionally volatile situation. Throw children into the mix and things were bound to get nasty. She never could work out how two people who had once loved each other enough to commit to a life together could get to that point of hate.

Her gaze drifted down the columns of type and snagged on a story toward the bottom of the page. She read the few lines of text.

"They found a body in a cave out at West Head a couple of days ago," she mused. "Actually, I think it's only a few bones." She glanced up at her father who gave no indication he'd heard. "I remember those caves. We used to go there all the time when I was a kid."

Her father frowned at her over his paper. "Did we?"

Mallory looked at him, filled with concern. "Of course we did. You used to take me exploring there every other weekend. You were the one who told me about the aboriginal paintings and entertained me with stories about how they came to be there. Surely you must remember?"

Her father merely shrugged and returned his attention to his paper. Mallory frowned. *How odd that he couldn't remember...* Okay, so it had been more than twenty years since they'd been there, but it was such a memorable part of her childhood. *How was it that he didn't recall it?*

A sense of misgiving shifted in her stomach. *Was her father getting dementia? Poor memory recall was one of the signs, wasn't it?* And then she chided herself. She was being silly. He might be nearly sixty, but he was as sharp as ever. He'd just told her about the billion-dollar property contract he and his client were only days away from finalizing. Someone losing their faculties wouldn't be able to manage a complex deal like that. She was sure of it. There must be some other explanation.

With a quiet sigh, she finished her cereal and returned her attention to the paper. She read the next line in the story about the cave bones and her stomach lurched.

"It says here the police speculate the body might have been in the cave for about twenty years." She stared pointedly at her father.

He glanced up at her again and shook his head. "Don't look at me like that, honey."

"Like what?"

"Like you think it's your mother. We both know what happened to her and she sure as hell didn't end up in a cave in the Ku-ring-gai Chase National Park. She didn't die. She left. Remember?"

Mallory grimaced at the harshness in his tone. Of course she remembered. She had been ten years old when her mother walked out on them, never to return. No one forgot something like that. Ever.

Her father continued to regard her over his paper. Slowly his expression softened. "I'm sorry, honey. I didn't mean to bring all that up again. The whole sorry mess is best forgotten." He paused and then added in a lighter tone, "How are things going with the Stone case? Have you managed to convince them to come to an amicable settlement?"

Mallory grimaced and shook her head. "No. There's nothing amicable about the Stone family. This is going to go all the way. It's the worst custody battle I've ever been involved in. Fraternal twin girls. Three years old. Being fought over like they're possessions. Dad wants one, mom wants one. No one seems to care about what's best for the children. The girls are too young to give evidence, but I'm certain they wouldn't want to be separated."

"Does one parent have a stronger claim over the other?"

"Not really. Both have their own successful businesses, nice cars, comfortable homes. Both live close to good schools. My client has a new girlfriend, but on the surface she appears to treat the girls well and they seem happy enough in her company. Mom lives on her own."

Mallory's father flicked her a glance and then returned his attention to the paper. "So what are you going to do?" he asked.

Mallory sighed. "I don't know. I can't help thinking about the welfare of those little girls if they grow up without their mother."

John Patterson lifted one graying eyebrow. Mallory hated when he looked at her like that. It made her feel like she'd said or done something wrong. Now was no different.

"Not exactly without her, Mallory," her father chided. "I'm sure you'll recommend generous visitation terms."

Mallory tamped down a burst of irritation. "It's not the same, Dad."

Her father lowered his paper. His expression filled with hurt. "Wasn't I enough for you?"

Guilt rushed through her. She pushed away from her chair and went to him. She gave him a hug of reassurance.

"Of course you were! I didn't mean that at all. It's just that... Well, after all this time... Twenty years... I must confess, I still miss her."

Her father patted her hand gently and nodded with understanding. Carefully folding his paper, he dropped it beside his place setting and stood. He was six foot three and still broad of chest and trim of hips. She only managed to come up to his shoulder. He bent his head and kissed her on the cheek.

"You'll be fine. Now, just so you know, I won't be home for dinner. I'm staying over at Alice's place tonight. Have a good day, won't you, honey?"

Mallory sighed quietly again, wishing they could spend a bit more time talking about her mom, but knowing it was never going to happen. Any discussion about Sofia Lopez Patterson was off limits. As it had been from the day her mother left.

"You, too, Dad," she said to his retreating back.

———

Detective Sergeant Rafe Connelly pushed back a hank of hair that had fallen across his eyes. He was long overdue for a haircut, but finding the time to get one was a bitch. As a senior detective in a busy homicide unit at the City of Sydney Police Station, it wasn't often he got time for such meaningless tasks as keeping his hair to a reasonable length. At the moment, it was long enough to curl around his ears and it covered most of the back of his neck. He didn't particularly like it that way, but right now, he was too busy to do anything about it.

He'd spent all morning in court, giving evidence against a man who was responsible for killing three people in a deadly shootout. The bloodbath had occurred in an old shed situated in the man's backyard. The argument had been over drugs. The victims were also drug dealers, but still, that didn't make it right. With a bit of luck, the judge would put the man away for a long time.

The door to the squad room swung open. Rafe glanced up to see his new partner, Detective Constable James Shepherd, enter the room. They'd been partners for only a matter of weeks, since Rafe's old partner had up and retired to the country.

From all accounts, James was a good cop and Rafe was pleased to be working with him. The two of them were close in age and were both determined to lower the crime rate in the city. James walked over to Rafe's desk and dropped a handful of papers on it.

Rafe looked up at him. "What's that?"

"Our new case. The boss handed it to me on my way up here. Told me to give it to you."

Rafe sighed quietly. His current case before the courts was winding down. With a bit of luck, it would be over by the end of the week. But there was always another one—as evidenced by the paperwork that had just landed on his desk. He reached over and flipped through the sheaf of papers.

"Does this have anything to do with the body discovered a couple of days ago in the Ku-ring-gai Chase National Park?"

James nodded. "Yep. I think that's the one. I only looked at it briefly on my way upstairs. The boss said something about a pile of human bones found in a cave north of Sydney." A grin tugged at Shepherd's mouth. "I guess we drew the short straw."

"I guess so," Rafe muttered.

He shuffled through the paperwork once more and paused when he got to the autopsy report.

"It says here the body is that of a Caucasian female aged somewhere between thirty and forty years old. They believe the bones have lain in situ for about twenty years. That would put her in her mid-fifties if she were alive."

James acknowledged his comment with a nod. "Whoever it is has been missing a long time."

Rafe kept reading. "She was found in good condition, considering. She was rolled up in a rug buried inside the cave. That protected her from the elements and the critters. The skeleton was largely intact. There was even some hair left behind."

"If we're lucky, we might get some DNA."

"They've already managed it. It says here that DNA was recovered from the victim's hair and bones. A DNA sample was also recovered from the rug our victim was found wrapped in. It's not the same as the victim's."

He looked at James. "Are you thinking what I'm thinking?"

"That our killer might have left something behind?"

"Yeah. It's definitely a possibility. Let's hope we can identify both samples. Knowing her identity is just as important as knowing who murdered her."

"We should be able to take advantage of the FaceFit Technology and have them do a facial reconstruction," James said. "That should help identify our victim."

Rafe sighed again and leaned back in his chair, stacking his hands behind his head. "I guess we also need to start searching historic records of missing persons and reports of potential murders where victims have never been located, especially if the crimes were thought to be committed somewhere in that area."

This time it was Shepherd who sighed. "We've got some work ahead of us," he said grimly.

Rafe nodded. "You betcha."

From the corner of his eye, Rafe noticed the wall clock across from him. He sat up with a start.

"Shit. It's three o'clock. I've got twenty minutes to collect Charlotte from school and get her to her dance rehearsal. The concert's on in three weeks. She'll kill me if I'm late."

James nodded. "I understand. I've got kids, too."

"Yeah?" Rafe replied, pulling on his jacket.

James pursed his lips. "Yeah. Two. A boy and a girl. Travis is two and Cindy is eight months."

Rafe eyed him solemnly. "I hope you're good to them."

James' expression filled with surprise and curiosity. "Of course, I'm good to them." Then he paused before adding, "Well, as good as I can be while I'm working fourteen-hour shifts more days than I can count." His voice faded away.

Rafe busied himself logging off his computer. He had no time to spend contemplating the drawbacks of life as a cop and he didn't want to, either. It reminded him of his own shortcomings as a father, not to mention his less-than-stellar childhood and the father he wished he'd never had. With that depressing thought, he grabbed his keys and left.

———————

By the time Rafe pulled up outside his daughter's school, he was ten minutes past the bell. The buses had long since departed and the school grounds were almost devoid of human life. It always brought a smile to his lips when he thought about how every kid he knew, himself included, was always busting to get out of school at the end of the day. It was like they couldn't take the confinement another second after the bell. He wished he'd known back then how easy his school days had been—a difficult home life notwithstanding.

He spied Charlotte standing outside the main gate. Her backpack hung over one shoulder and her arms were crossed against her chest. Her long braids had come loose and strands of dark hair lifted gently in the breeze.

She caught sight of him and shook her head. A frown marred the innocent beauty of her face. He grinned unrepentantly. She looked so much like her mother when she did that.

Khloe.

Rafe couldn't remember the last time he'd thought about Charli's mother, the first and only love of his life... She had midnight-black hair and a wildness about her that had made his teenage heart race. He still remembered the thrill he felt whenever he was around her. She also came from a broken home and with that in common, they'd gravitated toward one another, determined to block out the misery of their lives and rely on nobody but themselves. Rafe still had her name tattooed on his shoulder, decorated with a heart. He'd once thought they'd be together forever, but life and Khloe had other plans...

"Dad! Where have you been? The bell went

more than ten minutes ago! You know how embarrassing it is to be the only one left here! Even the bus kids have gone! I'm gonna be late for dance rehearsal."

His grin morphed into an apology. "I'm sorry, baby. I got caught up at work."

She rolled her eyes in the way only teenagers could, but offered him a reluctant smile. "So what else is new?" she muttered, the teasing light in her eyes taking the edge off her words.

"I'm sorry, Charli, I really am. I'll make it up to you. I promise."

"That's what you said last time," she murmured without rancor.

He grimaced. "Yes, and we went to Luna Park for the day and you ate so much ice cream you were sick, remember?"

Instead of the grin he expected, she shook her head again and gazed at him with a somber look in her eyes.

"Oh, Dad. I'm not a baby anymore. I'm thirteen. Ice cream's just not going to cut it."

He widened his eyes. "Since when?" he demanded with mock hurt.

Charlotte didn't reply. He pulled out into the traffic. The silence stretched between them until he broke it.

"Just so you know, you'll always be my baby."

He glanced across at her and caught another eye roll, but was relieved when it was accompanied by a grin.

"So, what are you working on?" she asked after a little while.

He shot her a quick look before turning his attention back to the road. "Do you really want to know?"

"Of course. You know how fascinated I am with the seedy underbelly of Sydney. I want to be a criminologist, remember?"

"I thought you wanted to be a dancer?"

She lightly punched his arm and smiled. "Dad!"

He widened his eyes innocently. "But you love dancing!"

"Yeah, but it's not something I want to do forever—like for a career. I want to solve crimes, like you. I want to make our world a safer place to live. I want to help people."

Rafe was filled with pride. He grinned. "That's very admirable, Charli. Following in your old dad's footsteps would make me very proud indeed."

He cleared his throat of a sudden lump of emotion. He couldn't believe how fast his little girl was growing up. Already she was thinking about a career, about life after school. The years were flying by too quickly.

"To answer your question, we found a body."

"Really? Who is it?"

"We don't know yet. All we know is that she's a woman. The forensic pathologist thinks she died about twenty years ago."

Charlotte's eyes widened. "Wow! And her body was still okay?"

"No. We only found bones and some hair, but her skeleton was complete and it's in good condition. She was wrapped in a rug and hidden in a cave. That protected her."

"Do you think she went there to die?"

Rafe negotiated a lane change and shook his head. "No. Her hands and feet were tied. The cable ties were still intact. There's no way she got there by herself."

Charli's eyes were wide with curiosity. "How are you going to find out who she is?"

"With a bit of luck, modern technology will help us out. The lab has managed to extract DNA from the bones and hair."

Charli's brow furrowed. "But won't you need to know her DNA already in order to match it?"

Rafe smiled. His daughter had always been in the top of her class, even in pre-school. Still, it never ceased to surprise him how clever she was.

"You're right, baby. If our lady's DNA isn't in the system, we still won't know who she is, but it's only one tool in our arsenal. We also have FaceFit Technology. You remember that story in the paper a few months ago? The one about the skeleton found on that farm in the far west of New South Wales?"

She nodded. "Yes. They discovered he was a drover, didn't they? He broke his leg while droving sheep in the outback and died before anyone could find him."

"Right. It wasn't my case, but it made the Sydney papers. Remember the picture of him in the papers? They recreated his face using his skull. The forensic pathologist entered his data into the FaceFit program and the computer recreated his face."

"That's really cool." Charli sighed.

"Yes. That's what we'll do with this woman and we'll hope someone out there recognizes her. Did you know each and every one of us has thirteen points of measurement on our head that determine what we look like?"

Charli's eyes widened. "Really?"

"Yes. And those measurements never change, no matter how old you are or whether you've suffered head trauma, or even if you've had surgery on your skull. The bones reform in the exact same position. It's what allows the computer program to know what you looked like previously. The program uses the measurements to recreate your face and it's fairly accurate, too."

Charli smiled. "You're pretty cool, Dad. Do you know that?"

Rafe grinned, abashed. His daughter's words filled him with warmth and love. She meant the world to him. He couldn't imagine his world without her in it. He didn't look forward to the day she left home to forge out a life on her own, but he knew it was coming—and faster than he could cope with.

"We'll also go over old missing persons cases and look for possible matches," he added in an effort to force his thoughts back to a more palatable topic. "There's a lot we can do to try and identify her."

Charli nodded. "Well, I hope you find out who she is. She might be someone's mom. I can't imagine having a mom and not knowing what happened to her. I might only know my mom from photographs, but at least I know where she is."

Rafe glanced across at his daughter in surprise. Though the details of his relationship with her mother weren't a secret, the two of them rarely talked about Khloe.

"Do you believe in heaven, Dad?"

The quiet question came from nowhere and took him even more aback than her previous comments. He quickly recovered.

"Of course, baby."

"Do you think that's where Mom is?"

Images of Khloe as he'd last seen her assailed him. Living on the streets, her body ravaged by drugs. She'd been found with a needle still in her arm. Overdose, the police had said. She'd been all of twenty-one. He blinked away the awful memories and forced himself to reply.

"Of course she is, baby. She had a hard life, but she was a good person and she loved you very much. I'm sure she's looking out for you, even now, just like she always did," he lied.

Charli smiled sadly. Rafe tried to concentrate on the road, but he was keenly aware of his beloved little girl seated beside him, quiet now.

He shot her a quick look. Silent tears rolled down her cheeks. He bit his lip hard against a rush of emotion. The last thing she needed was to see him cry.

"Would you like to go and visit Mom this weekend?" he asked gently.

Charli sniffed and wiped at her eyes. "Yeah. That would be nice. We haven't been for a while."

Rafe ignored the stab of guilt. "I'm off on Saturday. Let's do it then."

"I have swimming training until twelve on Saturday."

"Okay, we'll do it after that. I'll go to the market and buy some fresh flowers."

Charli smiled softly. "That would be nice."

Rafe took the next left and pulled up outside the dance studio. They were fifteen minutes late. Charli pulled out her phone and glanced at the time. She sighed quietly, but merely leaned over and pecked him on the cheek.

"Thanks, Dad. I'll see you in an hour."

"I promise I won't be late," he called out to her departing back. Without turning around, she gave him a casual wave and headed inside.

CHAPTER 2

Mallory glanced surreptitiously at the clock on the wall behind the mediator and swallowed a sigh. The court-ordered mediation of the custody dispute between Daniel Stone and Jessica-Mary Michaels had started only forty-five minutes ago and already it felt like they'd been inside the close confines of the mediation room for a lifetime. Things between the parties were not going well.

Mallory's client sat on her left. Dressed in a three-piece, custom-tailored suit and shiny leather shoes that cost more than her week's salary, Daniel looked every part the successful businessman. On Mallory's right side sat his father, Rupert Arthur Andrew Stone, a self-made media mogul. He'd come from humble beginnings on the floor of the newsroom and was now head of a multibillion-dollar company. Stone senior was the type who refused to take no for an answer.

It was obvious that cloistered together in the small mediation room, forced to listen to the words of advice from the mediator was pushing Daniel's father to the edge. Less than an hour in and Mallory saw the determined set of his jaw and that his fists were clenched beneath the table. It was taking all of his self-control to keep his mouth shut.

Fortunately, this wasn't his fight and even though he'd insisted on being present, Rupert hadn't been allowed to participate in the mediation. Mallory guessed he wasn't taking that decision well. Rupert Arthur Andrew Stone was a man used to getting his own way and today he'd been forced to play by the rules of the court. It was obvious he wasn't pleased.

Contrary to his father, her client remained cool and composed. The gossip around town was that Daniel had managed to double the family income in the five years since he'd taken over his father's business. Profits that used to be counted in the millions now had a few extra zeroes behind them. In the past, appealing to their wallet was a tactic Mallory used to get her clients to accept terms of settlement rather than have the court hand down a judgement after a hearing. Most people weren't in a position to continually throw money away on hefty lawyers' bills.

Unfortunately in the Stone case, money was no object and that tactic wasn't going to work. She had to find some other way to get Daniel and his father to listen to reason. The way things were going, this matter would end up in court, in a full-blown hearing. If that happened, no one came out a winner.

The mediator, George Koutsinous, cleared his

throat and looked at Mallory over his glasses. Mallory had been pleased when she heard Koutsinous had been appointed to preside over the Stone case. Koutsinous was a mediator with a wealth of experience. On top of that, he was fair. He had a reputation for being able to cut to the chase, to ignore the emotions that often ran high as well as the rhetoric from the lawyers, and get to the heart of the matter. He had a greater success rate than any other mediator for resolving difficult matters prior to them going to a hearing. He had a calm and mild manner that was laced with steel. People knew he meant business and most of them listened. In this custody case, however, his suggestions weren't going over well.

"Ms Patterson, has your client had the opportunity to look over the orders proposed by Ms Michaels?"

Mallory nodded. "Yes, thank you, Mr Koutsinous. Unfortunately, Mr Stone is not willing to relinquish custody of both of his daughters to the respondent. He has as much right to the children as Ms Michaels. We propose that each twin reside with one parent."

The mediator look surprised and faintly disappointed. Mallory flushed under his stern regard. "You'd advocate separating the twins, Ms Patterson?"

Mallory tried not to squirm. It was the last thing she wanted to advocate, but her client had been clear in his instructions and she was being paid well to follow them. She looked Koutsinous in the eye and replied, "Yes."

The mediator shook his head in obvious disapproval. "Then it looks like the parties aren't going to reach an agreement today. There are a number of issues that remain in dispute. Accordingly, I declare this mediation over. The matter will be listed for hearing in the Family Court. Previous custody orders with regard to the children will stand." He cast a somber gaze over the parties gathered before him and then turned on his heel and left.

Mallory waited for Koutsinous to gather his papers and leave the room before she turned to her client. The dark expression on his face told her everything she needed to know, but she refused to be harangued by either of the Stone men in front of her client's estranged wife and her legal representation. When Daniel's father opened his mouth, she quickly cut him off. "We'll speak outside," she said coolly.

If looks could kill she would have fallen over dead from the fury that shot in her direction by Rupert Stone, Even so, she was relieved when Daniel and his father departed in silence. Mallory took a few moments to gather her wits together.

To say her client and his hard-hitting father were pissed was an understatement. The upcoming confrontation wouldn't be easy. Still, she'd faced plenty of disgruntled clients before and no doubt would face many more in the future. Family law matters were like that. Emotions ran high. Often there was no discernible winner, no matter what result was achieved. It was something she'd learned to accept a long time ago.

Slowly, she gathered her files, pen and notepad and dropped them into her briefcase. She checked her phone for missed calls and messages and was relieved that there were none. Knowing she couldn't put things off any longer, she sighed heavily and pushed away from the table. Her client and his father waited for her just outside the door.

Rupert Stone immediately came at her. His face was a puce color. "You should have tried harder! That half-assed argument you put forward was bullshit. I was told you were the best! Now we're going to trial. How long is that going to take?"

Mallory regarded him steadily, silently counting to three. "It could be at least three or four months before we get a hearing date. The court dockets are full."

Rupert's old eyes blazed with anger. "Three or four *months*? And my granddaughters are allowed to live with that bitch all that time? I won't stand for it!"

Mallory glanced at her client, but Daniel's face remained rigid and tense, his gaze distant. There would be no support from that quarter. With an effort, she held her temper and addressed the senior Mr Stone.

"Unfortunately, Mr Stone, we didn't manage to convince the court your son's estranged wife *is* a bitch. The judge who initially presided over the case found that it was in the best interests of your granddaughters for them to remain together and to live with their mother, at least for now."

"That's nonsense," Daniel Stone said quietly, finally entering the fray. "You don't know what she's like, what she's capable of. She doesn't want those girls. The only person she cares about is herself. Why the hell do you think I left?"

Mallory swallowed a sigh and tried again. "Unfortunately, Mr Stone, you've failed to provide me with any evidence of her unsuitability to care for your children. You're also quite prepared for her to have custody of *one* of the twins. If the court were to be truly convinced of the unsuitability of your estranged wife to care for your children, you should have requested custody of *both* girls. On the evidence we've presented to date, the court has found Ms Michaels to be a perfectly adequate mother and they've decided your daughters should remain together with her. There's nothing else I can do."

Anger flooded Daniel's face. "I'm not going to take this lying down, Ms Patterson. They're *my* children. She is *not* going to take them away from me. I might be willing to leave one of the twins with her, but there's no way she's getting both."

Mallory was alarmed at his fury. In her line of work, she dealt with plenty of angry people, but Daniel Stone's countenance dictated something over and above. Coupled with his father's failure to see reason, she was afraid neither of them would listen to a word she had to say.

With an effort, she held her temper. When she spoke to her client again, her tone was placating and reasonable.

"Mr Stone, please calm down. Your getting angry will get us nowhere. Go and grab a coffee, maybe something to eat. We'll get together later and talk, formulate a new strategy." On impulse, she reached out and touched his forearm. "Just don't do anything stupid, all right? It won't do your case any good if you do."

Daniel glared down at her hand. She hastily removed it and tried to hide her embarrassment. He moved a few steps away and turned his back on her. A moment later, he spun on his heel to face her. Still breathing hard, his nostrils flared. He glared at her.

"Oh, yeah, we'll come up with a new strategy, all right," he snarled. "Starting with getting myself a new lawyer. You're fired."

Mallory stared at him in shock. Mouth gaping, her gaze switched to his father. A feral grin of satisfaction filled Rupert Stone's face. Anger stirred in her belly, but this was not the time or place. Besides, she wasn't disappointed to lose this client. The Stones were hell bent on a journey of self-destruction. They weren't prepared to compromise and they weren't prepared to lose and the last thing either of them was thinking was about the children. No one was going to come out of this custody battle a winner.

Keeping her tone pleasant, she replied, "That's your right, of course, Mr Stone. Let me know who you intend to instruct and I'll send over the file."

Daniel Stone gave her another hard look then turned and stormed away. His father glared at her and then followed his son out of the building.

Mallory sighed. *Great. Just great.*

Now she was going to have to explain to her managing partner how she'd lost a very lucrative client. So much for her hope for a promotion before the end of the year. Still, there was nothing she could do about it. She bemoaned the countless hours she'd already spent on the Stone case. Pointless hours going over evidence, interviewing witnesses, devising a strategy... It all seemed for naught.

Making her way down the stairs and exiting the court building, Mallory was still second-guessing her actions. *Should she have tried harder to pacify the Stone men? Would they have respected her more if she'd been a "yes" girl?* But she would have lost respect for herself and that would never do. She refused to relax her principles to suit someone else. That was never going to happen.

With her mind preoccupied, she didn't see the crack in the pavement until it was far too late. The four-inch heel of her strappy sandal caught on the uneven surface and brought her to a sudden halt. Losing her balance, with a cry of distress she fell in an ungainly heap on the ground.

This day couldn't get any worse...

Her face flamed with embarrassment. Busy pedestrians barely paused to walk around her, their minds focused on nothing but their destination. Picking up her briefcase from where it had landed beside her, she cautiously stood. Apart from a dent to her pride, nothing appeared to have been broken.

Thank goodness...

Then she went to take a step forward and her foot went out from underneath her again.

"Oh, no!"

The heel of her very expensive sandal had broken. Flailing, she would have fallen again were it not for a strong pair of hands that reached out and grabbed her before she lost her balance a second time. Flustered and relieved, she looked up into a pair of smiling eyes that were as blue as the summer sky above her.

"Whoa! Easy there! Are you all right?"

She glanced at her rescuer and then quickly looked away. Embarrassment heated her cheeks. Her belly flip-flopped with a rush of nerves at the sight of the good-looking man who stood before her.

His blond, tousled hair was longer than worn by most men who dressed in expensive suits. It curled down around his ears. His chiseled face could have graced the cover of a glossy magazine. The tie around his neck was two shades darker than his business shirt. Both items of clothing matched the color of his eyes and when he smiled at her again, it did weird things to her insides.

"Oh, I'm... I'm sorry," she stammered. "Thank you, I... I've broken the heel off my sandal." She pointed at the offending footwear where the heel now lay at an odd angle, barely hanging on by a thread.

His smile morphed into a grin. "I see. Yes, you certainly have. I'd nearly venture to say they're done for. How far do you have to go?"

With nerves still rushing through her belly and heat still suffusing her cheeks, she kept her gaze averted and shrugged. "Not too far."

He looked down at her feet with a dubious expression. "I'm not sure you're going to be able to walk any distance like that. Can you hop?"

Her gaze flew to his in disbelief. She caught the teasing glint in his eyes and relaxed. A reluctant grin tugged at her lips.

"You're right. The sandal is no more. It's my fault. I wasn't looking where I was going. I was thinking about...other things."

"I guess I could carry you," he offered, giving her another one of his disarming smiles.

Her eyes widened in alarm, not sure if he was joking.

"That is, if you don't have too far to go," he hastily added.

Another wave of embarrassment flooded her face. She noted his broad shoulders and muscular chest and the way his arms bunched beneath his jacket. He looked more than capable of carrying her. He looked like he could carry an elephant. Not that she wanted him to try. She gave him a tight smile.

"Thank you for your gallant offer, but I'll be fine."

She bent down and took off the offending sandal. It felt awkward to stand in four-inch heels when one of them was missing. Still, she did her best. Gathering what remained of her tattered pride around her, she gave him a curt smile of dismissal.

"Thanks again, Mr...?"

"Connelly," he supplied and held out his hand to her.

She shook his hand briefly and offered him another tight smile. "Thank you, Mr Connelly. I appreciate your help and your concern. But I'm fine. I promise."

"Mallory? My goodness! Are you all right? What happened to your sandal?"

Mallory turned and spied her best friend Sally-Ann Li coming toward her. Dressed in a power suit and laden with files and a battered leather briefcase, it was obvious Sally-Ann had also just come from court. Once again, Mallory flushed with embarrassment.

"Sally-Ann! Um... Hi."

Sally-Ann reached her side and gave her a quick one-handed hug. "Are you all right?"

Mallory nodded. "Yes. My sandal caught on the pavement and I've broken the heel. Fortunately, Mr Connelly here saved me from falling on my ass."

Sally-Ann turn toward the man who remained standing beside Mallory. Her eyes widened in surprise.

"Rafe! How are you? What brings you here this morning?"

Mallory frowned and looked from one to the other. "You two know each other?"

Sally-Ann smiled. "Of course we've been introduced. Rafe's a detective. He's just been partnered with my husband. They're in the homicide unit together."

Mallory nodded. She knew James Shepherd well. Sally-Ann was her closest friend. Mallory was one of the first people Sally-Ann had told when she and James got engaged. Now they were going on three years married and had two children. Time had gotten away from her.

Though Mallory loved Sally-Ann's kids to bits, she missed the long lunches she and her friend used to enjoy before the babies arrived. With her young family demanding more of her attention, Sally-Ann had cut back her hours to three days a week. It seemed like ages since Mallory had seen her.

"What brings you to the courthouse this morning?" Sally-Ann asked Rafe.

"I'm giving evidence in the Petrov trial. Been stuck in the witness box for the past two days."

Sally-Ann murmured sympathetically. Mallory silently commiserated with him. Two days giving evidence and being grilled by a defense attorney was no fun for anyone. The thought reminded her that she needed to get back to the office and make a start preparing her files for hand over to Daniel Stone's new attorney. She turned to Rafe.

"Thank you again for your help. It was very considerate of you."

His blue eyes captured her gaze. "No problem." He inclined his head slightly. "I didn't catch your name."

He stared at her with such frank interest, an instant spark of awareness shivered down her spine. She tried to sound as normal as possible when she replied. "It's Mallory. Mallory Patterson. I work with Sally-Ann at Sydney Legal."

His answering grin was slow and did funny things to her insides. "Well, it's a pleasure to meet you, Ms Mallory Patterson. And there's no need to thank me. I only did what any gentleman would have done."

Mallory fought off another wave of embarrassment. To her relief, Rafe turned his attention to Sally-Ann and after bidding her farewell, took his leave.

Sally-Ann peered at the sandal Mallory still held in her hand. "It looks like you've worn them for the last time," she said ruefully.

Mallory nodded. "Yes. It's too bad. Though they weren't exactly comfortable, they looked great with this suit."

"I have a spare pair in the cupboard in my office," Sally-Ann said. "You're welcome to borrow them. What size are you?"

"Nine."

"There you go. Same as me. I think I have the biggest feet of any Asian woman in the city." She laughed. "I'm not promising they're quite as stylish or comfortable as those, but hopefully they'll get you through the day."

Mallory smiled with relief. "Thanks, Sal. I really appreciate it. I wasn't sure what I was going to do."

"Hey, don't mention it. Besides, you've still got to hobble back to the office in one sandal."

Mallory took a couple of awkward steps forward and then giggled. She looked at Sally-Ann. "Oh, my goodness, I thought this day couldn't get any more embarrassing."

Her friend laughed. "At least you didn't land on your ass."

"As a matter of fact, I did."

Sally-Ann squealed. "Oh, no! In front of everyone! I thought you said Rafe came to your rescue? I thought you meant he'd caught you before you hit the ground."

At the mention of the sexy detective's name, Mallory's belly somersaulted once again. "He did," she explained. "The second time. I fell over when my heel caught on the pavement. It was when I got to my feet and tried to walk that I almost fell over again. Lucky for me, your friend was there."

Sally-Ann laughed until there were tears in the corners of her eyes. Seeing the funny side of it, Mallory reluctantly joined her. Together, they made it along the busy footpath toward the offices of Sydney Legal. With one shoe on and one shoe off, their progress was slow and awkward.

Sally-Ann cast her a dubious look. "Perhaps you'd be best to take off both sandals? At least then you could walk evenly."

Mallory glanced down at her feet and grimaced ruefully. "I think you're right." With that, she bent down and slipped off the remaining sandal. Then with her head held high, she walked all the way back to her office in bare feet.

Chapter 3

After collecting Sally-Ann's spare pair of shoes, Mallory managed to convince Sally-Ann to let her take her to lunch. After mild protestations, Sally-Ann allowed Mallory to drag her out of their building and lead her to their favorite café. With their lunch orders taken and coffees on the table in front of them, Mallory sighed quietly and tried to put the morning behind her.

"So, how are the kids?" she asked in an effort to distract herself.

Sally-Ann's face immediately broke into a grin. "What can I say? Travis is a typical two-year-old getting into anything and everything and causing as much chaos around the house as he can manage and Cindy's a little doll. She's the sweetest, most placid baby you could ever meet. I can sit her on the floor or in her playpen with a few toys and she'll happily stay there until I come and get her again. She'll be eight months old next week." Sally-Ann shook her head. "Can you believe that?"

Mallory nodded. "Oh yes, I can believe that. Time's flying by. It barely seems like I've started the day and it comes to an end. So, how's James? Is he still lining up for Father of the Year?"

Sally-Ann's expression softened and she got misty-eyed. "Oh, yes. I certainly got a good one when I chose him. I couldn't ask for a better father or a more supportive husband. He works such long hours and yet he still makes himself available to me and the kids. He changes nappies, does the laundry, cooks dinner if he's home early enough. He even makes time to ask me about my day. He's so sweet. I really got so lucky."

Mallory gazed across at her friend and stifled a tiny burst of jealousy. She was happy for her friend. She really was. She just wished *she* had a man in *her* life who was so supportive and made her feel warm and fuzzy inside.

Sally-Ann sipped from her latté. "So, what about you? How's life been? Are you still swiping left and right?"

Mallory poked out her tongue. "You're the one who encouraged me to join an online dating site!"

Sally-Ann grinned unrepentantly. "True. So, how did your date with Robert the accountant go?"

"Actually, he prefers to be called Bob." Mallory shrugged. "I guess it went okay. From what he'd written on his profile, we seemed to have a lot in common. The hard-working professional looking for love. Exactly like me. It's just... There was no spark. Unfortunately, that's not something you can tell by seeing someone on a screen. I knew from the moment we met that it wasn't going to work."

Sally-Ann sighed. "I'm sorry things didn't work out this time. But keep at it. Bob is only the fourth date you've had since you joined. I'm sure you'll find someone. Those dating sites are filled with people looking for love. It's a numbers game at the end of the day. You might get some wrong ones, but eventually you'll meet Mr Right."

She paused and then added with a teasing sparkle in her eyes, "Of course, I could always do a bit of matchmaking. The majority of James' work colleagues are male. Maybe I could introduce you to some of them? In fact, you've already met Rafe Connelly. You can't tell me he's not hot. I could invite him over to dinner—a barbecue. You could spend some time getting to know him; laugh about what happened today. Who knows what might happen."

Mallory chuckled good-naturedly, but shook her head. "Oh, my goodness, no! Please! No matchmaking! I can find my own dates."

Sally-Ann gazed at her with an amused expression. "Oh, yes. That's right. You joined a dating site. Come on, Mallory! What do you have to lose? Rafe's good-looking, single, about your age. Oh, I think he has a daughter. That's not a deal breaker, is it?"

Mallory shook her head. "No...I love kids, but it sounds like he probably has baggage."

Sally-Ann rolled her eyes. "Oh, please! He's thirty-something, Mallory. Who doesn't have baggage by that age? Come on! Say yes! I'll be sure to invite a few others over, too. It's not like he'll have any idea I'm trying to set the two of you up. Come on! It'll be fun."

The memory of the feel of Rafe's heated gaze locked on hers, flashed in her mind. Her belly tightened with nerves...and something else. He was definitely someone she was attracted to. They'd done nothing but look at each other and share some mindless conversation and she'd almost combusted from the flames.

Would it be worth it, getting to know him a little better? It was like Sally-Ann said: What did she have to lose?

Against her better judgement, Mallory found herself nodding. "Okay. I'll give it a go. But don't blame me if it doesn't work out."

Sally-Ann merely grinned.

———

Rafe stared down at the open files on his cluttered desk. It had been five days since the woman's body had been found secreted in the cave. They were waiting for a list of persons who'd gone missing during the time they believed the woman had been murdered. Rafe had put in the request and was assured by the records department they'd get it to him as soon as they could. That was three days ago.

In the meantime, Rafe and James had been kept busy with a spate of other serious crimes around the city. Earlier that morning, a man had been shot to death by his wife in what was alleged to be a domestic dispute. She was currently being interviewed by one of the other detectives and would no doubt be charged with murder. A day before that, there had been a gang-related stabbing at Darling Harbour. It had happened in the middle of the day with hundreds of witnesses present, and someone had supplied extensive CCTV footage covering every second of the deadly assault. It wouldn't be too hard for prosecutors to secure a plea. Not like the Petrov case which felt like it might drag on forever.

The squad room door opened and Rafe's partner filled the opening. In his arms, he held a pile of files.

"What do you have there?" Rafe asked.

James dumped the pile on Rafe's desk. "The records department came up with the list of missing persons. They apologized for the delay. I took the liberty of collecting the files. Each one of these relates to someone who went missing during the relevant time period. We'll have to go through them one by one."

Rafe groaned. "Who would have guessed there'd be so many?" He sighed. "At least we can eliminate any males and any females who aren't Caucasian."

"Yes. And anyone who isn't between the ages of thirty and forty years old," James added.

"Yeah," Rafe agreed. "Still, it's a huge pile to go through."

James halved the pile of files and took his half over to his desk. "Let's get to it. There's no time like the present."

For the next three hours, both men worked side-by-side going through the files, setting the possibilities to one side and eliminating those who couldn't be a match. It was late in the afternoon when James stretched his arms above his head and yawned. "I've had about enough of this for the day. My eyes are starting to cross over."

Rafe nodded. "Yeah. My back's killing me." He pushed away from his desk and twisted from side to side in an attempt to loosen his stiff joints.

"Oh, I almost forgot," James said. "What are you doing this Saturday?"

"Charlotte has swimming training until twelve. I promised her we'd go and visit her mother at the cemetery afterwards. We haven't been there in a while."

James slowly nodded. "Yeah, okay. What about after that? Sally-Ann and I are throwing a barbecue on Saturday night for a bunch of friends. We thought you might like to come over. Bring Charlotte too, of course."

Rafe thought it over for a few moments. It had been ages since he'd gone out and socialized. And he could take Charli. That always helped.

"Sure. Sounds good," he said, coming to a decision. "What can I bring?"

———

Rafe pushed through the turnstile at the local swimming pool and listened to the excited cries of the children as they splashed and played about in the water. He walked toward the bleachers down near the deep end where Charli usually trained. In her bright pink swimsuit and orange cap, she stood out like a beacon. He watched her dive off the blocks with confident grace and was filled with quiet pride. *He* was responsible for this young girl, the daughter he loved with all his heart.

Charli's mother had abandoned her shortly after she was born. Even all these years later, Rafe still couldn't understand that.

How could a mother who'd just given birth not want her baby?

Perhaps Khloe had been suffering post-natal depression, an illness that nobody paid much heed to in those days. Or maybe it was the drugs she'd been using right up until Charli's birth? Whatever it was, Rafe had been left feeling lost and confused. His world had been tossed on its end, but from the very first moment he'd spied his baby, he'd fallen madly and deeply in love.

The tiny scrap of humanity, all pink and squalling and soft was his daughter, his little girl. A miracle he could barely fathom. Despite the fact her mother had been a drug user, the doctors assured him his baby was perfectly fine. He might have only been eighteen, but without question he was immediately and eagerly willing to take on the responsibility of raising her. Charli would never know her mother hadn't wanted her. Rafe was determined to protect her from that. Besides, he had enough love for them both.

Rafe watched as Charli finished her lap and climbed out of the pool at the other end.

Grabbing her towel, she made her way toward him, grinning.

"Dad! Did you see that? I did a PB!"

Rafe pretended to frown in confusion. "What's a PB?"

She giggled and lightly punched his arm. "Don't be silly, Dad. You know what a PB is. A personal best."

"Oh, that's right. You did a PB? Well done!"

Charlotte's grin widened. "Yeah, I cut a full two seconds off my time! How about that?"

Rafe's heart filled with tenderness as he pulled her in close beside him. She tugged off her swimming cap and he ruffled hair.

"Dad!" she complained.

He laughed and they both headed toward their car. She spied the bouquet of fresh flowers sitting on the back seat and her eyes filled with tears. "Oh, Dad! You remembered!"

"Of course I remembered."

On the way to the cemetery, he told her about the barbecue they'd been invited to at the Shepherd house.

"Will there be any kids there?" she asked.

"Probably. The Shepherds have two, but they're a fair bit younger than you."

She turned him eagerly. "Babies?"

"Yeah. I think so. At least one of them."

Her smile widened. "Great. I love babies."

———————

Mallory set the hair straightener to one side and took a critical look at herself in the mirror. She'd taken the time to straighten her long red hair and had used dark colors to expertly shadow and highlight her green eyes. It was probably the thing she liked most about herself: her almond-shaped green eyes. Along with her red hair, she'd inherited her eye color from her mother.

Even though Sofia Lopez Patterson had been born in Argentina, she was part of a rare number of Argentinians who were born with red hair. Mallory's father had always joked it was probably a throwback to Sofia's Irish ancestors, rather than her being among the rare, one-and-a-half percent of the Argentinian population who had red hair. Whatever the case, Sofia Lopez had been a beautiful woman and had been known for her striking red hair.

Mallory's father had met her mother in college. Sofia had been studying medicine and her father was studying law. To hear him tell the story, he'd spied Sofia from across the crowded room, the beacon of her hair drawing him through the crowd.

It was something out of a Hollywood movie and Mallory had always loved the story. It convinced her that underneath his sometimes brusque manner, her father was a hopeless romantic. It was too bad her mother hadn't seen fit to hang around and live out the love story. Mallory would have enjoyed getting to know her.

As it was, her memories of her mother were through the eyes of a ten-year-old. There were times when she barely remembered what her mother looked like. If it weren't for the few photos she kept in her nightstand, she might have forgotten altogether.

One thing she hadn't forgotten was the feel of mother's arms as she drew her close and her kindness, her softness, her smile. Staring at her reflection in the mirror, Mallory couldn't help but notice how much she resembled her mother.

What had she done to drive her mother away?

The unwelcome thought was no less painful for its familiarity. Unwittingly, her eyes filled with tears.

"Oh, Mom! Why didn't you love me enough to stay? Were you that unhappy that you had to leave us? I was ten, Mom! A child! I needed you, Mom. I *still* need you. Where *are* you?"

The sound of her hollow voice in the silence, and the pointless questions that never went away, filled her with a gnawing pain. As the tears threatened to spill over and ruin her makeup, Mallory hastily blinked them away. Reaching for a tissue, she patted gently at the moisture until her eyes were once again dry. It had been twenty years since her mother had left. Twenty years without a word. Twenty years of not knowing where she was, who she was with, whether she was happy…

Forcing the sad thoughts aside, Mallory focused on the reason she was all dressed up: the Shepherd barbecue. Instead of making her feel better, she was filled with a sudden rush of nerves. The thought of speaking to Rafe Connelly again filled her with tension that was equal parts nervous anticipation and fear.

Fear? Really? What did she have to be afraid of? He was just a man. She'd met plenty of men, including good-looking ones like Rafe. In fact, she'd spent the past month going on coffee dates with one man after another. How hard could this be?

It was just that none of the men she'd met through the dating site had set her heart racing. None of them had filled her with shivery excitement from the moment he opened his mouth. And none of them had been as nice as Rafe Connelly. He'd stopped to help her when plenty of others had walked on by. He'd assessed her predicament with good humor and a smile. Oh yes, what a smile... Hell, he'd even offered to carry her so she wouldn't have to hop.

No, he'd been joking about that. But still, he'd made the offer and that meant something to her. He was a gentleman with good old-fashioned manners and that was refreshing in this day and age. She wanted to see him again... She wanted him to like her...and that was the reason for her nerves.

She was sure Sally-Ann wouldn't be obvious enough to invite just the two of them. This wasn't the first time Mallory had been to the Shepherd home for dinner. On the other occasions, there were a number of other people—couples, singles, families and a combination of everything in between. She was sure she wouldn't stand out and she hoped Rafe would be oblivious to Sally-Ann's matchmaking machinations.

Smoothing down the soft fabric of her green,

sleeveless linen dress, she took one last look at her reflection. She looked cool and calm and confident. There was no evidence of the turmoil inside her. She hoped she could keep up the façade all the way through dinner.

She collected her matching clutch purse from her bed and dropped her phone and car keys inside it and hurried from the room. She found her father in his den. The TV was tuned to a football game. The sound was turned low.

"You look nice, honey."

Mallory smiled. "Thanks, Dad."

"Where are you off to?"

"Sally-Ann invited me over for a barbecue. It's been ages since we caught up."

"That's good. I like Sally-Ann. She's a good lawyer."

"Yes, she is. Sydney Legal is lucky to have her."

"Listen, Mallory, I wanted to talk to you about Daniel Stone."

Mallory groaned. "Please, Dad. Not now. I'm on my way out. Besides, Frederick Wentworth's words of disappointment are still ringing in my ears. I don't think I can bear to listen to yours. Not right now."

Her father moved over to the sideboard and poured himself a finger of Scotch. "Yes, Wentworth told me he'd spoken to you," he replied with his back to her.

Mallory's shoulders slumped. The most senior managing partner and the head of Sydney Legal had talked to her father about how she'd lost a good client.

Great.

She didn't work under her father. He was a commercial lawyer. He had nothing to do with the family law department. Still, he was a senior partner and Frederick Wentworth was the boss...

"I can't believe Wentworth spoke to you."

Her father turned around to face her. "Yes. The thing is, Frederick had nothing but good things to say about you. He's proud of the way you conducted yourself. You stood up to Rupert Arthur Andrew Stone and told him what's what."

He moved closer and his tone softened. "Don't ever be ashamed of your courage, Mallory. I wish there was more of it in the world. Besides, old man Stone called Wentworth himself. He wants you back."

Mallory's mouth gaped open in shock. "What?"

"Yes. It turns out the esteemed Stone gentlemen made a few more inquiries and discovered you really *are* the best." Her father saluted her with his drink and grinned.

Mallory blinked in surprise and tried to take it all in. Shock and elation surged through her and then she remembered the reasons why she hadn't been all that disappointed to see Daniel Stone walk.

"I don't know that I want to represent Daniel Stone, Dad. He wants to separate his twins! Twins, Dad. It's cruel."

Her father took a sip of his drink. "That's not for you to decide, honey. All you have to do is take clear instructions from your client and present the facts to the court. Leave the rest to the judge. That's what they're paid to do."

She sighed and wished she felt so circumspect about it. As if reading her mind, her father spoke again.

"Chin up, honey! It's just a case. They come and go with monotonous regularity. You do your very best and the rest is up to the court. That's how it always goes. Now, go and kick up your heels and have fun with your friends. You deserve it."

Mallory managed a weak smile in reply. She leaned over and pecked his cheek. "Thanks, Dad. I'll see you later. Have a good night."

CHAPTER 4

Rafe twisted the top off a bottle of beer and took a healthy swig. The day had been unseasonably warm and he was glad for the cool, refreshing taste. The barbeque was in full swing and he'd already caught up with a couple of other detectives he worked with and their wives. The backyard was full of kids, playing and running and squealing, having fun. He noticed Charlotte chatting to a group of young teens. She said something and everyone laughed. He was relieved she was having a good time.

And then he saw her. The woman from the courthouse. *Mallory*. It was her trademark red hair that caught his attention—then and now. Of course, he knew she was a co-worker and friend of Sally-Ann's, but he hadn't expected to see her here. Then he noticed the baby on her hip and his spirits sank.

She was married. Or at least, she was in a relationship. The baby looked young. Less than a year, for sure. He tried to stem his disappointment.

And then he noticed Charlotte had broken away from her group and now stood beside the redhead. They shared a few moments of conversation and then Mallory turned and handed the baby to his daughter. Even from this distance, he could see the look of sheer delight on his little girl's face. It seemed like she really *did* love babies...

His gaze flicked to the infant and his eyes widened in surprise. The child was Asian. *Was she James and Sally-Ann's baby?* James had mentioned he had an eight-month old... Intrigued and unable to help himself, Rafe wandered over to the barbeque area where James was turning steaks.

"Hey, Rafe. How are you doing?"

"Good, thanks, mate. Do you need a hand?"

"No. All under control, I think." He turned a steak that was a little overdone and chuckled. "Well, maybe not completely under control, but who cares? There's always someone who likes their meat well done, right?"

"Right," Rafe agreed and took another swig from his beer.

"So, have you met everyone?" James asked.

"I caught up with Zane and Meghan Sullivan and a couple of the other guys. Who's the redhead over there?"

He kept his tone casual. James looked over to where he pointed. "Oh, that's Mallory Patterson. She and Sally-Ann are friends. She's a lawyer at Sydney Legal."

Rafe nodded and took another mouthful of beer. "Who is she here with?"

James flipped over another steak. "I think she came on her own."

"So she's not with anyone?"

"Not that I know of."

Rafe's spirits lifted, but he wasn't finished yet. His gaze returned to the group of women gathered around Charlotte. "Cute baby. Charli loves babies. Who does she belong to?"

James grinned with pride. "That would be my little angel. That's my little Cindy."

Rafe was hard pressed to hide his relief. *The baby wasn't Mallory's...* As far as James knew, she was single. Things were looking up. He drew in a surreptitious breath and with effort, kept his tone casual.

"She's gorgeous."

"Oh, yes she is. And growing more beautiful every day. Just like her momma."

James' smile was so filled with tenderness, Rafe was taken aback. And then he was immediately flooded with a yearning to have what his partner had. He wanted a wife and children. He wanted a happy home.

He had Charli and she was his world, but he'd never had what James had. A sense of belonging to someone, heart and soul, knowing they had his back. An adult to talk to, share his day with, his hopes, his fears, his dreams. He was thirty-one years old. He had a great career, a wonderful daughter, a good life. But he was lonely. And it was time to do something about that.

"Are you sure the redhead is single?" he asked.

James gave him a knowing grin. "Don't tell me you're interested?" he teased.

With an effort, Rafe managed to keep his embarrassment at bay. He gave a casual shrug. "A hot-looking babe like that? Who wouldn't be?" He chuckled and hoped it didn't sound forced.

James' grin widened. "Hey, if I wasn't a happily married man, I'd be interested myself!" He winked. "Come on. I'll introduce you."

Rafe opened his mouth to correct his friend's assumption that he and Mallory hadn't met, but in the end he remained silent. *What did it matter if James introduced them again?* At least it would give Rafe an excuse to talk to the beautiful and intriguing redhead again.

James called to one of his mates and asked them to tend to the barbecue and then turned to Rafe with another wink. "Let's go."

"You're a natural," Mallory said to the young girl who'd introduced herself as Charlotte. She watched the girl cradle baby Cindy to her chest. "Do you have any younger brothers and sisters?"

Charlotte shook her head. "No. There's just me and my dad."

"Well, you must have done some babysitting, then. Is that how you got to be so good at holding babies?"

Once again, Charlotte shook her head, but this time a smile tugged at her lips. "No, I guess it's just like you said. I'm a natural." A cheeky grin lit up her face and Mallory's heart clenched.

She was so carefree and beautiful... Just like a young girl should be. Just like *she* might have been if her mother hadn't up and abandoned her without so much as a goodbye...

Mallory watched as Charlotte lightly stroked the baby's black hair off her face. The dark color was almost identical to Charlotte's. The girl's hair was tied in two braids with pretty red polka dot ribbons at the end of each one. Her eyes were bright blue and shining. Her skin was clear. She was open and charming and confident. She was everything a young girl should be. Mallory wondered about the girl's parents. She seemed such a happy, well-adjusted child. They were obviously doing a fine job of raising her.

From the corner of her eye, she spied James heading toward them. A couple of steps behind him was Rafe Connelly. Mallory's heart skipped a beat and her pulse took off in overdrive.

Rafe Connelly...

She'd known he was going to be at the barbecue, of course, and had been preparing herself for their meeting all afternoon. But now she was about to come face-to-face with a man who set her heart racing and filled her dreams with impossible fantasies.

She did her best to ignore the men for as long as she could, but then they were there, right beside her and she was forced to acknowledge their presence. She half-turned to face them. Her gaze zeroed in on Rafe.

He wore a light blue polo shirt that matched the color of his eyes. The shirt was tucked into a pair of Levis that clung snugly to his hips. Long legs encased in denim seemed to go on forever. Mallory was tall for a woman, but this man towered over her. She hadn't noticed that the first time they'd met. Probably because she'd been concentrating so hard on maintaining her dignity while standing in sandals with a broken heel.

James made the introductions. "Mallory, this is a friend of mine, Rafe Connelly. We work together."

Mallory glanced at Rafe who'd stuck out his hand. She shook it. The warmth of his skin sent tingles of awareness along her arm. He had a nice firm handshake.

"It's nice to see you again, Mr Connelly, or should I call you Detective?"

James frowned. "Hang on, do you two know each other already?"

Rafe grimaced. "Yeah, mate. I didn't get a chance to explain. Mallory and I met the other day outside the courthouse. I…"

Mallory cringed at the memory of their first meeting and steeled herself against the embarrassment of what Rafe was about to reveal. Instead he surprised her by saying, "I helped her with her…files. She was having a little difficulty."

She gifted him with a grateful smile. He winked at her and her belly somersaulted with need. Heat rushed to her face…and to other areas. Flustered, she looked away.

"Well, I'll leave you two to get reacquainted," James said, and after bestowing a kiss on his baby daughter he returned to the barbeque.

"Dad, look at Cindy! Isn't she cute?"

Mallory blinked in surprise. *Dad?* She stared at Rafe as he moved closer to Charlotte and offered her a grin.

"See, I told you there would be at least one baby here, didn't I, Charli?"

The young girl grinned back at him. Mallory tried to adjust to the knowledge that the girl she'd been so recently admiring was none other than Rafe Connelly's daughter.

What had Sally-Ann said about the girl's mother? She wished she'd paid more attention. She shot a surreptitious look around the backyard where groups of guests had congregated, wondering which one of them might be Charlotte's mother. And then she decided to come straight out and ask. After all, she was thirty. Much too old for games.

"So, Rafe, it's nice to see you again. And your daughter is delightful. We've been bonding over Cindy."

Rafe smiled and it was sexy enough to curl Mallory's toes. Her nipples pebbled beneath her dress.

"Charli loves babies."

"I sure do," Charli agreed, softly brushing Cindy's cheek with her finger. A wistful expression filled her face. "I wish I had a baby sister—or even a brother."

A blush heightened the color in Rafe's face.

Mallory moved her lips into what she hoped was a smile. Standing so close to him she could smell his cologne and it was all she could do to ignore the invisible pull of attraction between them. She could barely concentrate on a word they were saying, let alone form coherent sentences in response. To her relief, Rafe filled the awkward silence.

"This is the first time I've met little Cindy." He leaned forward and captured the baby's fingers in his own. When she jiggled her hand up and down, Cindy gurgled with delight, staring at Rafe in fascination. Mallory understood exactly how the infant felt.

"How about you?" Rafe asked her. "Do you have any children?"

"No, no," she uttered. "No husband, no children."

"Are you a detective, too, Mallory?" Charli asked, her curiosity plain on her face. "Is that why you don't have a family of your own? My mom died when I was three. Dad always says he's too busy to find anyone else. He's a detective at the Sydney Police Station. He solves murders and all sorts of other crimes," she said proudly.

"He's trying to find out who that woman is who was found buried in a cave. She was murdered. She had her wrists and ankles tied together with cable ties. They were still intact after all this time. Can you believe that?"

Charli looked at Mallory with eyes that were wide with wonder. Rafe's blush deepened. To Mallory, it only made him more adorable.

"I'm sorry. Charli talks too much," he muttered.

Mallory laughed gently. "Don't be sorry. It's lovely to see a child speak so highly of her dad. You're her hero."

He shook his head, even more embarrassed. "I'm nobody's hero."

"Of course you are, Dad!" Charli protested. "You're my hero, just like Mallory said." The young girl turned to Mallory. "I like your hair. It's really pretty. I wish I had hair that color."

"But your hair is beautiful!" Mallory cried, gazing at the silken black braids.

Charlotte shrugged. "Thanks. I got my hair from my mom."

Mallory glanced at Rafe, taking in his dirty-blond hair. She leaned toward Charlotte and whispered, "So did I."

The young girl looked up and smiled. Baby Cindy waved her hands around and made goo-gahing sounds of pleasure. Everyone laughed. Something tightened in Mallory's belly. How wonderful it would be to have a family of her own... A baby to love and cherish, a husband to share her life—her hopes and dreams and disappointments.

"Are you all right, Mallory?"

Rafe's quiet question registered. She blinked hard, only just realizing she'd been staring at him. She must look like an idiot. Heat rushed up her neck. She prayed it wouldn't spread to her cheeks.

"Y-yes, of course," she stammered and cast around for something intelligent to say. She was relieved when once again he filled the awkward silence.

"So, what kind of law do you practice?"

Charlotte's eyes widened in surprise. "Oh, so you're not a detective?"

"No. I'm a lawyer, like Cindy's mom. I specialize in family law."

Rafe nodded, his expression filling with respect. "That's tough."

"Yes. Probably as tough as what you do. It can't be easy having to tell a family member that their loved one has been killed and then take on the responsibility for finding the person who did it."

"Yeah, it's tough. But it's rewarding, too. We found a body earlier in the week. We think it's been there for as long as twenty years. There's a family out there who's been waiting a long time to find out what happened to their loved one. I'm hoping to give them the answers they need."

Mallory swallowed against the lump that had lodged itself in her throat. All of a sudden, she was bombarded with memories, the endless questions driving her mad, and never any answers…

Rafe frowned. "Are you *sure* you're all right?" His voice was filled with genuine concern.

Mallory swiped a hand across her face and plastered on a smile. There was no way she was going to spill all her family's secrets to a complete stranger, no matter how good looking and kind.

"Yes, of course. I'm fine. I was just thinking how hard it would be to be one of those people—forever wondering where their loved one might be."

Charlotte watched the exchange with interest, her attention divided between them and the baby in her arms. Then a distinctly familiar smell wafted toward them. Mallory smiled. Charlotte's face went red and she held the infant away from her.

"Oh, Dad! I thinks she's..."

Instead of looking horrified, Rafe laughed. "I think you're right."

Charlotte held the baby out to him. "Here. Can you take her?"

Rafe made a move to accept the baby, but Mallory got there before him, pleased for the excuse to move away from him and the memories he'd unwittingly dredged up.

"I'll take her," she offered and lifted the baby onto her hip. Turning away from them, she made her escape.

———

Mallory found Sally-Ann in the kitchen setting out another plate of finger food. The small crackers decorated with cream cheese, salmon and dill looked delicious, but right now Mallory couldn't think about food. Her mind was still full of her conversation with Rafe and there was also a baby who needed attention.

Sally-Ann looked up and smiled. "Hi, baby! How's my little girl?"

Mallory screwed up her nose. "I think she needs a change." She handed Cindy over to her mother, who caught a whiff.

"I think you're right," she laughed. "We'll be back in a minute." Sally-Ann headed down the hall toward Cindy's nursery. Mallory followed.

Setting the baby down on the change table, Sally-Ann set about changing Cindy's diaper with an expert efficiency that spoke of great familiarity. Mallory watched in silence. Sally-Ann shot her a sly look.

"So, I saw you talking to Rafe. What do you think?"

Heat blazed across Mallory's face. Sally-Ann squealed in delight. "Oh, my goodness! You like him, don't you? I can tell! How fantastic!"

"It's only the second time I've met him!" Mallory protested, willing her embarrassment away.

Sally-Ann gave her a knowing grin. "Yes, but he's sparked your interest, hasn't he? After all, what's not to like? Good looking, smart, sexy. And a doting father, to boot. What more could you ask for?"

The heat on Mallory's face continued to burn. She cursed under her breath. She was thirty years old! Way too old to be blushing over a man.

"I don't know what to think of him," she muttered. "I don't even know him."

"But there's a spark, right?" Sally-Ann insisted.

"Okay, yes. There's a spark," she admitted grudgingly.

Oh, boy, was there a spark…

Sally-Ann's answering grin was triumphant. "I *knew* it! A spark is everything! You can't have a relationship without it, right? Isn't that what you've been telling me?"

Mallory gritted her teeth and offered a reluctant smile. "Yes."

Sally-Ann returned her attention to Cindy and finished adjusting the baby's clothes. She picked her up and cuddled her close.

"Rafe's working on that body found in the national park. I read about it in the newspaper. Did you hear about that?" Mallory asked.

"Yes. James mentioned it to me a few days ago."

"The police think she's been dead about twenty years." She glanced at Sally-Ann. My mom's been gone twenty years..." Her voice drifted off.

Sally-Ann looked at her in surprise. "Surely you don't think this could be your mother?"

"No, of course not," Mallory hurriedly replied. "My mother left us to return to Argentina. Dad drove her to the airport." She paused. "It's just that... In all these years, I've never heard from her. Not even once. Not a card or a phone call. It's as if she wiped me from her memory the moment she stepped onto that plane; like I ceased to exist." Her voice caught. "It still hurts. I don't even know if she's still alive."

Sally-Ann's expression filled with compassion. "I can't imagine how hard that must be for you. I'm so lucky both my parents are still alive. I love them so much. I can't imagine them not being in my life."

Mallory forced a smile. "I guess it's hard to miss what you never had. I was ten when Mom left. Of course, I remember her, but the feel of her, her smell, her touch… Those memories have faded. I'm scared one day I won't remember her at all."

Sally-Ann moved Cindy to her hip and gave Mallory an awkward hug. "You won't forget her. She's your mom. No one forgets their mom. I'm sure she has her reasons for staying away." She paused. "Have you ever tried to find her?"

Mallory shook her head firmly. "No. I wouldn't have a clue where to start. Besides, it would be disloyal to Dad. He's the one who loved me enough to hang around."

Sally-Ann regarded her steadily. "Yes, he did and he should get credit for that, but I'm sure he'll understand your need to make contact with her. She's your mother! He might even be willing to help you. He loved her once. Maybe he still does."

Mallory was suddenly bombarded with memories of the fighting between her parents in the months before her mother decided to leave. She shook her head.

"Things weren't good between them in those last few months. There was a lot of anger. Mom caught Dad cheating on her and from what I gathered, it wasn't the first time." She laughed without humor. "She might have walked out on him because of his infidelities, and he hasn't changed."

Sally-Ann shrugged. They both knew about her father's reputation around women. He dated regularly and was often seen out and about at social events with a glamorous woman on his arm. Right now, he was seeing Alice Simons, but next week it might be someone else. Some of them were younger than Mallory.

He was a love 'em and leave 'em kind of guy. She wondered if her mother's abrupt departure had influenced his own behavior in the years since. She was embarrassed to think about how often he changed his bed partners, but he was entitled to live his life on his own terms. She was just grateful he never brought any of the women home. She would have moved out long ago if that were the case. The thought made her frown.

Perhaps she was being selfish? Perhaps it was out of respect for her that he visited his lady friends at their homes? Was she the reason he didn't feel he could bring them home? Was he even now still loathe to dishonor her mother?

Even after her mother had left, her father never said anything to tarnish Mallory's memory of her. He merely said she was terribly homesick; she missed her family in Argentina; she had wanted to go home. He told Mallory how he'd begged her mother to stay even though things were a bit rough between them, but her mother had refused. She knew how much he loved their daughter and she knew Mallory would be okay. Her father loved her enough for both of them.

Mallory's thoughts turned to Charlotte. In some ways, Mallory envied the young girl. At least she had an acceptable reason why her mother wasn't in her life. Not like Mallory. Even now, it hurt to know her mother hadn't loved her enough to stay. Perhaps Sally-Ann was right. Perhaps it was time to find her mother and demand answers. As a long-forgotten daughter, she definitely had the right, didn't she?

A sudden surge of determination when through her. She looked at Sally-Ann. "You're right. It's time I stopped pretending it doesn't matter, and go and find my mother. It's time I got answers to all the questions that have just about driven me mad since the morning I woke to find her gone. She's had twenty years of being held unaccountable." She narrowed her eyes. "That's about to end."

CHAPTER 5

The sun had barely poked its head over the horizon when Rafe walked into the squad room on Monday. He'd come home after the Shepherd barbecue and he hadn't been able to get Mallory Patterson off his mind. They hadn't engaged in any further conversation, but he'd monitored her progress around the yard. She engaged easily with the rest of the guests and her laughter rang out loud and often. He liked her and he wanted to get to know her better.

The way he felt about her surprised him. He hadn't been seriously interested in another woman since Khloe. Oh, he'd had casual relationships that lasted a few weeks, but there hadn't been anyone who'd captured his heart. Not that Mallory had captured his heart either, but she'd certainly captured his interest.

For so long, he'd kept women at bay. It took him a long time to recover from Khloe. At the time, his heart had been broken. She was gone, abandoning him and their newborn and although he embraced the raising of his baby, he'd been more than cautious about putting his heart on the line again.

But Charli was now thirteen; no longer a baby and quite capable of looking after herself, as she frequently reminded him. She didn't need him to the extent she used to and that excuse had worn thin. She was often home alone while he was at work.

He was fortunate enough to have a friendly and reliable neighbor who was more than willing to look in on her if he was going to be arriving home late. Mrs Hubbard was a godsend, especially since his mother had died.

Even so, he never took on a night shift. It was an expectation of any cop and he knew that decision had held his career back, but Charli's needs had always come first. There was no way he was going to leave her alone all night.

But he couldn't deny there was something compelling about Mallory that attracted him and made him want to see where it might lead. The knowledge filled him with dread, littered with anticipation.

The door to the squad room came open and James came bounding in. His obvious good mood made Rafe smile. *If this is what a wife and children did for a man, he was all for it…*

"Hey, how was the rest of your weekend?" James asked, coming to a halt beside Rafe's desk.

"Yeah, good. Spent most of Sunday in the garden. It doesn't get near enough the attention it should."

James threw him a sly look. "I thought you would have spent it with the delightful Mallory Patterson. You two seemed to hit it off."

Rafe fought off a wave of embarrassment, but was pleased just the same. "You think so?"

"Yeah, I do. And Sally-Ann does, too. She was speaking to Mallory. I think the girl's interested."

Rafe's heart skipped a beat. He could hardly contain his grin. "Yeah?"

James winked. "Yeah."

Rafe thought for a moment. *Was he brave enough to take the next step?* He glanced at James and cleared his throat, suddenly beset with nerves. "Um, do you think you could give me her number?"

James gave a holler of excitement. "That's my boy! You go for it!" Then his excitement faded. "But I'm afraid I don't have her number."

"What about your wife?"

James brightened. "Of course! I'll call Sally-Ann. I'm sure she'll want to get Mallory's permission first before she hands over her number, but from what I saw on Saturday night, I'd say there's every chance you'll be able to call the woman before the day is out. Is that good enough?"

Rafe smiled. Nerves warred with excitement. "That's plenty good enough."

***

With one hand, Mallory spooned cereal into her mouth. With the other, she flicked through pages on her iPad. For once, the newspaper had been left on the kitchen counter. She had other things on her mind.

Her discussion with Sally-Ann had set off an avalanche of memories and had filled her with determination to find out where the hell Sofia Lopez Patterson had ended up. Mallory had spent most of Sunday on the Internet researching her mother's whereabouts. A simple Google search had thrown up a number of possibilities.

She'd started with the social media sites. Unfortunately, there were too many women by the name of Sofia Lopez on Facebook to distinguish which one might be her mother. Another complicating factor was that she didn't know what her mother now looked like. Sofia would be in her mid-fifties. The mother in Mallory's memory had dark red hair, like she did, but that had been twenty years ago. There was every chance Sofia's hair would be gray now. Particularly, if her mother had resisted the pressure to resort to an artificial means of coloring it.

Her father entered the kitchen and headed straight for the coffee pot. He was dressed for work in his usual impeccably fitted, wildly expensive, three-piece suit. A yellow-and-black striped tie Mallory had given him for his most recent birthday hung around his neck. Gold cufflinks, another birthday gift from his daughter, glinted in the morning light as he filled his mug.

"Good-morning. How did you sleep?" she asked.

He turned and gave her a cheery smile. "Great. I slept great. How was your weekend?"

She smiled. "It was good, thanks."

She'd wanted to ask her father about her mother the day before, but he hadn't shown up until late afternoon and he'd immediately sequestered himself in his office for most of the evening. He'd been quiet and introspective at dinner. She guessed he had a big case on his mind. He'd told her only a week earlier that he was about to sign off on a billion-dollar deal. She hadn't wanted to bother him then and had kept quiet about her sudden decision to search for her mother.

"How did the barbecue go?"

Her father's question interrupted her thoughts in an altogether unwelcome way. She immediately thought of Rafe. Heat crept over her cheeks. She hurriedly averted her face.

"Great," she managed. "It...went great. Sally-Ann and James have a precocious two-year-old and the cutest little baby. I also met some really interesting people."

"Good," her father replied. "Anyone I know?"

Once again, her thoughts zeroed in on Rafe. She'd thought about him all Sunday, even while she was supposed to be focused on finding her mother. She couldn't remember the last time she'd been so interested in a man. She only hoped the interest really was reciprocated. *How unfortunate it would be if the first man she'd felt attracted to in a long time wasn't the least bit interested in her.*

"There were a bunch of lawyers from Sydney Legal, mostly from Sally-Ann's department. And there were a few cops who work with James. I'm not sure if you'd know any of them."

With mug in hand, her father took a seat opposite her at the kitchen table. She spooned more cornflakes into her mouth and chewed slowly. Her father seemed like he was in a good mood and for the next few minutes, she had his attention. He spent so much time with his current girlfriend, she wouldn't know when he might be present like this again.

Perhaps now was the time to raise the subject of her mother? After all, her father was the best person to ask. He might even be able to help identify Sofia from the long list of possibilities Mallory had found on Facebook.

Taking a breath, she plunged in. "Dad, I've been thinking… I'd… I'd like to find my mother."

Choking and spluttering on his coffee, her father's mouth gaped. His eyes widened in concern. "I beg your pardon?"

Mallory forged on. "I can't stop thinking about it, Dad. I want to find my mother. I want to know why she left. I want to ask why she didn't bother to contact me, not even once. I'm her daughter! I deserve to know!"

The initial shock on her father's face faded and was replaced by resignation. "It's been twenty years, Mallory. Why now?"

Mallory sighed. "It sounds strange, I know. Twenty years is long time to let things go unanswered. What you don't know is that I've spent most of that time pushing everything that happened to the furthest reaches of my mind. I've even refused to allow myself to think about her, let alone wonder where she might be or why she left."

She paused and then continued. "The discovery of that woman's bones in the national park has triggered something inside me. She might have been someone's wife, mother, daughter… Who knows? The fact is, the police believe she's been missing for twenty years. All that time, no one knew where she was. I don't want the first news I receive of my mother to be a notification of her death. I want to know where she is, how she's been, I want to talk to her again. There're so many questions I want to ask."

Her father's eyes filled with compassion. "Oh, honey. I'm so sorry you've felt that way. I wish I'd known what you've been dealing with all these years. Your mother left because she didn't love either of us enough to stay. It still pains me to tell you that, but it's the truth. There's nothing she can tell you to change the way it was. I was there. I remember it like it was yesterday."

He reached over and patted her hand. She sent him a look to tell him she appreciated his wordless act of comfort.

"Sometimes we're better off not knowing the truth, honey," her father continued in a gentle tone. "Or at the very least, not having it tossed in our face by the person meant to love us the most. I want to protect you from that. I've *always* wanted to protect you from that. I know there's nothing your mother can say to make it right between you. It's the reason I haven't encouraged you to go and look for her. It's why I don't think this notion of yours is a good idea. I don't want her to hurt you anymore."

"I understand what you're saying, Dad, and I appreciate that even now, you're looking out for me, like you always have. But I still want to find her. I still want to hear her say it, offer an explanation, give me *something* to understand the reasons why she left and never came back."

Father shook his head slowly, his eyes full of sadness. "Oh, Mallory. I don't know what you want me to say. I thought I'd done a good job of raising you, of being both Mom and Dad. Now I discover you've found me lacking all these years. You've broken my heart."

Guilt surged through her at his words. She cried out in distress. "No, Dad! No, you're wrong! Please don't think you weren't enough. I know how much you love me and how hard you worked to compensate for the fact my mother left. It's not that you weren't enough..."

She struggled to make him understand. "It's more that there's been a part of me that's been empty ever since she left and nothing anybody does can fill it up. I need to talk to her."

Her father's expression closed. "I think you're on a foolhardy mission and I'm sorry, but I can't support you in this."

Tears burned behind Mallory's eyes. She blinked them away. This was what she'd been afraid of— hurting her father; hurting the one parent who loved her with all his heart. Still, now that the idea had taken root, she couldn't let it go. Determination surged through her.

"I'm going to find her, Dad. With or without your help. It sounds crazy and I'll probably drive myself around the bend and end up nowhere, but I have to try." She pleaded with her eyes for him to understand. "If there's any chance she's still alive, I have to find her. I need to know why she left."

Sudden anger ignited in her father's eyes. He banged his fist down hard on the table, startling her.

"Haven't you been listening? You *know* why she left!" he shouted.

The tears that had threatened now filled her eyes. "Right. She didn't love us enough to stay. I get it, Dad. But, the thing is... I... I need to hear her say it, Dad. I need to know if she ever thought about me at all... If she has any regrets..."

She was crying in earnest now. With the backs of her hands, she wiped the tears off her face. Her father sighed. All at once, his anger was gone. Pushing away from the table, he stood and gave her a hug. He pressed a soft kiss against her hair.

"I'm sorry, honey. I didn't mean to yell. I know this has been hard for you. Hell, it was hard for me, too. I might not have been an angel while your mother and I were together, but I still loved her. I was as devastated as you were when she left."

He sighed again. "I just don't want you to be disappointed, or hurt all over again. I assume by now she's made a new life for herself. She might even have another family. How will you feel if you discover she turned her back on you, only to start all over again, as if what she had with us didn't matter?"

Mallory hiccupped. Tears still blurred her vision. "I know what you're saying, Dad and I appreciate your concern. The thing is, I accepted a long time ago that Mom willingly abandoned me. It took me a long time to come to terms with that, but I think I have. That's no longer important. Having her say those words now…telling me she didn't love me enough to stay… They no longer have the power to hurt me. I've grown up knowing that's how she felt."

She paused and drew in a shaky breath. "I just want to know where she is, make contact, maybe call and talk to her every now and then. Is that too much to ask?"

"Oh, honey! I'm so sorry. I wish there was something I could do. I'm scared that confronting her might be worse than you could ever know. I don't have a good feeling about this. Why can't you leave things be?"

Mallory shook her head slowly, feeling more determined than ever. "I wish I could, Dad. But I can't. I have to know. Are you sure you won't help me?"

For a long moment, her father remained silent. He stared off into the distance. Finally, his shoulders slumped on a heavy sigh. As if weighed down by an anchor, he slowly regained his composure. When at last he looked at her, the expression in his eyes was bleak.

"I'm not sure there's anything I know that could help you, Mallory. I haven't seen or heard from your mother since she left."

Encouraged by his willingness to talk to her,

Mallory pressed forward. "You said you drove her to the airport. Do you know where she was going?"

"As far as I know, she was going back to Argentina. To her family. At least, that's what she said. Who knows if that was the truth?"

"Did you ever meet any of her family?"

"No. She came out to Australia on her own."

"Tell me again how you met."

A smile slowly transformed her father's face. "We met in college. She was an international student studying medicine. I was studying law. I spotted her in a crowd. It wasn't hard. The bright red hair. Just like yours." He smiled at her fondly.

"And you fell in love the instant you laid eyes on each other," Mallory finished, having heard the story many times before.

Her father winked. "Of course. Who wouldn't? She was the most beautiful woman I'd ever seen."

"But you didn't get married right away, did you?"

"No. We couldn't afford to. We were both students, struggling to pay our college fees and keep a roof over our heads."

"Then I came along and that changed everything," Mallory said.

"Yes, then you came along. Your mother came to me on the eve of my graduation to tell me she was pregnant."

"You were thrilled, of course." Mallory grinned.

"Of course. We still didn't have much money, but I'd managed to get an internship at Sydney Legal and your mother was accepted into the

Sydney Harbour Hospital's new graduate program. We were doing okay.

"We found a little place in Stanmore, not far from the city. Back then, it wasn't the trendy suburb it is today, but it was convenient to the hospital and to my work—and best of all, it was affordable."

He paused. "We didn't have a lot of money, but we had some good times." His eyes became distant, as if he was caught up in his memories.

"What happened?" Mallory asked softly.

Her father shrugged, his expression filled with sadness. "Life, I guess. I was working long hours. We both were. You spent more time in childcare centers than you did at home. We were both bright and ambitious and worked hard in our quest to climb to the top. We were earning more money than we thought possible. In five short years, I'd made junior partner."

"You put so much effort into your careers, you forgot about each other," Mallory murmured.

"Yes. I often worked late. Your mother did her share of night shifts, too. We barely saw each other. I was lonely."

"So you had an affair." Mallory tried to keep the accusation from her voice, but wasn't completely successful.

Her father raised his hands in surrender. "Yes. I had an affair. Michelle was my secretary. In my defense, I spent more time with her than I did my wife. She was young, attractive and eager. She wanted me. I'm not making excuses for my behavior, but we all need to feel wanted, loved."

"Don't you mean your ego needed that?" Mallory asked with a caustic edge to her voice. She knew all about her father's past infidelities, but they still upset her. She couldn't help but think if he'd remained faithful to her mother, maybe she'd have stayed with them.

No, it was futile thinking like that and unfair to her father. After all, he was the one who'd stayed behind to raise her, to love her, to give her everything she had. The devastation she'd experienced growing up without a mother wasn't on him.

She sighed quietly. "So she never tried to call you, or write?"

Her father's expression filled with resignation. "I wish I could tell you differently, but no, honey. The truth is, she never did."

CHAPTER 6

A knock on her office door brought Mallory a welcome distraction from the files that were piled high on her desk. She looked up and saw Sally-Ann fill the opening and smiled.

"Hi, there. What brings you down here?"

Sally-Ann specialized in children's court matters. Her team of dedicated lawyers all had offices on the tenth floor.

She smiled back at Mallory. "Oh, I thought I'd slum it down here for a while with you family law attorneys. You could probably do with a break from the endless bickering you must endure, and I'm not just talking about your clients."

Mallory grimaced. "Yes, you have that right. Their lawyers are just as bad. No one wants to give an inch. It always shocks me how two people who at some point declared undying love for each other now want to tear each other to shreds. There's no such thing as a win in the family law arena. By the time I get to see the client, they're already at the point where they don't want their ex-spouse to get a single penny and we both know that's beyond realistic."

She sighed and set aside the file she had open on her desk. "But enough of that. I'm sure you didn't drop by to listen to me moan about the quality of my clients. What can I do for you?"

Sally-Ann moved closer to Mallory's desk and sat in the vacant chair opposite. "Well," she said, dragging out the consonants. "I just had a phone call from my husband."

Mallory shrugged, failing to see the significance of Sally-Ann's announcement. "Okay. How is James?"

"He's fine. Busy at work. You know how it is."

"Oh yeah," Mallory said dryly. "Don't I ever. Just like the rest of us with our noses to the grindstone. One day is pretty much the same as the next, right? Oh, by the way, thank you again for having me over on Saturday night. I had a great time. Your kids are adorable and it was a really nice crowd, don't you think?"

Sally-Ann grinned at her knowingly. "As a matter of fact, I do. That's why I'm here."

Mallory frowned in confusion. "Sorry, I'm not following."

"Remember Rafe Connelly? He was at the barbecue."

Heat immediately rushed across Mallory's cheeks. Of course she remembered Rafe Connelly. Playing it cool, she kept her voice casual.

"Rafe Connelly… Yes, I remember him. The detective I first met outside the courthouse. The one you invited over for me to meet…again."

Sally-Ann laughed. "Good. I'm glad you remember him because he certainly remembers you."

Butterflies fluttered in Mallory's belly. "He does?"

"Yep. In fact, he asked James for your number."

The nerves in Mallory's belly intensified. Her blush deepened. All she could do was smile.

"He did?"

Sally-Ann's grin turned triumphant. "He absolutely did. See? I told you he looked interested. How about that? Am I the best matchmaker in the world, or what?"

Mallory grinned ruefully. She was thrilled Rafe had asked for her number. "Yes, Sally-Ann, you might very well be. We'll have to wait and see."

Sally-Ann *whooped* her excitement. "So you're okay if I let him have your number?"

Mallory took a moment to consider. "Yes," she said, nodding slowly. "I am."

"Yay! So the fact he has a daughter isn't a deal breaker?"

"No, not at all. I met Charlotte at the barbeque. She's a nice kid."

Sally-Ann squealed in delight. "Oh, I don't believe it! The two of you are just going to be perfect together! I just know it! I'll call James back right away and pass on your details. I wonder when Rafe might call you? *Ooh*, I hope it's soon."

Mallory rolled her eyes and grinned at her friend. "Okay, Mrs Matchmaker, are you done now? I have a heap of work to do."

Sally-Ann stood and smoothed down her skirt. "Oh, yes. I'm done. I got exactly what I came for!"

With a wink, she turned on her heel and sashayed across the room toward the exit. She paused a few feet from the door and turned back to face Mallory.

"Oh, how did you do with your search and rescue mission? Any progress?"

Mallory frowned. "You mean, the search for my mom?"

"Yes. Did you have any luck finding her online?"

Mallory shook her head. "Not yet, but the good news is, Dad's onboard to help me."

Sally-Ann's dark eyebrows flew upwards in surprise. "So he wasn't as put out about the whole thing as you feared?"

Mallory grimaced. "He wasn't exactly thrilled when I first told him, but he's come round. He's happy to share whatever he knows with me—which unfortunately, isn't much."

Sally-Ann shot her a sympathetic look. "Well, hopefully his information might lead somewhere. I can understand how you want to know what happened to her and where she is. I'd feel the same way. Good luck with it, okay?"

Looking at her friend, Mallory was filled with a rush of emotion. It was nice to know she had the support of people she counted on.

"Thanks, Sal. I really appreciate it."

Sally-Ann grinned wickedly. "You'll appreciate me even more when you receive a call from a certain hot detective. Your love life is about to heat up!"

Mallory merely laughed and shook her head. Sally-Ann waved good-bye with a jaunty jiggle of her fingers. She opened the door and closed it quietly behind her.

Mallory blew her breath out on a sigh. From the moment she'd arrived at work that Monday morning, she hadn't had a second to contemplate furthering the search for her mother. The work on her desk had kept her fully occupied, not to mention a number of phone calls that had come in. In fact, she hadn't even thought about her mother until now.

She bit her lip, wondering silently if she was wasting her time. *What if she ran into a dead end? How long was she prepared to spend finding a mother who might or might not want to be found?* People who didn't want to be found could stay hidden forever.

That thought sparked another: *Had her father ever tried to discover her mother's whereabouts?* He was under the impression she'd returned to her home country, but had he ever tried to contact her there? Ask her how she was? Or asked her to return?

Mallory understood that he didn't want to hurt her and she would have been hurt if she'd known he'd begged her mother to return only to have the woman refuse, but had he conducted any enquires in secret? He was a man of means. He could afford to hire a private investigator. Perhaps he'd done all that and had come up empty—or worse, found his runaway wife only to be told again their life together was over. It would be like reopening a wound barely healed over.

Was that the reason he'd told her he hadn't

had any contact with her mother? Even after all these years? Sadness and disappointment lodged like a rock in her belly, hard and unyielding. Was she going on a wild goose chase? If her mother really wanted a relationship with her daughter, she could have reached out long before this. After all, they still lived in the home Mallory had been born in. It wasn't like Sofia didn't know where to find them. And yet, she'd chosen to keep her distance.

The knowledge filled Mallory with pain, but it was an old and familiar pain that she'd grown used to over the years. This was the first time she'd given serious consideration to finding her mother and demanding answers. Was she hell-bent on a path of self-destruction? Would it be best to do as her father advised and leave things well enough alone? Could she live the rest of her life without knowing anything more about her mother? What about when she had children? Could she bear the thought of their grandmother never knowing anything about them, even their very existence?

The questions kept coming and with each one, there were no answers. Hell, she didn't even have children, and that wasn't likely to change any time soon. It wasn't that she didn't want to be a mother, but it still took two for that to happen. She wasn't the kind of woman who sought out the services of a sperm bank. Having grown up without one of her parents, she wouldn't willingly do that to her child.

Thoughts of Rafe crept into her mind, unbidden. Good-looking, smart, and a secure job made him perfect father material. Besides, it was obvious he was devoted to his daughter. At her age, he probably could have left her at home while he went out and enjoyed time with his friends. Instead, he'd brought her with him and had been considerate of her needs.

They seemed to have a good relationship and that wasn't easy these days. Mallory should know. She spent enough time talking to the children of her clients. Kids didn't always get on with their parents. In fact, most often, it was quite the opposite.

On top of that, Rafe was doing the parenting thing all on his own. Charlotte had mentioned her mother died when she was three. It must have been tough for Rafe. Grieving the loss of his wife while being forced on his own to take on the responsibility of a young child. Her respect and admiration for him went up another notch.

She wondered what Mrs Connelly had died from. The woman had obviously been young. Had it been cancer? A car accident? Or something even more tragic, like being trapped inside a house fire... Mallory couldn't think of anything worse.

And then she shook her head and forced her thoughts in another direction. Whatever the cause of Rafe's wife's death, it was of no business of hers. If he chose to tell her the details sometime down the track, then so be it. Until then, she'd keep her curiosity in check. And hope like hell he called.

———————————

Leaning across his balcony, Rafe barely noticed the light breeze that lifted his hair and caressed his cheek like a lover's touch. In his hands, he held the piece of paper James had given him. It had Mallory Patterson's number on it. He'd folded it in half and half again and had lost count of the number of times he'd stared down at those digits and willed himself to call her.

One thing that gave him some reassurance was the fact Sally-Ann had asked Mallory for permission to give him her number. It meant she knew he had it. He'd had it for two days, in fact. Two whole days in which he'd gone over the pros and cons about what taking the next step would mean as he tried to work up the courage to call her. Now he was hiding out on his balcony with his phone so Charli couldn't hear.

He blew out his breath on a nervous sigh. He wiped sweaty palms against his jeans. He didn't have much practice asking girls out. In fact, the last time he'd properly asked someone out he was in high school. Even then, he'd stammered and stumbled until Khloe eventually took pity on him and agreed to go out with him even before he'd gotten all the words out. That scene was embarrassing to recall now.

He was only eighteen when Charli was born. Overnight, his social life had come to an end. Khloe took off within days of Charli's birth and he was literally left holding the baby. Then Khloe died and even though they were no longer together, it had been a tremendous shock. He knew then that he was the only parent his little girl would likely know.

Between him and his mother and his younger sister, the three of them had raised Charli together and he was proud of the job they'd done. She was a super kid, smart, pretty and kind. He wished his mum and Breanna were around to see it...

No sense going there... Nothing was going to bring them back. It was a good reminder of how short life was. Both his mother and his sister had been taken away well before their time. He should be outing aside past hurts and disappointments and making the most of every day. After all, he'd promised his mother exactly that as she lay in that hospital bed, dying from cancer.

A surge of determination went through him. He'd make good on his promise. Starting right now. With a deep breath, he tugged out his phone and dialed Mallory's number.

Seated on the sofa in the living room with the night gently folding around her, Mallory stared down at the old photographs of her mother spread across the coffee table. Her father had left a message on her voicemail telling her he wouldn't be home tonight. Though she missed his presence, the solitude also gave her the opportunity to pull out the photo album and immerse herself in the few memories she had of her mother, something she was loathe to do when he was around. Looking at the photos, she recognized herself in her mother's features and, of course, there was no mistaking the bright red hair.

Each photo represented a fleeting snapshot of their time together, but little by little, Mallory's memories were fading. She couldn't remember the smell of her mother's perfume or the sound of her laughter. Had it been loud and contagious, or something softer and more subdued? Maybe there hadn't been too much laughter in the last few months she'd lived there? Maybe that was the reason Mallory couldn't recall it.

Whatever the reason, it saddened her to know there would be other things she was bound to forget as the years went on until the woman in the photographs was nothing more than a stranger from her past...

The sound of her phone ringing interrupted her thoughts. She glanced at the screen. It was a blocked number. She was tempted to ignore it. After all, anyone who couldn't reveal their number was probably someone she didn't need to speak to. Then she remembered Sally-Ann asking if she could pass along her number to Rafe.

Rafe.

The hot detective; smart and kind, who loved his daughter beyond measure.

Rafe.

The man who made her pulse leap and her mind spin with possibilities.

Rafe.

The man with whom she felt an instant spark of attraction and she knew firsthand how rare that was.

Dammit. She answered the call.

"This is Mallory."

"Mallory. It's Rafe. Rafe Connelly. We spoke at the Shepherd barbeque on the weekend."

Her heart skipped a beat at the sound of his voice. Deep, masculine, husky... It sent shivers of desire down her spine. *Oh yes, there was definitely a spark...*

"Of course! Rafe! H-how are you?"

"I'm fine. I hope you don't mind me calling. Sally-Ann gave me your number."

"No, no. Of course not. She told me you'd asked for it. I was...happy to give it."

"Great." There was a pause and then he said, "Umm... I was wondering...if you'd like to...go to dinner?"

Mallory's heart leaped and her belly flooded with nerves. She should play it cool, make him sweat, make him wonder. *What the heck?* She was already thirty. She liked him. And he seemed to like her, too. He'd asked for her number, hadn't he? And now he'd asked her out. There was no time to waste.

"I'd love to," she replied.

"Great. Seven at Ally's on George tomorrow night? Is that all right?"

She heard the relief in his voice and bit back a smile. He'd mentioned the name of a popular French restaurant in the city. If there was one thing Mallory loved, it was French cuisine.

"It sounds good. What about Charlotte?"

"Charli should be fine. She has dance rehearsal until eight. One of the mothers of her friends has offered to drop her home. I'll have my neighbor check in on her afterwards."

It seemed he had everything sorted. She liked that he'd taken care of arrangements ahead of time. It showed a degree of confidence and that was one trait she liked in a man.

"Okay," she replied. "I guess I'll see you then."

"Great. I'm looking forward to it," he said.

Rafe ended the call and couldn't hold back a wide grin. A thrill of excitement raced along his veins. *He'd asked Mallory Patterson out to dinner and she'd accepted!* He couldn't remember the last time he'd felt so good.

"Who was that?"

He turned and spied Charlotte standing just inside the doorway that led out to the balcony. Despite himself, he blushed.

What the hell? He had nothing to hide. He was determined to be honest with her. He cleared his throat.

"I was speaking to Mallory Patterson. You remember her?"

Charlotte nodded. "The lawyer from the barbecue, right? With the red hair?"

"Yes."

"Do you like her?"

Rafe blushed again and was pleased for the dimness that hid the color that heated his cheeks.

"So, do you?" Charli insisted.

Rafe contemplated his answer for a couple of seconds and then responded. "Yes."

"Cool. Are going out with her?"

He held Charli's gaze. "Yes. Is that okay?"

She grinned. "Of course it's okay!"

He smiled with relief. Charli came all the way outside and gave him a hug. "I've been telling you forever to start dating, Dad. You've been on your own for far too long."

A wave of love and tenderness washed over him. He hugged her close. "I want to be there for my little girl."

She gave him an exaggerated eye roll. "Dad, I'm *thirteen*. I'm no longer a little girl. I'm quite capable of taking care of myself. *You're* the one I worry about. You work so hard. Who takes care of you?"

Tears burned behind his eyes. He couldn't believe she was his, this angel. She'd been born so little, underweight as a result of her mother's drug use. For a few days, the doctors weren't sure she'd survive. But she was a fighter and he loved her with all his heart. He pressed a kiss on her forehead, his chest tight with emotion.

"Thanks for your concern, baby, but I don't need anyone taking care of me. I've been doing it for a long time now."

Her expression remained somber. "Yes, but for a long time you had Grandma. It's been three years, Dad. Three years since she died and left you alone."

"I'm not alone!" He protested. "I have you."

"Of course you do, but you need another adult,

someone you can talk to like adults do. You used to talk to Grandma, but ever since she's been gone... Who *do* you talk to?"

Rafe averted his eyes from her much-too-knowing gaze. "I don't need anyone to talk to, baby."

"Of course you do, Dad. Everyone does," she insisted.

He shook his head, unable to believe how mature she was or how insightful and sensitive to his needs. The truth was, she was right. He was lonely. It had been so long since he'd had a girlfriend, a partner to share his day, his life; someone he could love. Not since Khloe, had he felt anything close to that and it was only after Khloe had dumped him so spectacularly that he realized what they'd shared hadn't been love at all.

They'd been two desperate teenagers, both trying to escape violent homes. They'd come together out of necessity and had mistaken comfort and an element of safety and security for love. He could see that now. On some level he'd always known it.

Khloe's suicide three years after their daughter was born had shocked him, and saddened him to the core, but it had also filled him with a determination to do all he could for his little girl. He'd vowed there and then, standing over Khloe's grave, that his daughter would know every day of her life she was loved and wanted and he'd never, *ever* stray down the path his father had.

His father.

Michael Connelly. The huge bear of a man who could out drink and out fight anyone who was stupid enough to take him on. As Rafe knew all too well… His gut tensed with remembered anxiety. Hiding in his darkened bedroom, waiting for his father to arrive home; he'd waited for the inevitable explosion…

With a conscious effort, he thrust the bad memories aside and forced his fists to relax. His daughter knew nothing of her grandfather and that's the way it would stay. Rafe hadn't set eyes on his father since he was fifteen and he darn well liked it that way. For all he knew, the man was dead.

Good riddance.

CHAPTER 7

Mallory checked her watch and cursed under her breath. *She was late.* If Rafe was punctual, he'd been at the restaurant at least ten minutes. To some people, ten minutes off the mark might not even register as late, but for Mallory who prided herself on her punctuality and took it as a personal insult if people disrespected her time by being late, it was a big deal.

She reached the restaurant and pushed open the door, breathless from the quick pace she'd maintained for more than a block. Traffic was heavy and she'd asked the cab driver to drop her off almost half a mile from where she needed to be. She was sure she'd make it faster on foot. Now she did her best to catch her breath and straighten her jacket and hair and try and make it look like she hadn't just almost galloped the distance.

She spied him at a table on the far side of the room. He was dressed in another casual polo shirt coupled this time with tan chinos. His hair was still wet, as if fresh from the shower. It curled around his ears in a way that made her fingers itch to touch it. She silently scolded herself.

As if sensing her scrutiny, he looked up and smiled. The motion crinkled his eyes. Her heart skipped a beat. He was so good looking… And then he stood and waited for her to make her way to his side, pulling out her chair as she reached him.

Good manners and good looks. Could he get any better?

She took a seat and waited for him to return to his seat across from her. "I'm so sorry I'm late," she started without preamble. "I got caught up at work. As you can see, I didn't even have time to go home and change. My case ran overtime and when I got back to the office, I had a client waiting to see me. It was just one of those days. I'm sorry."

He laughed away her apology. "Hey, don't sweat it. I know how work can get in the way. I'm sure it was important."

She grimaced. "I wish I could say I was busy seeking justice like you, but I'm a family law attorney. It's never as noble as that. In fact, justice is often the last thing I achieve."

"Hey, I'm just happy to see you. I thought for a moment I might have been stood up."

He followed his comment with a chuckle, but she could see the vulnerability in his eyes. For all his good looks and confidence, this man was still as uncertain about her as she was about him. Okay, so they'd accepted that they liked each other, but where did they go from here?

She made a sound of annoyance in the back of her throat and silently admonished herself. This was their first date. They were a long way from even thinking about forever. She needed to relax and let it happen. If she came on too strong, she'd frighten him off.

"Of course I wasn't going to stand you up. I'm glad to be here."

He smiled in relief. The waiter appeared and took their orders. A glass of house red for Mallory and a Budweiser for Rafe. They both skipped the appetizers and went straight for a main.

"I want to leave room for dessert," Mallory explained.

Rafe's eyes twinkled with good humor. "Ah, a woman after my own heart."

"What's your favorite dessert?" she asked.

"Crème brulée. And yours?"

She took a moment to think about it. She had a terrible sweet tooth. She'd forgo a main meal for a dessert every time.

"I think it's a toss-up between tiramisu and crepe suzette with lashings of cream and ice cream."

His eyebrows rose. A teasing light glinted in his baby blues. "Cream *and* ice cream? That's beyond decadent."

"You've got that right. I'm a woman who *loooves* her dessert."

His gaze roved over her. Taking his time, he examined her from head to toe and back again.

Heat blazed in a trail that followed the passage of his gaze. Her nipples tightened under his scrutiny.

"You don't look like a woman who spends every meal eating dessert."

The desire in his eyes ignited a corresponding need deep inside her. Flustered, she lowered her gaze and tried to think of something to say.

"S-so, how was your day?"

The teasing expression in his eyes told her he knew exactly why she'd changed the subject. Once again, a shiver of need ran down her spine. It was madness to be so instantly attracted to a man she barely knew, but there wasn't a thing she could do about it.

"It was busy," he replied with a smile. "Working in homicide always is. Although perhaps not quite as busy as the drug squad."

"How are you doing with the unidentified bones?"

Mallory fought to keep her voice casual, but she waited on edge for his answer. No matter how much she told herself the woman couldn't possibly be her mother, she was driven to find out for sure.

"We don't have any leads as yet. No one's come forward to claim her. We're putting together a 3D picture of what we think she might have looked like. That picture will then go out in the media—newspapers, TV, online. Hopefully someone might recognize her."

Mallory tilted her head to one side, intrigued. "How do you know what she might have looked like? You only have bones, right?"

"Right. But we have this thing called FaceFit. It's an amazing new technology. We can enter the data we have, such as facial measurements, DNA and other information and the computer generates an image."

"That sounds fascinating. How accurate is it?"

"It's remarkably accurate. Using the technology we've managed to identify a considerable number of people who otherwise might have remained nameless forever. It helps to give people closure, supply answers that are long overdue." He shook his head slowly. "It's changed peoples' lives."

"Wow," Mallory breathed, duly impressed. "Are you able to use this technology to determine what a person might look like now if they were still alive?"

"What do you mean?"

Mallory paused. *Was she ready to disclose to this man who was almost a stranger one of the greatest secrets of her life? Could she trust him with the information?* She almost laughed. He was a law enforcement officer. He knew all about keeping secrets and maintaining confidentiality, just like she did.

The fact was, Rafe might be able to help her. As a detective, he had access to so much more than she did. He might be able to track down her mother through other means that were completely out of her reach. *Could she afford to turn her back on such a possibility?* Coming to a conclusion, she drew in a deep breath and told him about her mother.

They'd finished their main meal and were halfway through dessert before she finished. Rafe looked at her with understanding and compassion. His response brought tears to her eyes. Here was a man who was sensitive to her feelings, who listened without interruption, who didn't judge. From time to time he asked her a question, but for the most part, he let her speak.

"I know this body can't be my mother, but I just can't help wondering what happened to her. I want to find her. Fortunately, with the arrival of the Internet, the world isn't such a big place anymore."

Rafe nodded. "The Internet is a great place to start."

Mallory told him about the hours she'd spent searching through the social media sites. In some cases, there were no photographs of the account holder, making it impossible to know if it was the Sofia Lopez she sought.

Rafe took a mouthful of crème brulee and swallowed it before replying. "If you're willing to come down to the station and fill in a missing person's report, I could help you."

Her eyes widened. She'd hoped he'd make such an offer, but it still came as a nice surprise. After all, he didn't owe her any favors. It was just another indication of how sweet and kind he was.

"Really?"

He nodded. "Yes. I can't do anything unless you lodge an official report, but once you do that, I can search through databases, issue search warrants on bank accounts—all the usual stuff. I can probably do more to find her than you can, although the social media sites are definitely a good start. We use them, too."

Warmth filled her belly. She stared at him. Excitement filled her veins. With Rafe's expertise in her corner, she had a real chance of finding her mother, of finally getting the answers she needed. And it all came down to the man who sat across from her looking more delectable than any man had a right to.

She wanted to kiss him.

Not just because of his offer to help her, but because of *him*. She wanted to touch him, to taste him, to get to know every inch of him. Her feelings were so foreign they confused her, but at the same time, she couldn't deny they were exciting and real.

Without thinking, she leaned closer. Her mouth opened and her tongue stole out. She nervously wet her lips. Rafe's eyes darkened with desire. His gaze fixed on her mouth. The emotions he evoked were so erotic, she could barely catch her breath, felt overwhelmed by them.

Almost in slow motion, Rafe moved until his lips were almost touching hers. Their breaths mingled while hearts pounded. Eyes dilated with need. She closed the slight distance between them and brushed her lips against his. The sensation was electrifying.

Then reason stepped forward and in a torrent of heat and confusion, she pulled back. Embarrassment flamed across her cheeks.

"I-I'm sorry. I shouldn't have done that," she

stammered. She could barely bring herself to look at him.

"Don't be sorry," came his soft reply. "I wanted to kiss you, too."

Her gaze tangled with his. The desire that turned her insides to mush was reflected in his eyes. She bit her lip in an effort to stem the turmoil.

"Is it too soon?" he asked.

She gave a jerky nod. "Probably. Yes. But I like you, Rafe Connelly. I like you far more than I should."

Once again, his eyes darkened with emotion, but apart from a single nod, he remained silent. A few moments later, he signaled to the waiter and asked for the bill. He held out her chair while she stood and then helped her with her jacket.

"It's a nice evening. Would you care to take a walk along the harbor?"

Mallory smiled. She was also loathe to see the night come to an end. "That would be lovely."

Rafe took her hand and led her out of the restaurant. It felt so natural, walking side by side, her hand in his. They walked the rest of the way down George Street until they came to the boardwalk that ran alongside Circular Quay. The water lapped gently at the wharf. The smell of salt filled the air. Despite the late hour, there were still diners in the restaurants that littered the pier. Laughter, conversation and the tinkle of glassware filled the night.

"Thank you for dinner, Rafe. It was lovely. And thank you for listening to me for so long. I didn't mean to go on about my mother, and to tell you the truth, I've managed to avoid thinking about her for a lot of the past twenty years, but there was something about the article I read in the paper about the bones found in the national park that triggered something inside me. I couldn't help thinking about the woman—how she was someone's wife, mother, sister, friend... Someone has been missing her all these years and finally they get to know where she is and what happened to her. They get answers. It's something I've been denied for so long."

She turned to him. "Is it wrong of me to want to know why my mother abandoned me? Why she couldn't bring herself to contact me, not even once? I was a child! She must have known what it would be like for me to have my mother leave without so much as a good-bye? How could she do that to me?"

To her embarrassment, her voice broke with emotion. Tears burned in her eyes. Rafe stepped forward and took her in his arms, pressing her close against the warm strength of his chest. Being held by him should have felt strange and unfamiliar, but instead she felt like she was home. It was a feeling she'd never had before.

She wanted so much to lift her head and kiss him once again, but things were moving way too fast. She might feel like she'd known him forever, but the truth was, she hadn't. They needed to slow things down, take their time, get to know each other. If what she felt for him was real, they owed it to one another to take it slow and savor every moment.

As if sensing her thoughts, Rafe pressed a kiss against her hair and tightened his arms around her. He held her in silence as they stared out across the water, surrounded by the sounds of the night.

Rafe stared at the computer screen in front of him and tried to concentrate. He was already onto his third cup of coffee and had just been handed a new case, but his thoughts kept returning to Mallory. He'd spent most of the night tossing and turning, re-living their evening. Their date.

Their date. Yes, that's exactly what it had been. He'd asked a woman out on a date and she'd enjoyed it as much as he had—at least, that's what she told him when he dropped her off outside a beautifully restored circa 1920s bungalow at an equally impressive eastern suburbs address.

She explained the house belonged to her father and appeared only slightly embarrassed when she admitted she still lived at home.

"Hey, you don't need to justify your living arrangements to me." He laughed. "I'd take this place over my aging terrace house in the inner west any day."

She smiled at him and it turned his insides into mush. Then she leaned across the gearstick and pecked him on the cheek.

"Thank you again for dinner, Rafe. I had a lovely evening." And with that, she climbed out of his SUV and disappeared up the cobblestone path that led to the front door.

Rafe stared after her, his body aflame. The feel of her lips on his was seared into his mind. Her sweet perfume still lingered on the air. It was a long time afterwards that he finally cleared his senses enough to drive home.

She'd provided him with her mother's basic details: full name, date of birth and address. She'd also given him a photograph she fished out of her purse. He'd been taken aback by Mallory's likeness to her mother.

"This was taken twenty years ago on the day of my tenth birthday," she told him. It was the last time she'd seen her mother.

He assured her he'd take care of the photo. As soon as he got to work, he copied it and tucked the original into the pocket of his jacket. He'd return it to her the next time he saw her. It would give him an excuse to see her again.

Earlier, she'd telephoned him to confirm she'd attended the police station and had filed a missing person's report, giving him the authority he needed to get started on the search. Now, instead of dealing with the new case his boss had handed to him that morning, he was using his time to dig into her mother's past.

He could have passed the matter off to the missing person's unit. In fact, that's probably what he should have done. He was a homicide detective. Locating a missing person wasn't in his job description. But this was Mallory's mother. He didn't want to hand it over to anyone else.

He dragged his keyboard toward him and ran Sofia Lopez Patterson through the police database. He wasn't surprised when he didn't get any hits. It told him she was a law abiding citizen with no prior arrests. The next thing to do was to check with immigration about whether she'd left the country when Mallory thought she did. He reached for his phone and put in a call. After being put on hold for what seemed an interminable amount of time, he was finally transferred to someone who could help him.

He relayed the details of his request and was assured it would be dealt with as soon as possible. When he pressed for a more specific timeline, he was given the usual spiel about being short staffed, a lack of resources, et cetera et cetera. It was the same for every government department. He held onto his patience and thanked the woman for her assistance before ending the call.

The next step was to contact Interpol. Unfortunately, he didn't have the necessary clearance to call Interpol directly. But Clayton Munro did. Clayton was an officer in the elite Australian Federal Police force and also a good friend. They'd met through mutual police acquaintances and had cemented their friendship when Clayton had presented a workshop in Sydney about getting into the mind of a serial killer.

As a New South Wales homicide detective, Rafe had attended the conference. He and Clayton had renewed their friendship and had spent time bonding over beer. Though they didn't see each other often, he was sure Clayton would be willing to help him out, if he could.

To his relief, Clayton answered his phone on the second ring.

"Detective Superintendent Clayton Munro."

"Superintendent, is it now? Somehow I missed that. Clayton, it's Rafe Connelly. How are you?"

"Rafe! How're you doing? I haven't heard from you in years! What's going on, mate?"

"Oh, busy as usual trying my best to put the bad guys away, only to have the courts give them a slap on the wrist. You know how it is."

"For sure," Clayton commiserated. "Nothing ever changes."

"So...Superintendent? Wow! That has a nice ring to it. Congratulations on the promotion!"

In his usual humble way, Clayton brushed off Rafe's admiration and downplayed his recent promotion. Rafe would have none of that. No one got promoted to superintendent without just cause. He was sure Clayton had earned the prestigious award. After spending a bit more time swapping stories of their lives, including the fact one of Clayton's kids was now in high school, Rafe got to the point.

"Listen, mate. I was wondering if you'd do me a favor. I need to track down a missing person. The best information I have is that she departed Australia twenty years ago. I'm waiting on immigration to confirm that, but in the meantime, I thought I might get Interpol involved. They might be able to shed more light on her movements."

"Of course. Happy to help," Clayton replied. "Where was she headed?"

"Argentina."

Rafe heard Clayton's sigh on the other end of the phone. "Is that a problem?" he asked.

Clayton sighed again. "Unfortunately, the South American authorities are notorious for being rather slow to take action on this kind of enquiry. They're hesitant to look into the lives of private citizens."

"Afraid of what they might dig up?" Rafe asked dryly.

"You guessed it. But put in the request and we'll see how we go. I can't promise anything, though."

"I understand. And thanks, Clayton. I appreciate it."

"Don't mention it, mate. We'll have to catch up for a drink. It's been too long."

"Yeah. For sure. Let's do that. Call me when you're free. I kind of like the idea of having a drink with a superintendent."

With Clayton's chuckle ringing in his ears, Rafe ended the call. He looked up in time to see James coming toward him, coffee mug in hand. He came to a stop beside Rafe's desk.

"How's it going?" James asked.

"Good, mate. I was just talking to a buddy at the AFP. A friend of mine asked me to look into the disappearance of her mother. She was last known to be heading overseas. I've put in a request for the AFP to contact Interpol. See if she shows up anywhere."

"How long has she been missing?"

"Twenty years."

James' eyebrows rose. "And your friend is only now starting to look for her?"

Rafe shrugged and averted his gaze. "People have their reasons."

James's gaze slid to the photocopied picture of Sofia Patterson nee Lopez which Rafe had left lying face up on his desk. He cursed beneath his breath.

A knowing grin tugged at James' lips. "This friend wouldn't happen to be one very delectable family law lawyer, would it?"

Despite himself, Rafe blushed. He couldn't help it. Though thoughts of Mallory had consumed him since their date, he wasn't ready to share his interest in her with anyone—not even his partner.

He liked her and she liked him. Her kiss had set him on fire. *But would it lead to anything permanent?* He didn't know yet and until he did, he'd keep their budding relationship to himself.

Picking up Sofia's photo, he turned it over and changed the subject. "So, how are you doing with Jane Doe?"

The expression on James' face told Rafe his partner knew exactly what he was doing, but to Rafe's relief, James didn't press. Instead, he stood and began to pace slowly back and forth in front of Rafe's desk as he updated him on his progress.

"I've spent the past few days going through our list of missing persons. I've managed to narrow them down to fourteen. All of our MPs have DNA samples on record, collected from various personal items when the initial missing persons' reports were made. We need to compare these

DNA results to the DNA extracted from Jane Doe. That will narrow things down fairly quickly."

"Good," Rafe responded. "How soon do we expect the results?"

"I called the lab earlier this morning. They're backlogged as usual, but they hope to have something to us in the next couple of weeks."

"I guess that will have to do. I'm heading to the morgue later this afternoon to meet with Samantha Wolfe. She's been working with an embalmer and an artist on the FaceFit image. She expects to have something we can use before the end of the week."

James nodded. "Great. Then we'll have something to give to the newspapers."

"Yeah. Between what you're doing to match our woman up to known missing persons and the FaceFit image, we might just get Jane Doe identified. Maybe as early as next week."

"Good. Although I guess there's no real hurry. Whoever this woman is, she's been missing for twenty years. Another week isn't going to make much difference."

Rafe nodded in agreement. Sliding the photocopied picture of Mallory's mother into a file, he pushed away from his desk and reached for his jacket.

James lifted his coffee mug in salute. "Here's cheers to coming up with an identification, partner." He winked. "On both counts." With that, he turned and headed toward his desk.

CHAPTER 8

Mallory glanced at her watch and swallowed a sigh. She'd been sitting in the courtroom for most of the morning, waiting with her client for their turn to be heard by the judge. Daniel Stone's estranged wife and her legal team sat on the opposite side. Tension was thick in the air. Neither party was looking at the other. The whereabouts of the twins was unknown. Mallory wondered if their parents would have behaved any differently if the children were there, witnesses to the petty games their parents insisted on playing.

The thought of separating the twins still filled Mallory with horror. *What kind of parent would do that to a child?* It was a move calculated to hurt, only it wasn't just the adults involved who'd be maimed.

Mallory was an only child, but she could imagine what it would be like to be separated from a sibling, and a twin, at that. It was cruel and unusual punishment and she could see why the court refused to support it.

They'd been summoned with the intention of bringing the parties together to see reason. The success or failure of that was yet to be seen. It would be handy to have their case called before the day was over, that was for sure. She had a pile of things to do at work.

"Stone versus Michaels," the clerk called.

Mallory got to her feet and made her way to the bar table. She motioned toward her client for him to take a seat behind her. His father watched on, grim-faced, from the public gallery.

Nerves fluttered in Mallory's stomach. She'd done this kind of hearing hundreds of times before, but never under so much pressure or such close scrutiny from a client who was altogether hostile. It was Rupert Arthur Andrew Stone who'd insisted she come back on board as their attorney. Daniel Stone, the twins' father hadn't been given a say. It was obvious her hefty bills were being paid for by his father. Knowing she didn't have her client's full support made her uncomfortable.

Still, she was there to do a job and she'd do it to the best of her ability and if her client continued to refuse the court's instructions, who was she to blame? In the meantime, she'd console herself with memories of her date with Rafe.

Even the thought of him brought a smile to her face. He was so good and kind and gentle. He'd listened to her pour her heart out and he'd offered his support. To top it off, he was drop-dead gorgeous and got her heart racing like no other man had. What was there not to like? He was perfect. And she was almost certain he felt the same way about her. If it weren't for the dark shadows surrounding the whereabouts of her mother, she'd be on top of the world.

"Ms Patterson, are you ready to proceed?"

The judge's question interrupted her musings. Quickly, she regained her focus and nodded.

"Yes, Your Honor."

The judge turned to the other team of lawyers. "And you?" he asked.

"We're ready to proceed, Your Honor," Michaels' lawyer replied.

"Good. Well, you all know my feelings on this matter. I hope you've seen common sense. Does Mr Stone wish to amend his application?"

Nerves rushed to block off Mallory's breathing. She hastily cleared her throat. "No, your Honor. I've been instructed to continue to press forward with our case as it is. Mr Stone is adamant that it's in the best interests of his children for them to live apart. That is, one twin with each parent."

The judge's face flushed with anger. Mallory briefly closed her eyes, awaiting the anticipated explosion.

"Do you mean to say, after everything I said the last time we were here, you're still insisting on this ridiculousness?" the judge shouted.

Mallory winced at the anger in the judge's voice. She glanced toward her client. His face was a mask of granite. He certainly lived up to his name.

One of the members of Michaels' legal team got to his feet, puffing up with righteous indignation.

"Your Honor, this is preposterous! They're twins, for heaven's sake! Apart from that, these little girls are three years old! They need to be with their mother."

Mallory silently agreed. She wished she could blink her eyes and all of this would be over. Most of the time, she loved her job, but this was one instance where she wished she could make her client understand and have this whole sordid episode go away.

The judge eyed her sternly. "You know my attitude on this, Ms Patterson. I suggest you talk some sense into your client before you next come before me. I'm adjourning this matter for another week."

His narrow-eyed glare was directed firmly at Mallory when he added, "Let this be a warning. I'll not stand for any such nonsense as this. No child of that age shall be separated from her sibling. I suggest you work it out."

With that, the judge banged his gavel down hard and pushed away from the bench. Those present in the courtroom stood as he stalked out. When the way was clear, Mallory sank down in her seat and tried to gather her courage for yet another face-off with her client and his equally intractable father.

Her phone vibrated in the pocket of her jacket. Putting off the inevitable confrontation for just a few more minutes, she tugged it out and checked the screen. It was a message from Rafe.

I'm in the neighborhood. Do u have time 4 coffee?

Her heart skipped a beat of excitement. She had so much more on her mind right now, but the thought of seeing Rafe again got her pulse racing. Quickly, she sent off a reply.

"In court. Give me twenty minutes. I'll call u." She finished it with a smiley face.

———————

Rafe spied her the moment she entered the café. The lunch crowd had finished and only a scattering of people remained. That enabled Rafe to secure a table by the window, where they could watch the world go by.

He'd messaged Mallory at the spur of the moment on his way back from the morgue. Samantha Wolfe and the experts she'd called in to help her were still working away on creating an image of the dead woman they'd found. Sam was confident they had enough to work with to enable them to get a decent image, but this kind of thing took time. He understood. Besides, like James had said, the woman had been missing for twenty years. A few more days, even another week wouldn't matter.

Mallory looked around the café. She smiled when she saw him. He smiled back and waved her over, standing as she approached.

"Hey, it's great to see you," she said and leaned over and gave him a quick kiss.

It seemed to come to her so naturally. He didn't bother to hide his pleasure. "Thanks for joining me.

It's great to see you, too."

She pulled a face. "Ugh! What a day! You have the most perfect timing! You wouldn't believe what I've had to go through today!"

"Tough day in court?" He sympathized.

"Tough doesn't begin to describe it."

He reached over and squeezed her hand, offering wordless comfort. Once again, the gesture seemed so natural. The waitress appeared and took their orders. Both of them ordered double-strength lattés. Mallory also ordered a piece of apple pie.

"With cream and ice cream, if you don't mind," she added.

Rafe shook his head fondly and grinned. "You weren't lying when you said you had a sweet tooth."

She grinned. "Why would I lie about that?"

"Oh, I don't know. Most women are worried about their figures." He let his gaze linger on her tidy curves. "It's refreshing to be with a woman who doesn't give a toss."

She laughed and shook her head. "Oh, no, you have it all wrong. I definitely give a toss. I work off the extra pounds in the gym. If I didn't, I'd be the size of a house." She laughed and shrugged. "It's the tradeoff, I guess. But one I'm certainly prepared to make. After all, what's not to love about apple pie?"

She winked and then broke into laughter. His gut tightened with need. There was something so darn attractive about a woman with a good sense of humor. Laughter was something that had been sorely missing from his life. And not just in recent years after burying his mother and his sister before that. He couldn't remember any laughter in the home he'd shared with his dad.

Refusing to let the dark memories intrude on his time with Mallory, he forced the grim thoughts aside.

"So, how's your day going?" she asked.

"Good. Since you filed that missing person's report, I've been able to make some enquires about your mother."

Her eyes widened, the expression in them warring between caution and excitement. "Have you found anything?"

"Not yet." He explained how he'd run her mother's name through the system and come up with nothing.

"I guess that's a good thing that she hasn't been arrested since she left, but it doesn't get us anywhere, does it?"

"No. But if she left the country and never returned, I wouldn't expect to find her in our database."

Mallory's shoulders slumped. Rafe nudged her with his foot. "Hey, don't lose heart. It's early days, yet. There are plenty of other avenues for us to try."

"Such as?"

"Well, I've put in a call to immigration, for starters. I want to check the date your mother left Australia and confirm her destination."

"But I already told you she—"

He held up his hand. "Yes, but what sort of investigator would I be if I didn't double check the information? I'm not saying you have it wrong. I'm just being thorough."

She nodded. "I understand." She paused and then asked, "What else are you going to do?"

He told her about his call to Clayton. "He's a good investigator and a top bloke. He's promised to do what he can to help. With Interpol involved, we'll be able to track her movements. Or at least each time her passport was used. She left here for Argentina, but that was twenty years ago. She could be anywhere now."

"You're right. She could even be back here."

He studied her. Mallory's expression turned distant and Rafe could only imagine she was thinking about what it would mean, what it would feel like to know her mother was in Australia, had maybe even been here for many years.

The waitress arrived with their coffees and Mallory's apple pie. She smiled in delight when she saw the generous serving of ice cream and whipped cream.

"Oh, that looks delicious," she said, grinning at the waitress. The woman merely smiled and moved away.

Rafe took a sip from his coffee. He'd had more than his share of caffeine that day, but still, this one tasted good. Or maybe it had something to do with the woman who sat across from him, devouring her pie?

"Oh, this is sooo good. Total ambrosia! You must try some."

She grinned and lifted a piece onto her fork and brought it to Rafe's lips. He opened his mouth and took the morsel onto his tongue. His eyes locked on hers.

The intimacy of the moment wasn't lost on either of them. Mallory stared at him. His heart began to thump. Her eyes deepened to the color of emeralds. He heard the little catch of her breath and saw a pulse flutter at the side of her neck. He knew exactly how she felt.

"You're right," he murmured, his voice husky with need. "Delicious."

"Oh."

Her lips formed a perfect circle. His heart beat fast. They'd met only eleven days earlier and yet he'd never wanted a woman like he wanted this one. And it wasn't just that she was gorgeous. She was smart and warm and funny. She was good around kids. She loved pie.

A tiny dot of cream clung to the corner of her mouth. He reached over and wiped it off with his fingertip and then put his finger in his mouth. All the while, their gazes remained locked as if neither one of them could look away. That was certainly how he felt.

And then he needed to touch her again and this time he reached out and traced the soft line of her mouth. Her lips were full and sumptuous; made for kissing. The chaste kisses they'd shared to date had only whetted his appetite. He yearned to kiss her properly, thoroughly, until they were both begging each other for more.

Blood pounded through his veins and centered in his cock. He was so hard, it was painful. And still, he couldn't stop touching her. With the pad of his thumb, he pressed down on her lower lip and almost cried out when her tongue came out and flicked across his skin.

Her eyes deepened to the green of a midnight forest and her breath came in short, sharp gasps. Her tongue swiped a second time across the pad of his thumb and he thought he might come in his pants. With his other hand, he cradled her cheek in his palm and gently extricated his thumb. Any more of that and he'd embarrass himself. She made a little moue of disappointment.

"Later," he rasped. It was all he could manage.

———————

It was a whole lot later than either of them envisaged before they caught up again. Rafe had asked her to meet him for dinner that evening and she'd eagerly accepted. Things were moving fast, but neither of them wanted it any other way. Then Rafe called just before she left the office and told her they'd have to re-schedule. She tried to hide her disappointment.

"Oh, too bad. I was looking forward to dining out with you again," she teased. "Especially with you paying."

"Hey, I have no problem with paying. I wish we could go out again tonight, too. It's just that Charli's called me. She's not feeling well. Apparently she had a headache all day at school. Now she says she's burning up, but at the same time she feels cold."

"Oh, poor baby!" Mallory replied, at once sympathetic.

"Yes, it sounds like she's coming down with something. We'll have to do dinner another time. I need to get home."

"Of course you do. Is there anything I can do? Would you like me to run to the store and get some paracetamol?"

"Thanks, that's very kind of you, but I'm sure we have enough painkillers at home. You're probably best to stay away in case it's contagious."

She chuckled. "I'm not afraid of a few germs. Are you sure you're going to be okay? I can come over and keep you company, if you like?"

There was a pause and then Rafe said, "Would you really do that?"

"Of course. I like you, Rafe. I like you a lot. I like spending time with you. So, we can't go out to dinner, but I could always bring dinner to you. How about it?"

There was another pause and then he sighed quietly. "That sounds great." He gave her his address.

She smiled and tried to contain her excitement. He was tending his sick child, for goodness' sake.

"Great. I'll see you in a little while. Do you like Chinese?"

CHAPTER 9

The address Rafe had given her was in a part of Newtown that was just beginning to see gentrification. All around his, Mallory saw evidence of progress, where developers had come in and restored the old terrace houses to their former glory, but Rafe's house wasn't among those. She didn't know if he rented or whether he owned the place, but as she made her way up the cracked pavement toward the front door, it was obvious the place was in need of some tender loving care.

Peeling paint hung off the exterior. The window frames had warped. Though there was a well-tended garden off to one side that burst with summer color, it wasn't enough to hide the fact that this once-grand home was suffering from serious neglect.

Not that it mattered to her where he lived. It didn't change him as a person. People usually chose to live where they could afford to live. It was often as simple as that. Besides, it was close enough to the city to enjoy spectacular views of the city skyline and it was also close to Rafe's work. No doubt Charlotte attended one of the schools in the vicinity.

Mallory knocked on the door and waited for Rafe to answer it. Butterflies filled her stomach. It seemed like every time she was around him, she felt nervous, fluttery and excited. The feelings were so new she wasn't sure how to handle them.

She felt like a giddy teenager on her first date. In fact, she couldn't even remember feeling this giddy on her first date. It was strange and yet it was wonderful and it all came down to Rafe.

The door opened and there he was, smiling at her in greeting. She held out the two sacks of Chinese food and he took them from her, along with the bottle of red wine she'd bought from the liquor store on the corner.

"You come bearing gifts. You're my kind of visitor. Food *and* alcohol," he teased.

She grinned. He wore a cream-colored sweater over a pair of jeans. The fabric of his clothing conformed to his muscular shape. She stood there and drank him in.

"Coming in?" he asked.

She blushed and hurried across the tiled foyer and through the open doorway. Once inside, she took a moment to look around. They were in a long, narrow hallway. High ornate ceilings were surrounded by crown molding, both painted a blinding white. The walls were a beautiful heritage green that fit perfectly with the period of the house. Elegant light fixtures gave the place a timeless feel. Despite the shabbiness of the exterior, inside it was all warmth and comfort and grace.

"You have a nice place," she said.

"Thanks. It's taken some doing, one room at a time, as funds allow. But I'm almost there. Next, I start on the outside." He grinned. "You might have noticed it's not quite up to scratch."

She laughed. "Oh, my goodness, you did all this yourself? That's amazing! You're a man of many talents."

She stepped into the front room and gazed around with admiration. These walls were a soft blue. Once again, the high ceilings with their crown molding were painted white. His furnishings had also been chosen with care. The vintage gold sofa looked right at home against the pale gray wall. The red cedar antique coffee table also looked like it was meant to be there.

Rafe led her out of the front room and into the kitchen. He set the boxes of Chinese takeout on the counter and turned to her.

"Can I pour you a glass of wine?"

She nodded. "Yes, please."

She looked around the small space. Compact, but homey, it had also been furnished with love and care. From the old-fashioned copper tea kettle that sat on the stove to the framed patchwork picture that hung on the wall. She shook her head and smiled.

"What are you smiling about?" Rafe asked with a grin.

"You," she said.

"What about me?"

She moved closer until her sleeve brushed his and then tried to ignore the rush of heat that filled her body. "You're an enigma."

"Really? And here I was thinking I'm a pretty straightforward kind of bloke."

She reached out and scraped her finger along the smooth expanse of his cheek. "You're good-looking enough to be a Hollywood front man. You hold down a responsible job. You care about what happens to people and not just those you're related to. You like antiques and you also like taking care of old houses, even when they're money pits."

He rolled his eyes. "Aren't they all money pits?"

"*Shh,*" she admonished, smiling. "I'm not finished."

"There's more?"

She slapped him playfully on his arm. "It takes a good deal of patience and perseverance to restore a house such as this. It says a lot about a man who does. Not to mention the fact you canceled a hot date to be at home with your sick child."

She shook her head slowly back and forth. "You sound too good to be true, Rafe Connelly. You sound like someone I could fall in love with."

His eyes darkened momentarily with emotion and then he grinned. "Wow, you got all that from the first five minutes in my house? I would have invited you over here long ago if I'd known it would have that effect."

She laughed and he laughed with her. It felt like they were a couple, sharing a private joke. She liked it.

He handed her a glass of wine and then poured himself another. "Cheers," he said and gently touched his glass to hers.

"Cheers," she murmured.

They both took a sip and then his expression sobered. "All jokes aside, thanks so much for coming over, Mallory. I really appreciate it."

"Of course. I'm happy to. How's Charlotte?"

"Right now she's asleep. I gave her some medication to bring down her fever. I checked on her a while ago. She feels cooler, thank God."

The relief on his face was visible. She could see how much he cared for his little girl. It filled her with warmth and only reinforced the growing belief that standing before her stood a good and decent man.

As if aware of her thoughts, their gazes tangled and held. The moment seemed to go on forever. Her heart beat hard against her chest and blood thumped in her ears. Slowly, slowly, he drew her closer. She tilted her head. Their lips met and melded in the most exquisite kiss.

Breathless and with her heart pounding, they slowly drew apart. She stared up at him, glad to see he looked as affected as she felt.

"Wow. That was... That was amazing."

He smiled gently. "I'm glad you think so."

Their gazes held a moment longer until Rafe broke the spell. He turned around and reached for the cartons of Chinese food. Quietly and efficiently, he opened them and found plates and utensils in the cupboard.

"This smells delicious," he said. "Thanks again for coming around."

She smiled. "Thanks for having me."

They piled their plates high and took them to the small wooden kitchen table. Four matching chairs with yellow-and-white checkerboard patterned cushions sat around it.

After their delicious meal, they sat on the couch and it was comfortable and companionable. Rafe checked on Charlotte a couple of times and in between, they held hands and talked about all sorts of things. And all the time, Mallory felt herself falling for this man with the gentle smile and the quiet way he had about him.

Finally, she extricated herself from the couch and stood. "It's getting late. I should go."

He stood and took her in his arms. He held her tightly against him for a few moments and then gently set her aside. "Thanks again for coming over. It's been a lovely night."

"I'd like to do it again sometime," she whispered.

Coming up on her tiptoes, she pressed her lips against his and was instantly rewarded with his response. The peaceful companionship that had surrounded them only moments earlier evaporated. All of a sudden, they were both burning up with need.

His lips moved over hers with increasing pressure, kissing her like he couldn't get enough. Her arms came up around his neck and she clung to him, pressing herself against him. Her nipples were hard, her breasts ached with need, her core burned with fire.

His hands ran down her sides and then gently cupped her ass. He pressed her to him and she felt the unmistakable bulge against her belly. It thrilled her to know he wanted her as much as she wanted him.

But slowly, slowly, their kisses softened until at last he lifted his head and eased her away from him.

"Thank you for a wonderful evening, Mallory."

She nodded, respecting his decision to take things slowly. It was a refreshing change from the guys she usually dated who couldn't wait to get her into bed and who assumed every date would end that way. Besides, holding back and waiting would only serve to build the anticipation. She could live with that.

"I had a lovely evening, too, Rafe. I hope Charlotte is feeling better soon. Good-night." With that, she gathered up her handbag and left.

The phone at Rafe's elbow rang, interrupting his thoughts. He'd only just returned from interviewing witnesses in his current homicide case and was sorting through his notes. His mind had been constantly on Mallory, which hadn't helped. He hadn't seen her since the night she'd come over. She'd been busy and so had he. Apart from a few text messages, they'd had no contact.

Was it because he'd called a halt to their lovemaking? Had that turned her off? Hell, he hoped she knew he found her attractive. The last impression he wanted to give was that he wasn't interested.

It was just that she was special. He'd known it right from the start. He wanted them to get to know each other better before jumping into bed. It seemed these days everyone slept together before they'd barely traded names. It had cheapened the whole act, made it a whole lot less extraordinary, as far as he was concerned.

Mallory was more than a casual fling. He wanted to start things off with her the right way. Slowly, respectfully, so that when they did make love, it would actually mean something.

The sound of the phone still ringing finally registered. Distractedly, he picked up the receiver and answered the call.

"Homicide. Detective Connelly speaking."

"Detective, It's Rashid from the immigration department. You put in a request a few days ago regarding the passport of Sofia Mary Lopez."

Rafe at once became alert. He sat up straighter in his seat and reached for a pen and notepad. "Yes, that's right. What can you tell me about her?"

"I understand your enquiry was with regard to a departure from Australia twenty years ago, but according to our records, the last time this passport was used was to enter Australia."

"To *enter* it?"

"Yes. And it was thirty-five years ago."

Rafe frowned in confusion. "Excuse me?"

The immigration officer sighed on the other end of the phone. "I said, your information is incorrect. This woman didn't leave Australia twenty years ago. At least, not using her own passport."

Rafe blinked. His mind spun. Mallory had been sure her mother left the day after her tenth birthday, and even if she got the dates confused, she sure as hell couldn't have gotten twenty years mixed up with thirty-five. He didn't know how old Mallory was, but he'd bet she wasn't even alive thirty-five years ago. Besides, she'd been told her father had driven her mother to the airport, bound for Argentina. Something didn't add up.

Either Mallory's father had lied about taking her mother to the airport, or Sofia Lopez was dropped off at the airport and then failed to catch her plane. Had it all been part of her plan to disappear? To leave a life she no longer desired? Had she hoodwinked her husband into thinking she needed to return to her home country, only to start a new life somewhere down the road?

Perhaps she'd been living in Australia all this time? It was possible. She hadn't left the country. Her passport told them that. The only other possibility was that she was traveling on a different passport.

Rafe grimaced. As a law enforcement officer, he knew only too well how easy it was to get hold of a fake passport if you had enough money and you knew the right people. Governments around the world worked hard to combat such fraudulent activities, but the truth was, there were some very clever people in the world with access to even smarter technology who could and would do anything if there was enough money to be made.

After thanking the immigration officer for his information, Rafe hung up the phone. He thought of Mallory and how she would feel knowing that there was a strong likelihood her mother had never left Australia. Rafe knew how she'd feel. She'd be devastated. There was a good chance her mother was still alive and well. After all, Sofia Lopez would only be in her mid-fifties. Unless she'd been struck down by a terminal illness, there was every chance she was still living life to the fullest.

Knowing the hurt that would cause Mallory gave Rafe pause. He was unwilling to cause her any further needless pain. At least, not until he was in possession of all the facts. There was no need to tell Mallory it was quite possible her mother was still living in Australia until he knew for sure where the woman was. He needed to find out where Sofia Lopez was living now and where she'd spent the past twenty years. Unless she left on a fake passport, she must still be in the country. She might even be living in Sydney. People often didn't stray far from their roots.

Yes, he'd keep quiet about what he'd discovered from immigration until he had something more concrete to go on. He needed to track down Sofia Lopez, or at least eliminate the possibility she was still living in Australia. The first place to start was the banks. No one could get by for long without money.

With that thought in mind, he dragged his keyboard toward him and began to prepare search warrants. It was a time-consuming and tedious task. There was nothing for it but to issue a warrant against each and financial institution in Australia. It was quite a long list, but without knowing who Mallory's mother banked with, it was the only course of action available to him.

When he was finished, there was an ache between his shoulder blades and a faint headache had made itself known. He pushed away from his desk in search of caffeine before he attended upon a magistrate and received the required approval to have the warrants issued. He didn't anticipate any problems, but even if the warrants went out the next day, it would be at least a week or two before he received responses from the banks. For now, all he could do was wait.

The morning sunlight filtered through the curtains and landed on Mallory's face. She squinted and brought her arm up over her eyes to block the brightness. And then she remembered. It was Sunday. *She would see Rafe!*

It had been more than a week since she'd had dinner with him. She might have been feeling paranoid that he didn't like her as much as she thought, except for the fact he'd kissed her with a passion that couldn't be faked and she'd felt the evidence of his desire against her stomach. It was just that he'd been busy and she'd been busy and there had been no time for them to catch up. There was no way he didn't like her. In fact, he'd told her so more than once.

They'd spoken on the phone and had texted every day since she'd spent the evening with him at his house. Short, funny messages, designed to make each other laugh. She'd discovered that not only was Rafe good and kind and compassionate, he also had a great sense of humor. She felt herself falling for him a little harder every day and there was nothing she could do about it.

Not that she wanted to do anything about it—apart from get her hands on him. She asked him why he'd pulled back when it was obvious she was ready and willing and able to go the whole way. He'd explained how he thought they had something special between them and he wanted to make sure when they finally came together, it would be beyond amazing for both of them.

He wanted them to get to know each other better, spend time together without the pressure of sex. He was quick to assure her it wasn't that he didn't *want* to sleep with her, but he thought they owed it to each other to do things this way. They lived in a fast world where the journey was often forgotten in the quest to reach the destination. He wanted to experience the journey with her, savor every step. By the time they slept together, they'd be making love and it would be on a whole different level. He assured her it would be worth the wait.

She was touched by his explanation and realized yet again how special and unique he was. He was a keeper, there was no doubt about it and she was excited to see where things went. That didn't mean she wasn't impatient for his touch, or feeling a little frustrated. With the weekend looming, she'd called to see if he wanted to catch up on Saturday.

"Oh, I'm sorry, but Charli has swimming training in the morning and then a birthday party to attend out at Concord. We're going to be out all day."

Mallory had swallowed her disappointment and assured him that was okay. He had a daughter to take care of. She understood.

"I wish I could, though," he added. "I miss you."

Her heart skipped a beat at the depth of emotion that filled his voice. She had no doubt he meant it.

"I miss you, too." Her voice was husky with emotion. She had to clear her throat. "What about tomorrow, then?"

"Sure. Only, Charli has a dance rehearsal in the morning. They're practicing for a concert which is coming up next week. The rehearsal finishes at eleven. I could swing by and pick you up afterwards, if you like. We could go to lunch. A picnic, perhaps?"

Mallory smiled in relief and anticipation. "That sounds great, Rafe. I'd really like that."

"Do you mind if Charli comes along?"

There was only the slightest hint of uncertainty in his voice. She hurried to reassure him.

"Of course not. You and Charli are a package. It's okay. I get it. I'd love to have her come along."

Now the morning had arrived and it looked like it was going to be a bright and sunny day. A perfect day for a picnic. Feeling better than she had in days, Mallory pushed aside the blankets and climbed out of bed. Stretching and yawning, she made her way into the bathroom to begin preparing for her lunch date with Rafe.

She found her father in his study, immersed in a book. "Good-morning, Dad. How was your night?"

"Fine."

He didn't look up as he said it. She frowned at the brusqueness of his tone. "Is everything okay?"

He glanced at her briefly and then returned to his book. "Of course it is. I have a headache, that's all. Too much scotch last night, I think."

Mallory nodded. "How's Alice?"

Her father looked up. Frown lines creased his forehead. "Oh, didn't I tell you? Alice and I broke up."

Mallory blinked in surprise. "Oh, I thought the two of you were getting on well. You've been together almost a year and were spending a lot of time with her."

Her father offered a wry grin. "You're right. A record for me. But things weren't working out. She wanted something more permanent. She kept bugging me to commit. As if sleeping in her bed three or four nights a week wasn't a commitment."

He shook his head and made a derisive sound in the back of his throat. "Women. I'll never understand them."

With great restraint, Mallory managed not to roll her eyes at his comments. She shouldn't be surprised. Her father had been unfaithful to her mother and in the years since she'd left, he'd had a string of women in his life. It was like he couldn't be on his own, but neither did he want one permanently in his life. It was strange. But that was the way he was.

She sighed and moved over to plant a kiss on his forehead. "Well, I hope you're okay about the breakup. I'm on my way out to lunch."

Her father raised an eyebrow. "Anyone I know?"

"No. He's a detective. I met him at Sally-Ann's barbeque the other week."

Once again, her father frowned. "A detective? You don't normally date that kind of guy."

Mallory gave a short laugh. "What kind of guy, Dad? At least I met him in the normal way and not off a dating site."

Her father waved away her reply as if it were of no consequence. "Yes, well, you know full well how I feel about those dating sites."

She threw up her arms in frustration. "What would you have me do, Dad? Spend my life alone? Or have casual hookups that never last, like you? I want a husband, Dad. And children. I want a family of my own. I want a man who loves me above all others. A man who wants to spend his life with me. Is that so hard to understand?"

She hated the tremor in her voice and the tears that threatened behind her eyes. Her father's expression softened. He beckoned her closer. With a sigh, she moved into his comforting embrace.

"I'm sorry, honey. Of course you want to find love. We all do. And I understand why you want a family. Yours was stolen from you by a mother who said all the right words, but when it came down to it, she really didn't care at all. You've had a difficult time of it and you've come out of it so well. You're a beautiful, successful, talented woman and I'm so proud of you."

The tears that had threatened now welled up in her eyes. She blinked hard to keep them at bay. She'd spent a long time on her eye makeup and Rafe was due any minute. She didn't want to open the door to him with smudged mascara and eyeshadow running down her cheeks.

"Thanks, Dad," she murmured and patted away her tears.

"I'm here for you, honey. I'll always be here for you. I want you to know that."

She nodded and bit her lip to hold back another surge of tears. A knock on the door caught her attention.

"That will be Rafe. Thanks again, Dad. You take care. I'll see you later."

CHAPTER 10

Closing the front door behind her, Mallory greeted Rafe with a smile. He looked good in his chambray shirt and chocolate-colored chinos. Brown leather boat shoes sans socks completed his casual look.

"You look beautiful," he murmured, admiring her knee-length, floaty summer dress. "That color matches your eyes. It makes them look like emeralds."

She laughed, pleased, and they made their way down the paved path that led to the gate. He ushered her into the front seat of his SUV. She immediately turned around and greeted Charli in the back.

"Hi, Charli. How was dance practice?"

The young girl smiled. Her shiny black hair was pulled back in a bun, making her appear older. She had the remnants of eyeshadow, rouge and lipstick on her face. Dressed in a white T-shirt with the Nike logo emblazoned across the front and a pair of casual, apricot-colored shorts, Mallory guessed she'd changed out of her dance gear at the studio.

"It was great thanks, Mallory. The girls are all really coming together. Are you going to come to the show?"

Mallory glanced at Rafe, who'd climbed in behind the wheel and was now pulling out into the traffic. He shrugged, but gave her an encouraging smile. She looked back at Charli. "When is it?"

"Thursday week. At eight. Dad's going to be there, of course. It would be really great if you could be, too."

Mallory felt an overwhelming sense of warmth and belonging. Just like that, Rafe's daughter had included her in their family. It felt so good. It felt so right.

"I think I could probably manage that," she replied.

Charli *whooped* in delight and grinned. "Great. All the other girls have mothers there. This will be the first time for—." She stopped abruptly and her cheeks turned red. She ducked her head. "I-I mean..." she stammered.

Mallory took pity on her. "I know what you mean, honey. And it's okay. I'd never try to replace your mother, but I'm happy to be your friend. Is that okay?"

Tears shone in Charli's eyes, but she nodded and even managed a smile. "That's more than okay."

The rest of the afternoon passed in a blur of good food, good conversation and good company. They found a spot on the grass by the water. With the sun shining and surrounded by the harbor on one side and the botanical gardens on the other, it made for a wonderful day.

Rafe kept his promise and supplied a sumptuous picnic basket filled with deviled eggs, ham sandwiches, cherries, grapes and strawberries dipped in chocolate. He'd even remembered a tub of clotted cream.

"These are delicious," Mallory enthused, dropping another chocolate-coated cream-dipped strawberry into her mouth.

"I hope I've done enough to satisfy your sweet tooth, at least for now," he teased.

Mallory grinned. On impulse, she leaned over and pressed a kiss against his mouth. He tasted like orange soda and strawberries.

Though momentarily taken aback, Rafe returned the pressure of her mouth in a soft and sensual kiss. When they finally broke apart, her heart was racing.

Charli coughed into her hand and laughed. "So, I guess this means you and my dad really like each other, right?"

Mallory blushed, but Rafe merely chuckled. "I guess so, baby. Is that all right with you?"

Charli looked from one to the other. "It's more than all right." Her expression sobered. "I love that you're so happy, Dad. It's been a long time since I heard you laugh."

A lump formed in Mallory's throat as she watched Rafe and his daughter communicate without words. She wasn't aware of the circumstances surrounding the death of Charli's mother, but she knew it had happened when Charli was three. It couldn't have been easy for either of them.

Rafe didn't come across as still nursing a broken heart, but still, the woman had been the mother of his child. She'd always hold a place in his heart. And that was fine, as far as Mallory was concerned.

Like Sally-Ann had said, by the time anyone made it to thirty, they tended to come with baggage. It was just the way it was. She just hoped Rafe would let her into his heart in the same way he'd managed to get into hers. She wanted him in her life. She hoped they could make things work.

"How's work?" she asked, as they began to pack up the picnic things.

He frowned. "Busy, as usual. The cops get smart and the criminals get smarter. At least, that's how it feels some days." He sighed.

"Poor baby," she murmured. "All work and no play makes Rafe a dull boy."

He laughed and she was relieved to see it chased the shadows from his face. "Have you had any time to put into my mother's investigation"?" she asked.

He glanced at her and then turned away, reaching for their plates. "No. Not really. I made a few enquiries, but I don't have anything concrete yet."

Mallory swallowed her disappointment. She knew these things took time and it wasn't as if Rafe didn't have anything else to do. He'd just told her how busy he was. She forced a smile.

"Sure. I understand. I appreciate that you're doing anything at all. You could have passed it onto someone further down the line. I'm sure following up on a missing person's report isn't normally how you spend your time."

He stood and gently pulled her to her feet and drew her up against him. Folding his arms around her, he held a close.

"You're right. Missing persons are not my thing. We have a whole separate department for that. But this is *your* mother who's missing and *you're* the one who's needing help. That's important to me. *You're* important to me. I promise I'll do what I can to find her. It just takes time, that's all."

She nodded, touched by his answer. "Thank you. You're a very special man, Rafe Connelly. Have I told you that?"

He bent down and pressed a kiss against her lips. Soft and sensual and loving, it brought tears to her eyes.

"Yes, you have," he whispered. "And just so you know, I feel the same way about you."

"Who wants to play Frisbee?" Charli shouted and then took off at a run across the flat.

Rafe looked at Mallory. She grinned. "I'm game if you are."

With their arms around each other's waist, and feeling more content than she had in a long time, they headed over to where Charli stood.

———

The door to the squad room opened. Rafe looked up in time to see James shoulder his way through. In his hands, he held two large Styrofoam cups of coffee. He deposited one beside Rafe.

"Thanks, mate. You're a lifesaver."

James grinned. "I thought you looked like you could do with a hit. How's the investigation going?"

"Which one?"

"Oh, that's right. You're trying to locate Mallory Patterson's mother, too. How's that coming along?"

Rafe sighed and filled him on what he'd discovered so far.

"So she didn't leave when she said she would?" James asked.

"It appears not. The only other explanation is that she traveled on a false passport."

James nodded. "Which can be accomplished far easier than our government would like us to believe. Still, she's the wife of a prominent lawyer. If she looks anything like her daughter, she's a stunner. It wouldn't be so easy for her to go undetected or to even know the kind of people who know the people who do this sort of thing. What's your gut telling you?"

Rafe regarded James steadily over his coffee cup. "My gut's telling me she's still here. I don't think she went anywhere."

James whistled and shook his head. "Wow! That takes some courage. Walking out on your husband and child, your life—and starting afresh. I wonder what she was running from?" he murmured.

"According to Mallory, her parents' relationship was rocky in the months before her mother left. John Patterson was having an affair. Sofia caught him out. They argued. Things got tense. You know the story."

James compressed his lips, looking grim. "Yeah, all too well. At least she got out before it turned deadly. Not everyone is as lucky as she is to have escaped."

Rafe frowned. That was one angle he hadn't yet considered. The ramifications left him cold. *Could John Patterson have murdered his wife? Was that the reason she never left Australia?* Misgiving stirred in his gut.

"Have you checked her bank accounts?"

James' question interrupted the somber train of Rafe's thoughts. He cleared his throat. "Yes. I issued search warrants more than a week ago against all the banks. I hope to start getting responses in the next few days."

"Well, if she's still living here, she must have access to money. Let's hope you get a hit. In the meantime, I have news on Jane Doe."

"Good. Have you got her identified, yet?"

"No. But I know who she isn't. I got the DNA results back on all of our missing persons. None of them are a match."

"Damn," Rafe cursed quietly. It would have been too simple if one of their historical missing persons had matched the woman in the cove. It seems they weren't going to get off this case so lightly.

"Yeah," James agreed. "I guess that means we're going to have to rely on the public for an identification and we both know how fraught with danger that is."

Rafe grinned. "Every weirdo in the country will come out of the woodwork claiming the woman as their own. It never ceases to amaze me what some people will do for their five minutes of fame."

"What about the DNA found on the rug?" James asked.

Rafe shook his head. "It doesn't belong to anyone in the system. Just another unknown someone we need to identify."

"How long before you expect to get the FaceFit picture?"

"I'm expecting a call from Samantha any day. In the meantime, you can do me a favor and chase up those banks. I haven't told Mallory yet about what I found out from immigration. I want to be able to tell her where her mother is, not where she's not."

James nodded. "I understand." He moved away toward his desk. "I'll start making calls; put a rocket up the ass of those banks. It's time they got off their asses and worked a bit for those hefty salaries. Starting right now."

Rafe grinned, relieved. With James on the job, he was more likely to receive speedier responses. Withholding his findings from Mallory didn't sit well with him. He wasn't exactly lying, but when she'd asked him if he'd found out anything, he hadn't told her the truth. He hoped she'd forgive him if she ever discovered his deceit. He might have withheld the information in her best interests, but she might not see it that way.

He blew out his breath on a sigh. He'd have to face that hurdle if and when it came his way. In the meantime, he had work to do.

Mallory groaned as she frowned down at the court orders she'd drafted and redrafted at least fifty times. Well, maybe not that many times, but that's what it felt like. No matter how she phrased it, the judge wasn't going to like her terms. Her client continued to insist on seeking the custody of just one of the Stone children and nothing she said to either Stone men seemed to make a difference. As for the judge's dire warning, Rupert Stone had arrogantly laughed it off.

"Don't you worry about Judge Mason, Ms Patterson. I play golf with him every Friday. You leave him to me."

It turned Mallory's stomach to think that someone like Rupert Stone, someone with wealth and power and influence, could corrupt a member of the legal fraternity, and one who held such a high and honorable office. She wanted to believe that people who had taken an oath to apply the law and uphold the truth were above that kind of thing, but apparently not. It made her feel disillusioned with her profession, to say the least. As for the moral values of her client and his father... She couldn't even bring herself to think about that.

The sound of an incoming text on her phone registered in the silence of her office. She reached for her handbag where she'd stowed it beneath her desk and tugged out her phone. Checking the screen, she smiled. Sally-Ann had sent her a message.

If I don't get out of this office, I'm going 2 go insane. Do u have time 4 coffee?

Mallory's smile widened to a grin. She knew exactly how her friend felt. If there was one thing she needed right now, it was a break. She hurriedly sent a reply text.

YES!!! B downstairs in 5.

Sally-Ann was already waiting for her when she stepped out of the elevator. They hugged briefly and then headed outside. The afternoon sun was warm on Mallory's face. A light breeze, tinged with salt, ruffled her hair. That was one thing she regretted about having an office job. She didn't spend enough time in the fresh air. Still, there was nothing to be done about it now. She'd chosen her path and she was happy about it most of the time. She was just glad she was able to take time out every now and then with friends, like she was doing now.

"You happy to go to Ronnie's?" Sally-Ann asked, referring to a popular café nearby.

"Sure. They do good coffee there."

The two of them crossed the street at the lights and headed toward the café. They were about halfway there when Sally-Ann shot her a sly look.

"So, tell me about Rafe Connelly."

Despite herself, Mallory blushed. "What do you want to know?" she replied playing it cool.

Sally-Ann grinned. "Come on, now, Mallory. Don't be shy. James told me everything."

Mallory's eyes widened in surprise, but she was secretly pleased to know that Rafe had talked about her to his friend. "Really? And what did he say?"

Sally-Ann shrugged. "Oh, this and that. You know how boys are. They only have the barest of information. They never ask any questions, dammit!"

The mock outrage on Sally Ann's face sent Mallory into a fit of giggles. It felt good to laugh; to let go of the stress of the day.

"Okay, so what do you know?" she asked.

"All James told me was that Rafe is into you. So, are you into him?"

Mallory laughed again. Sally-Ann was nothing if not direct. They arrived at the café and as they made their way to an empty table. Mallory used the time to formulate an answer. *Was she ready to share personal details with her best friend? What if things went sour with Rafe and she had to tell Sally-Ann it was all over? Could she bear that?*

But this was her friend, a trusted confidante. Besides, she was dying to tell someone. She pulled a chair out and sat down. Sally-Ann did the same.

"Okay, spill all," Sally-Ann demanded, her eyes twinkling.

Mallory drew in a deep breath. A fluttering of nerves and excitement filled her belly. This was it.

"Okay, you asked for it. Yes, I'm into Rafe Connelly."

Sally-Ann squealed. A couple of other diners looked their way and then returned to their meals.

"Oh my goodness!" Sally-Ann cried in a slightly less high-pitched tone. "Are you *kidding* me? You and Rafe Connelly? That's fantastic!"

Mallory smiled at Sally-Ann's enthusiasm. Her cheeks still burned with embarrassment. "I'm glad you think so."

"So, are you guys dating?"

Mallory nodded. "I think so. We've been out a few times. And he invited me over to his place for dinner once, but that was because his daughter was sick and he couldn't go out," she added.

Sally-Ann gazed at her with speculation in her eyes. "*Mm*, interesting. So, have you kissed?"

Mallory averted her gaze and tried to stem the fresh wave of heat that crept up her neck. "Yes. Is that okay?"

"Of course it's okay! I love that you've met someone you're really into. It's been so long. I haven't forgotten how hard you've been trying with all those Internet dates. Each and every one of them was a dud, remember?"

Mallory rolled her eyes. "Of course I remember! I was the one having to sit across from each of them, pretending I was totally engrossed in their conversation. Besides, you were the one encouraging me to keep going! It's a numbers game, you said, remember?"

Sally-Ann giggled unashamedly. "Yeah, yeah, yeah. Okay, maybe I was wrong. But if you're into

Rafe Connelly and Rafe Connelly is into you, your nights spent wasting time on Internet losers is over. See? It's worked out well for everyone and you have me to thank for it," she said smugly.

The waiter arrived and they both ordered coffee. After the waiter departed, Sally-Ann leaned forward. "I'm so *proud* of you, Mallory. You like this guy and you've just gone for it. It's fantastic! What's even better, is that he feels the same way. At least, that's James' take on it."

"What did Rafe say to him?"

"I'm not sure he actually said anything, but James could just tell. It's a guy thing, apparently. James is sure Rafe's interested in you. That's all you need to know."

Mallory took a moment to consider Sally-Ann's comments. Although it didn't come as a surprise to hear Rafe liked her, it was always good to get confirmation from someone else.

And then a sly expression came over Sally-Ann's face again. "So, you kissed." She waggled her eyebrows. "What else have you done?"

Mallory gasped in mock outrage. "Sally-Ann! That's none of your business! Besides, there's nothing to tell. We're saving ourselves, okay?"

Sally-Ann frowned. "Saving yourself? What the hell is that supposed to mean?"

Mallory patiently explained Rafe's reasoning and how important it was to him that they wait. Sally-Ann looked suitably impressed.

"Wow! Who'd have thought this day and age men like that still existed? You scored a good one, that's for sure. I always liked Rafe Connelly and now I like him even more. I knew you two would be good together. I just *knew* it."

Mallory laughed and regarded her friend with affection. "Yes, you're right. And I guess I have to thank you for your part in this. You played the matchmaker perfectly. So far, things are working out."

Sally-Ann grinned. "I feel so so good for you two. I'm so excited for your future. It thrills me to bits that I brought the two of you together. I'm so glad to see you happy."

The waiter arrived with their coffees. As Mallory stirred cream and sugar into hers, she contemplated asking Sally-Ann about Rafe's family. Mallory knew his wife was dead and, of course, she knew Charli, but he'd never mentioned any other family members. His mother, for example, or his father or siblings.

"Do you know any of Rafe's family?" she asked.

Sally-Ann shook her head. "No. Not really. I know his mother died three years ago. James wasn't working with him then, but all the detectives are pretty tight. Word gets around."

"Oh, I feel so sad for him. First his wife, then his mother. Do you know what she died of?"

"Cancer, I believe. And I don't think Rafe's been married before. I think he and Charli's mother were still boyfriend and girlfriend."

Mallory absorbed the information. "What about his father? Or brothers and sisters? Does he have any?"

"I'm not sure he has any siblings. I've never heard him mention any. As for his father, come to think of it, I haven't ever heard him talk about him, either. Even when his mother died, a bunch of us went to the funeral. I don't remember seeing his father there. Of course, there were a lot of people in attendance. He might have just been lost in the crowd. I don't know," she said thoughtfully. "Maybe you could ask him?"

Mallory nodded. "Yes. I will. I just thought you might know something about his family. He doesn't speak of them. And now, come to think about it, I didn't notice any family photographs in his house."

Sally-Ann sighed. "Well, I guess you don't get to choose your family. Some of us talk to them and some of us don't. Some of us have none at all. I'm sure you're the last person to judge someone on their family, or lack thereof."

She said the words lightly, but they still hurt. Mallory blinked back a sudden rush of emotion.

"I'd never judge him because of his family," she said quietly. "I was just curious. We both know what happened to my mother. The only family I've ever felt like I had was my father. I just wondered if Rafe had other loved ones in his life."

Sally-Ann reached over and squeezed her hand. "Hey, I didn't mean to upset you. I'm sure Rafe will tell you about his family in his own time. In the meantime, just enjoy each other's company and look forward to the wedding night." She winked. "It's going to be one hell of a wild ride."

CHAPTER 11

Rafe gulped down the last of his coffee and then grimaced. It had gone cold. He'd been so immersed in finalizing the last of the witness statements in his most current homicide case, he'd lost track of time. Thankfully, the shooting murder of a woman by her estranged husband had occurred in broad daylight outside her place of work. There were a large number of eyewitnesses who had all given sworn statements to support the charges that had been laid against Simon Croft. There were also countless statements from friends and family members of the estranged couple, indicating that prior to the homicide they had misgivings about Croft's mental status and concerns he might turn violent.

It gave Rafe no joy to accept their misgivings had come to fruition. Nor was it any comfort that Angela Croft had sought and was given protection under a Domestic Violence order. The terms of the order had prevented her husband from coming within one hundred yards of her place of abode or entering her place of work. In this case, the defendant had shot her as she left the building. He was fifty yards away, concealed behind a tree, armed with a high powered rifle.

It was just another sad episode in the lives of a family that had already been torn apart. One thing Rafe was thankful for was that his father had left before inflicting fatal violence on his family. Of course it didn't excuse the other kinds of violence Michael Connelly had engaged in on a regular basis—the heated arguments that inevitably ended with his mother sporting a black eye; the emotional and financial abuse; the humiliation.

That was the reason Rafe found himself virtually living on the streets before he turned fifteen. It was the reason he had been drawn to Khloe. She offered him safety, security, and love. If he'd had a more normal, peaceful upbringing, they might never have met. Still, then he wouldn't have Charli and he wouldn't give up his daughter for anything.

James shouldered his way into the squad room with a Styrofoam coffee cup in one hand and a pile of letters in the other. He came up to Rafe and dropped the envelopes on his desk.

"Looks like my pointed conversations with the bank staff worked some magic. From the logos on the envelopes, these look like they've come from them. Mary-Sue in the mailroom asked me to give them to you."

Rafe's heart leaped with excitement. With a bit of luck, Sofia Lopez Patterson had a bank account with at least one of the financial institutions Rafe had contacted. He tore open the first envelope with enthusiasm and quickly scanned the contents. It was from the National Australia Bank. Unfortunately, Mallory's mother was not one of their customers.

That was fine. There were plenty of others. He tore open the next envelope. Once again, the bank was sorry to advise Sofia Lopez Patterson did not have an account with them. Rafe went through four more letters, each with the same result. He was becoming despondent until he opened one from the Commonwealth Bank. He scanned the typed text.

"Yes!" He punched the air. He'd hit pay dirt.

James looked over from where he sat at his desk. "I take it you've had success?"

Rafe grinned. "You betcha. Sofia Lopez Patterson has an account with the Commonwealth Bank of Australia."

"That's great," James replied. "That should help narrow the search down."

"Yes. Let's hope so."

Rafe pulled his keyboard toward him and quickly typed in the necessary instructions to pull up the search warrant page. Now that he knew the Commonwealth Bank held an account in Mallory's mother's name, he could seek approval from the court to issue another warrant requesting details of the account. It meant waiting a little bit longer for the information he was anxious to receive, but at least he knew he was on the right track.

Almost as an aside, he went through the

remaining envelopes. Each of them returned the same answer: Sofia Lopez Patterson was not known to this institution.

Still, it didn't matter that she was only a customer of one bank. A lot of people stayed with the same bank for all their financial dealings. Rafe did. His savings account, credit card and house mortgage were all at the National Australia Bank. There was nothing unusual about that.

Quickly filling in the details of the warrant, he hit print and pushed away from his desk. Collecting the warrant off the printer, he signed it, folded it and tucked it into his shirt pocket. He returned to his desk and pulled on his jacket.

"I'm going to put this in front of a magistrate and then hand deliver this to the Commonwealth Bank in Martin Place so they can get started on it right away."

James nodded. "No problem. Any headway on the Croft case?"

"I've finished the last of the witness statements. They're all in the system. Feel free to look over them, if you like. I don't think the prosecutor will have any difficulty securing a conviction. I'll be back soon."

It was nearing lunchtime and the streets were busy with pedestrians and heavy traffic. There was talk of removing vehicles from the downtown area, but it hadn't happened yet. Rafe couldn't imagine what it would feel like without the constant noise of traffic. Still, it was definitely worth considering. The congestion in the city was beyond a joke.

Picking his way through the crowds, he continued to make his way to the local court precinct. A magistrate was required to approve the issue of any search warrant prior to it being executed. The court precinct was a decent walk away from the station, but he appreciated the chance to get out of the office and take in some fresh air. Well, as fresh it could be with thousands of cars and nearly five million people living there.

Still, he couldn't complain. He'd been to other cities in the world and in his opinion, Sydney ranked among the cleanest. Okay, he might be biased about his hometown, but when the wind blew in from the harbor and cleared away the morning smog, it was just beautiful. Just like it was today.

The light breeze felt cool against his skin. It lifted his hair and reminded him that he was well overdue for a haircut. If he had time, he'd try and squeeze it in this week, before Charli's concert. She'd teased him more than once about his long hair. It would please her to see that he'd made an effort to tidy it up.

He came to a halt at an intersection and waited for the traffic lights to change. He pulled out his phone, intent on checking emails when he heard someone call his name. He looked up and turned and saw Mallory walking toward him. His gut immediately clenched with nervous anticipation.

She was dressed in a smart, tailored business suit. The charcoal-gray jacket hugged her curves and contrasted nicely with the color of her hair.

The matching skirt fell to just above her knees and drew attention to her shapely calves. The restraint he'd held himself under was sorely tested. All he wanted to do was take her in his arms and bury himself inside her and forget the world even existed.

Which was ridiculous really... They were standing on a crowded street in the middle of the day. Beyond ridiculous...

"Hi," she said a little breathlessly and leaned over and pecked him on the cheek.

Her sweet perfume wafted toward him and filled his nostrils. It was all he could do not to kiss her back, properly, this time. Instead, he merely smiled and returned her greeting.

"Hi, yourself. It's good to see you."

"What are you doing here?" she asked, curiosity evident in her green eyes.

He patted his pocket. "I'm heading to the local court to get approval to issue a search warrant."

"Oh. Anything interesting?"

He debated for a few seconds about what to tell her. It still didn't rest well with him that he hadn't brought her up to date on the findings of the immigration department. Still, his reasons for keeping quiet hadn't changed. He still didn't have any concrete evidence about her mother or where she might be. He decided to play it safe.

"It's just a regular search warrant. Looking at a person's bank records can help us narrow down their location. Nobody can last long without money, right?" His chuckle sounded forced.

She smiled. "Is that something you'd use in my mother's case? Is that a way we could use to locate her?"

The hope in her voice was reflected in her eyes. It caught him off guard. He couldn't keep pretending anymore. He needed to come clean, at least about the warrant.

"As a matter of fact, this search warrant is for your mother's account. Apparently she held an account with the Commonwealth Bank. The warrant will give me access to the details."

Mallory's eyes widened in surprise. "Oh my goodness! You mean, you might even find out the last time she accessed her money? That's fantastic!" she added without waiting for his reply. "I mean, we all use ATMs, right? And you guys can pinpoint the exact time and place, right?"

Her voice rose with increasing excitement. Rafe hated to be the one to bring her back down to earth, but he had no choice.

"Yes, you're right. We can pinpoint the exact location where money was withdrawn out of an account, but that only works if the account has been active. That is, if there have been any transactions."

A frown marred the smooth skin of Mallory's forehead and confusion filled her eyes. "But my mother couldn't possibly be living without money, unless she found some rich sugar daddy to support her." Her laugh was devoid of humor. "If she has a bank account, she must be using it, right, no matter where she's living?"

"You'd think so," Rafe agreed, wanting to give

her as much reassurance as he could. "I guess will have to wait and see."

"How long will it take?"

"You mean to get the information from the bank?"

"Yes."

"It's up to them, of course, but I'm hopeful I might have access to the information by this afternoon. I could get lucky."

"This afternoon? That's wonderful! That means we might even know where Mom is living by then."

"Please don't get your hopes up," he said quickly. "It doesn't always work out like that. Just because your mother accessed an ATM in a certain location, doesn't mean she's living there. It also depends how long ago the transaction occurred. If it occurred a week ago, or even a month ago, who knows where she might be?"

"Yes, but it will help you to narrow it down, surely?"

"Yes. It'll definitely be of some use."

"And it will also confirm which country she's living in, right?"

"Yes, unless someone else has access to her account."

Mallory shoulders slumped on a sigh. "Oh, why can't this be easy? For so long, I didn't want to even think about where my mother might be living. I tried not to think of her at all. But she still has an Australian bank account! That information must mean something. Now that I've started down this path, I just want to know. Do you understand?"

Her eyes pleaded with his. Compassion and tenderness flooded through him. He drew her close and gave her a brief hug. Drawing slightly away, he framed her face with his hands and kissed her.

"I *do* understand. And you've been so brave and patient." He laughed at her expression of surprise. "Okay, maybe not so patient, but I understand. I get it. I really do. It's like when we make up our mind to do anything. We want to see results straightaway. This is no different. I promise I'll do the best I can."

Mallory nodded. "It does seem a bit strange though that Mom would still have an account opened in Australia, don't you think? I mean, she left the country twenty years ago. Why would she still have a bank account here?"

Rafe shrugged. "Perhaps she forgot to close it? She might have left in a hurry. Maybe she just made up her mind one day to leave and that was that. If she's spent all this time overseas, it probably hasn't been a priority for her to file the necessary paperwork to get it closed."

He looked at his watch. As much as he enjoyed talking to Mallory, he needed to go.

"Anyway, I'd love to stay and chat, but I need to get going. I'll have no chance of getting the information if I don't get the warrant."

She nodded. "Me, too. I'm on my way back to the office from the courthouse. My secretary will be wondering where I am. I have client appointments booked in all afternoon."

He grimaced. "Too bad. I was hoping we might be able to do lunch."

She shook her head. "Unfortunately, I'm booked solid. I'm planning on grabbing a sandwich on my way back."

"How about later? Tonight, maybe?" he asked hopefully.

She smiled and the brilliance of it took his breath away.

"I'd like that."

"Do you eat Italian food?"

"I love Italian food."

Great." He smiled. "I'll pick you up at seven."

With his head still full of Mallory, and with a barrage of phone calls to return, Rafe's afternoon sped by. He was formulating a reply to an email when he noticed one had arrived from the Commonwealth Bank. Immediately, he was filled with anticipation. He finished the message he was on and then clicked on the email from the bank.

The information was contained to one page. Sofia Lopez Patterson held two accounts with them. One was a savings account. The other one was for a credit card. Rafe scanned the information. The more he read, the lower his spirits sank.

According to the bank, neither of Sofia Lopez's accounts had been touched for twenty years. There was a nil balance owing on her credit card.

The last transaction on her savings account was a withdrawal of one-hundred-and-fifty dollars from an ATM five days before she disappeared. The account still had a balance of three thousand six hundred and seventy-five dollars and forty-five cents.

Rafe stared at the screen. Cold, hard dread settled in his gut. The woman's passport indicated she was still living in Australia and yet her bank account and credit card hadn't been touched. Unless she'd found someone to support her and look after her every need, like Mallory had jokingly suggested, the lack of activity on her bank account appeared more than ominous. If the information had come in for anyone but Mallory's mother, he would have already formed suspicions that the woman might be dead.

Scrubbing his hands through his hair, he blew out his breath on a heavy sigh. This was the second piece of information that didn't bode well for Sofia Lopez. He was having dinner with Mallory tonight. *Should he tell her what he'd discovered?* She already knew he'd been on his way to issue a search warrant on the bank. No doubt she'd ask him if he'd heard back. *Was he prepared to lie outright to her?*

He compressed his lips, feeling grim. No, he didn't want to lie to her again. The first time he'd been evasive. This time, he might be forced to tell a straight-up lie. He didn't want to do that. At some point, she'd be told the information, anyway. He didn't want the fact he'd withheld it from her to cause problems between them.

He liked her. He really liked her. He could see a future for them. He wouldn't jeopardize that over something like this. Whether he disclosed his findings to her or not, it wasn't going to change the facts about her mother. And that was that.

He looked over to where James normally sat and saw that his chair was empty. It was after five. No doubt he'd gone home to his family. Just like Rafe should.

With that, he shut down his computer and made an effort to straighten the papers on his desk. He called Charli and told her about his date with Mallory, but assured her he'd be home soon with some takeout.

"Can you get some Thai food, Dad? Mussaman beef and rice. And don't forget the money bags. Oh, and some chicken satay skewers. That would be great."

Rafe smiled. "How many people are you feeding?"

"Just one," came the pert reply. "But this way I'll have leftovers to take to school tomorrow. See?"

He laughed. "Okay, you win. I'll see you at home soon. Be good."

CHAPTER 12

With their hands casually laced together, Rafe led Mallory up the stairs to the restaurant he'd chosen for dinner and tried to forget, for tonight at least, what he knew about her mother. Sighing quietly, he held the door to the restaurant open and followed her inside.

Icebergs was housed inside the Bondi Icebergs Surf Club and was a bar and dining room perched on top of the Bondi cliffs. It had been established by Italian restaurateur Maurice Terzini in 2002. Terzini had a long history in the hospitality industry and his restaurant had become an iconic dining venue in Sydney. Twenty years later, it was still at the forefront of the Australian culinary landscape.

With an ever-changing menu focused on modern Italian cuisine, the dining room had been arranged to take in the famous view of Bondi beach. It didn't matter whether you dined there during the day or at night, the dining experience was unforgettable. Rafe didn't go there often, but when he did, he always enjoyed himself. It was a special place and one he wanted to share with Mallory.

"I've never been to Icebergs before," she commented.

He turned and smiled. "I'm glad I'm with you for your first time, then. You're in for a treat."

She smiled and Rafe's heart turned over. He was falling hard for this woman. He was pleased the thought didn't make him panic. He was ready to find love again, to settle down with a woman and share his life. He'd been lonely for a long time without realizing it. It was time to turn things around.

The maître d' greeted them on their arrival. Rafe had phoned ahead and had been lucky enough to secure a table on the balcony that overlooked Bondi Beach. It was early enough that there were still people swimming in the ocean and surfers on their boards further out. The beach was littered with joggers and people walking dogs and others who were just taking in the beauty of the ocean and the golden sand.

"Wow, what a beautiful view," Mallory breathed, as the maitre'd showed them to their table.

Rafe agreed. "This place is beautiful anytime. You wait until the sun sets and the lights come on. It's magical."

She shot him a grin. "You really are a romantic, aren't you, Rafe Connelly?"

He blushed.

She quickly added, "Don't be embarrassed. I like it. I like it a lot," she added softly.

They were seated at their table and a waiter appeared to take their drink orders. Rafe asked to see the wine list and after a quick consultation with Mallory, ordered an aged Merlot. He gave the waiter their order.

Mallory nodded in approval. "You really are the man about town, aren't you? Good-looking, sexy, hard-working and a man who knows his wines. Is there anything you can't do?"

"From what I can tell, you have more than your fair share of gifts, too," he said with a smile.

His gaze rested on her meaningfully and then slid lower. She was dressed in a long silky black sleeveless dress that was snug around her breasts and waist and then flowed out gently over her hips. The plunging neckline gave him a good view of her cleavage. The thought of touching her, kissing her, sucking her nipples had been driving him wild ever since he'd collected her outside her door earlier that evening. He wondered if she'd worn the dress on purpose.

Although she respected his decision to take things slowly, she'd made it clear from the passion in her kisses that she was willing to go as far as he would let them. It excited him to know she was a warm and passionate woman who was willing to give everything of herself to her man and he couldn't wait to make love to her.

All of a sudden, it seemed foolish to make her wait. After all, they both wanted it. And it wasn't like this was their first date. He felt he'd gotten to know her well enough to take things to the next level. He was almost certain she felt the same.

Still, it was a little complicated. The logistics weren't quite as easy as all that. He had a thirteen-year-old daughter in the bedroom right next to his. She still lived with her father. The thought of paying for a hotel room to consummate their relationship was singularly unappealing, but did they have any other choice?

And then there was the information he had about her mother. At the station, he'd pretty much come to the conclusion he would tell all this evening, but now they were here in this beautiful restaurant, enjoying the night and each other's company, he didn't want to spoil things.

She wouldn't take the news well. No one would. The implications were just too devastating. And the problem was, he still didn't have any real answers. He still didn't have any idea where her mother was.

Dread and anxiety settled like concrete in his gut. He blew out his breath on a sigh.

"Are you okay?"

The concern in her voice warmed him. At the same time, he forced a smile. "Of course. Why wouldn't I be? I'm dining out in a wonderful restaurant on a lovely balmy night with a beautiful woman by my side. What could I be unhappy about?"

She continued to regard him solemnly. "I don't know. But you've been sighing quite a bit tonight. Is it work? Is that why you're so distracted?"

He grimaced. He hadn't realized his feelings had been so obvious. He thought he'd done a good job of concealing his disquiet. Or maybe she was just a little more perceptive than most. Whatever it was, he wouldn't enjoy his dinner until he told her.

He opened his mouth, but the words wouldn't come. His courage deserted him.

"I was just thinking about Charli's concert," he said instead. "It's on next week. Are you still keen to come? Don't think you have to," he added quickly, not wanting her to feel she was obligated just because Charli had put her on the spot.

"Don't be silly. Of course I want to come. I love going to concerts."

Rafe lifted an eyebrow. "It's a kid's concert. They're not exactly a professional performance."

She laughed. "It'll be great, I'm sure. And I think Charli would like to have me there."

He nodded. "You're right. She would. Her mother died when she was so young. She has no memories of her. It must be hard for her to see all the other girls with their mothers... I guess I never really gave it too much thought." The words immediately filled him with guilt.

"Well, you've been busy making a life for the two of you, and you've done a great job of it. Besides, the death of Charli's mother is probably something you prefer not to dwell on. Most people would feel that way."

He saw the frank interest in her gaze and wondered if this was the time to tell her about Khloe. If they ended up in bed together, she'd see the tattoo of Khloe's name on his shoulder. He didn't want her to wonder about the woman's name he had marked upon his skin. Besides, it would distract him from the other news he had.

"Charli's mum and I got together when we were teenagers."

Mallory's eyes went wide. "Wow! So you were together for a long time."

"Not really. We met when I was fourteen. Khloe was the same age. She was already living on the streets. I spent more time with her under the bridge than I did at home."

He paused for a moment, lost in his memories. "I was seventeen when Khloe fell pregnant with Charli. It came as a shock. I guess I should have realized it was a possibility, but you don't really think of things like that at seventeen, do you?"

He gave her a half-smile and continued. "I turned eighteen a month before Charli was born. I was preparing for my final school exams. On top of that, I was a new father. It was a little overwhelming."

Mallory's expression was full of sympathy. "That must've been tough. I can't imagine how you coped."

Rafe grimaced. "Don't worry, it got worse. Khloe abandoned Charli a few weeks after her birth. She wasn't interested in being a mother."

Mallory slowly shook her head, her eyes filled with compassion. "Oh goodness. You poor boy! What did you do?"

Rafe sighed. "I was lucky I had my mother and my younger sister. They helped a great deal when Charli was young. My mother, in particular, was an angel. I couldn't have done it without her."

Mallory cleared her throat. "Sally-Ann mentioned something about your mother's death."

Rafe felt a burst of surprise that she'd been talking about him with her friend, but he was also pleased. It showed she cared. "Yes, she died three years ago. Cancer."

"I'm so sorry," Mallory murmured.

Though they were just words, he took comfort from them, from *her*. Even now, the thought of his mother's death upset him. They'd been through a lot together. They'd been very close. As if sensing his emotions, Mallory reached over and squeezed his hand.

"You mentioned a sister. Does she live in Sydney?"

Rafe drew in a breath and let it out on a sigh. "No. I probably shouldn't tell you this, because it might make you run a mile, but the thing is, we've had a lot of tragedy in the Connelly family. My sister, Breanna, died when she was twenty-two. She was killed in a car accident."

Mallory's face filled with horror. She put a hand up to her mouth. "Oh, Rafe! No! How terrible for you! Goodness, you're right. So much tragedy, so much grief. I can't believe how well-adjusted you are, how well you seem to have coped. It would be enough to send anyone over the edge."

Her words drifted over him, soothing, calming, comforting. From someone else, they might have been meaningless, but from her, they meant a lot.

"Thank you," he said gruffly. "It's been a long time since I discussed my family with anyone."

"I'm honored that you chose to share it with me."

The waiter arrived with the bottle of wine. After getting Rafe's approval, he filled their glasses. Rafe took a sip. The wine was rich and mellow. Perfect.

Mallory looked at him. "What about your father? Are you still in contact with him?"

Mallory watched the color leach from Rafe's face and wondered at its cause. He'd hinted at an unhappy childhood. After all, no one spent more time on the streets than they did at home unless there was good reason and that reason usually involved fear. Domestic violence occurred often enough that Mallory wouldn't be surprised to discover that was the cause. She waited for him to answer.

He took another sip of his wine, as if buying time. While he'd told her about his mother and his sister, he'd made no mention of his father. If Mallory were to have a future with this man, she didn't want any secrets between them, including the ugly ones.

"Rafe?" she quietly encouraged.

His expression remained closed. "You're better off not knowing about him," he said gruffly. "He wasn't a nice man."

Mallory gaged his response and decided to ask another question. "Is he still alive?"

"Who knows? I don't rightly care, either way. He lost the right to be called my father a long time ago."

The anger in his voice was reflected in his eyes. His fists were clenched above the table and his breath came fast.

"Please, Rafe. Talk to me. You won't shock me, I promise."

He raked her with his gaze. "My father was a nasty drunk. He took pleasure from beating my mom. If I never see him again, it will be too soon. Is that enough for you?"

Tears burned behind Mallory's eyes. She was overwhelmed with sadness for the young boy he used to be and the hardened man he'd become. It was a miracle he had it within himself to love anyone. She guessed his little girl had a lot to do with that. Without her to be responsible for, his life might have taken a very different course.

The waiter returned to their table to take their orders. Mallory took a few moments to study the menu. Rafe did the same. The menu was largely written in Italian, with English translations on the side.

"I'll have the hand-cut spaghetti with the Moreton Bay bug and tomato and verbena butter, please. And I'll have the mascarpone mousse, with the espresso, meringue and marsala sponge for dessert."

A slight grin lifted the corners of Rafe's mouth. "Good to see I haven't put you off your dinner."

Mallory was pleased to see his good humor had returned. She reached over and gave his hand a comforting squeeze. Rafe placed his order and after the waiter had departed, he took both her hands in his.

"I'm sorry I was short. I don't like talking about my father. Too many bad memories."

"I understand. Dredging up bad memories is the last thing I want to do. Let's forget about it for now and enjoy this beautiful evening."

They both looked out toward the ocean where the sun had almost set. The pinks and oranges and purples were fading as the night moved in. The day had come to an end.

"I love the ocean," Mallory murmured.

"So do I. One day, I hope to be able to afford a place somewhere around here."

"Me, too."

He smiled. "You live a lot closer to the beach than I do."

She laughed. "Yes, but the house belongs to my father. I really need to find a place of my own."

"Why haven't you?"

"I guess there's never been a need. We keep each other company and we respect each other's space. Dad is often out overnight, anyway. He has a number of lady friends."

She thought she'd offered the information in a non-judgmental tone, but Rafe must have picked up on something.

"Do you think he's being disloyal to your mother?"

"No, of course not. She's been gone for years. No doubt she moved on from their relationship a long time ago."

Their meals arrived and silence fell between them as they took the time to enjoy the artful display of food before them. Mallory put a piece of Moreton Bay bug in her mouth and almost drooled at the taste of the succulent lobster.

"*Mm*, this is so amazing. I love what they've done with the sauce. It's like nothing I've ever tasted."

Rafe scooped out an oyster. "You have to try one of these. Absolutely delicious." He leaned across and she opened her mouth and took the small morsel on her tongue. Watching her closely, Rafe's eyes darkened.

"*Mm*, you're right. They *are* delicious."

"Absolutely," he replied, his gaze on her mouth and his voice husky.

Her tongue came out to catch the juices and she heard him groan. Her belly somersaulted with desire and heat spiraled down to her core. All of a sudden, the air crackled with sexual tension.

The rest of the meal was completed with only the barest of conversation. It was as if the two of them had simultaneously come to an agreement that tonight was the night they were going to be intimate. Mallory barely tasted her dessert and quickly declined coffee. Rafe did the same. After paying the check, he took her hand and guided her back outside.

His face was in shadows, but there was warmth and strength in his hand. She squeezed it tightly.

"Would you like to go for a walk along the beach?" he asked in a gravelly voice.

What she wanted was to go somewhere

private and tear his clothes off, but she restrained herself from making the suggestion and merely said, "Yes. That sounds lovely."

Rafe tugged off his shoes and socks. Slipping off her high heels, Mallory dangled them from one hand and dug her toes into the sand. It was cool and coarse and invigorating.

"Let's go down to the water's edge," she suggested on a laugh. Not waiting for Rafe's response, she took off to where the waves lapped against the shore. The tide was on its way out and miles of golden beach were exposed to their gaze. There was just enough light from the moon to illuminate their way.

"I love the smell of the salt spray," Rafe confessed, as the waves rushed over his bare feet.

"Me, too."

He put his arms around her and drew her close, pressing his body up against hers until there was no mistaking his desire. A rush of liquid heat burned through her, centering in her core. She came up on her tip toes and draped her arms around his neck, mindful of her sandals. At the same time, she brought his head down for a kiss.

It started out slow and sensual and quickly turned hot and hard and fast. She clung to his shoulders, he tightened his hold and still the fire burned out of control. They kissed each other mindlessly. She wanted this man. She'd fallen in love with him. She couldn't imagine her life without him.

The knowledge both scared and exhilarated her. It was frightening to give someone so much control over your happiness, but it was also wonderful knowing he felt the same. He hadn't actually said the words, but she had no doubt from his actions that he was well on the way to feeling as deeply for her as she did for him.

His hands slid up from around her hips until they caressed her breasts. With the pad of his thumbs he stroked her nipples. They pebbled beneath his touch.

"Oh, Rafe. That feels so good," she moaned, breathless for more.

He bent his head and spreading wide her neckline, lifted one breast to his mouth. She felt the heat of him even through her bra and was anxious to feel his skin on hers. She wished they were somewhere more private, where they could explore this right to the end.

He pulled slowly away and lifted his head and stared down into her eyes. They were both breathing hard. She reached up and loosened his tie and undid the first few buttons of his shirt. Spreading the fabric wide, she planted her palms against his broad chest and reveled in his muscular strength.

With just the lightest scattering of hair, he was perfect in every way. His pectoral muscles were sculpted. His abdominals were well-defined. Desperate need poured through her. She wanted this man so badly. She thought she might simply combust if she couldn't have him.

As if reading her mind, he took her hand and placed it on the large bulge in his pants. He was hot and hard and huge.

"Feel how much I want you," he said, his voice rough.

"I want you, too," she breathed.

"You do things to me that I've never felt with anyone else."

She nodded. "I feel the same."

He crushed her to him once again and they kissed like they were starving. Eventually, they came up for air.

"I think we should go home," she gasped.

He stared down at her, his eyes dark and unfathomable. "Is your father there?"

She held his gaze as she replied. "No. He's out for the night. What about Charli? Will she be all right?"

"My neighbor will sit with her until I get home. I arranged for some takeout to be delivered for them."

Mallory slowly grinned. The stars had finally aligned. "Let's do it then."

CHAPTER 13

At the look in Rafe's eyes, Mallory's heart beat faster. They'd made it to her father's house in record time. She unlocked the front door and led him straight into her bedroom. Tugging his shirt out of his pants, she undid the rest of his buttons and spread his shirt wide. He shrugged it off his shoulders. At last, she could gaze on his male perfection.

He was bronzed and sculpted and beautiful. She gazed at him in awe. Tentatively, she reached out and ran her fingernail down his chest. The muscles jumped beneath her finger. She smiled, loving the power she had over him. Then she noticed his tattoo.

Khloe.

His first love. The mother of his child. She was glad he'd told her about the woman or she might have felt more insecure. As it was, she ran her finger lightly over the heart that encircled the name and then moved lower to concentrate on his nipples.

Small and brown, she traced the nubs with her finger and then leaned forward and touched them with her mouth. His sudden gasp was gratifying. *Oh, she was going to enjoy this!* For weeks he'd been holding her at a distance, wanting to take things slowly, driving her insane. Now it was her turn to push him to the edge.

She switched her attention to his other nipple, all the while fondling his chest. Then she upped the ante and kissed her way down to his pants. On her knees now, she reached for his belt and then the button. The zipper slid down with only a little difficulty. His manhood bulged behind Looney Tunes briefs, but it wasn't enough. She needed to see him. *All* of him.

Reaching up, she drew down his pants and briefs simultaneously. He stood still and then assisted her by stepping out of them. When he was completely naked, she sat back on her haunches and stared.

He was even more perfect than she'd imagined. She told him so. He looked embarrassed. His humility only served to endear him to her more. Coming up on her knees once more, she wriggled close enough so that she could hold his cock in her hand and take him into her mouth.

He groaned and buried his hands in her hair. She licked the top of his cock, down the sides, around his head and then did it all over again. Then she took him into her mouth, as far as she could go and sucked him in a rhythm that was calculated to drive him wild.

"Mallory," he gasped. The single word held a wealth of meaning. "I'm going to come if you keep that up."

She merely looked up at him, grinning wickedly. "Don't worry. I'll make sure I'm right there with you before that happens."

He groaned again and with his head thrown back in abandon, gave himself up to her ministrations. She kept loving him with her hand and mouth until she tasted his salty fluid. Just enough to let her know he truly was hanging on the edge. With that she pulled back and stood.

His eyes flew open and he reached for her. Spinning her around, he slid down the zipper of her dress and she was thankful she hadn't worn anything with buttons. In no time at all, he had her dress up and over her head and tossed it aside.

She wore lacy black underwear. She'd dressed with care that evening, even though she wasn't sure if Rafe would discover what was underneath. Now she was glad she'd worn her best lingerie. Slowly, he turned her round to face him. From the look on his face, it had been well worth the effort.

"You're so beautiful," he rasped.

She smiled. "I think that's my line."

They moved toward each other, then Rafe bent and picked her up as if she were weightless and deposited her on the bed. A quick glance confirmed the bed was made and the room was passably tidy. She swallowed a sigh of relief. She was pretty sure Rafe was fully occupied with other things, but still... She didn't want him to think she was a slob.

And then he was kissing her again and all thoughts of the cleanliness of her room were swept from her mind. His lips were full and soft and supple. He kissed with confidence and she liked that. Her arms crept round his neck and she held him to her.

He deepened the kiss and their tongues entwined and it was a dance as old as time. The kiss seemed to go on forever, until at last he pulled away. But he didn't go far. Instead, he kissed his way down her neck and then lower still. When his mouth fastened around one of her nipples, she gasped and almost came off the bed.

Just like she had, he licked and stroked and suckled until she was wild with need. Blood pounded through her veins, rushing through her ears and igniting nerve endings she hadn't known existed. He loved one breast and then the other and then continued his descent.

He kissed his way across her stomach, pausing to dip his tongue into her belly button. She squirmed and then tensed when he moved lower and flicked his tongue over her clit. With fists clenched, she endured his sensual onslaught, knowing he was merely doing to her what she'd done to him. He drew her to the point where she was about to scream and then he moved away and came back to cover her with his body.

She felt his erection, hard and hot and needy, pressing against her femininity. And then she remembered protection.

"We need a condom."

He tensed above her and then relaxed. "Do

you have any? I'm afraid I stopped carrying one in my wallet."

She smiled, warmed by his admission, and then reached over to the drawer on her nightstand. She found a condom and handed it to him and within moments, he was sheathed. He positioned himself at her entrance and she silently urged him on. And then he thrust forward and she gasped as he buried himself inside her.

"Oh, God. You feel so good," he murmured on a groan.

"So do you."

And then he began to move and all conversation was over. Slowly at first; as the pressure inside her built, so did the speed of his movements. She clung to his shoulders, riding each wave, until she couldn't stand it a moment longer. She reached the peak and cried out, digging her nails into his skin. As her muscles contracted around him, he thrust harder and faster. A moment later, he climaxed and collapsed against her.

Slowly, she got her breathing under control and Rafe rolled off her and sighed. "Oh, Mallory. I hope you think like I do and agree that was worth the wait."

He looked at her and smiled and she grinned back. "Oh, yes. It was definitely worth the wait."

With that, Rafe moved away and stood and pulled on his clothes. Mallory sat up, at once feeling bereft.

"Where are you going?"

"Charli's at home. I need to go."

Mallory tried to stem her disappointment, but she completely understood. It was one of the disadvantages of dating a man who had a child.

When he was fully dressed, he came back over to where she had pushed herself up against the pillows. She tucked the sheet around her. He sat down on the edge of the bed.

"Thank you for dinner," she said quietly.

"I had a great night, Mallory. There's nothing I'd rather do than spend the whole night with you, but unfortunately, I have to go."

"It's fine, Rafe. I understand. Don't worry about it for a minute. Some day in the future, I hope we're in a position where you can stay the night. Or maybe I could stay at your place. Whatever. We'll work it out. In the meantime, thank you again and I'll see you soon."

He bent over and kissed her softly on the lips. "I'll call you tomorrow."

Rafe let himself quietly out of Mallory's house and climbed into his car. He checked the time.

Half-past ten.

It was later than he'd wanted to be out. Charli would be asleep. Still, he wanted to be there for her during the night in case she woke and needed him. It hadn't happened for a long time, but she was his little girl, his baby and she was far too young to be left alone.

Mrs Hubbard was there, but that wasn't the

same. It wasn't fair to expect the woman to spend the night in his home. And yet, he hadn't been lying when he told Mallory he wished he could stay with her the whole night. He was torn between his baby girl and the woman he'd come to care for deeply. Hell, he felt more than that. He was falling in love. He needed to think hard and make some decisions and he hoped everything worked out all right.

And he still hadn't told Mallory about her mother...

Tomorrow. He'd tell her tomorrow. Switching on the ignition, he pulled away from the curb and drove away into the silent night.

Mallory stared hard at Daniel Stone and his father and tried not to feel intimidated. The two angry, intense men seated across from her were demanding assurances she wasn't prepared to give.

Great.

They'd been going round and round in circles for so long she was exhausted. The Stone men remained adamant they wouldn't let up on their quest to seek custody of only one of the twins. Despite the countless meetings she'd had with them and the warnings from the judge, both men still refused to listen to reason or accept the likelihood the court would refuse their application to separate the girls.

The last time Mallory had seen her client, Rupert Stone had assured her all would be well. He had friends in high places and his influence over them was not to be discounted. But he'd just advised her that his plan to get Judge Mason on side had gone awry.

"It seems the esteemed Judge Mason has had an attack of conscience," Rupert sneered. "I offered him a considerable amount of persuasion in the form of unmarked hundred dollar bills, however, he turned me down and now he seems to have taken fright."

All Mallory knew was that Judge Mason had been reassigned to another case and they now had a new judge to convince, apparently someone who wasn't in Rupert Stone's pocket.

"Gentlemen, we're getting nowhere," Mallory said. "This case comes back before the court in three days. Judge Ticehurst is not known for pussyfooting around. He'll want to know what's going on with these children and why no one seems to be considering their best interests. I've told you over and over again. Our best course of action is to seek custody of both children. If we ask for both, we have a fair chance of success."

The expression on both of the men's faces remained stoic. It was as if she hadn't spoken at all. Impatience and irritation surged through her. She seared both men with her gaze.

"What's the problem? Why is it such a big deal for you to seek custody of both children? If I didn't know better, I'd think it was your way of showing some kindness toward your estranged spouse—

that is, rather than one of you missing out on your children altogether, you share one each. Except I'm not buying that. Your animosity toward Ms Michaels has been demonstrated on more than one occasion. This ridiculous position you've taken has nothing to do with being kind."

Daniel Stone averted his gaze and squirmed in his seat. His father remained silent. Her gaze remained unrelenting. She was through with playing games.

"So? What is it? There must be a reason. I want to hear it. *Now.*"

"I-I... The truth is, I-I don't get on with Isabelle," Daniel stammered. "She's a weakling. Always crying about something. I only have to look at her and she bursts into tears. We don't understand one another. I look at her and can't work out what went wrong. Now, Zoe is the perfect child: smart, pretty, funny, pleasing." He smiled. "She's so much like me. She's everything I could wish for in a daughter. She's the one I want."

Mallory sat back in shock, not even bothering to hide her reaction. This was madness! Daniel Stone was insane. *What kind of father makes judgements about his children, and such harsh ones at that, and then chooses between them?*

She looked at Rupert to gage his reaction, hoping to see something in his expression that even loosely resembled the shock and dislike she felt for his son. But there was nothing. His face was as hard as granite and his lips remained tightly compressed. It was clear he had no intention of commenting or passing judgement against his son.

Mallory stared at both of them, aghast. She'd known right from the outset this case was going to be difficult and would test her to her limits, but she'd had no idea how hard it would be. And now she'd had enough.

"Gentlemen, listen here and listen well. I'm not going to say this again. I refuse to seek an application to separate those girls. I don't care that you like one more than the other and quite frankly, your reason for wanting Zoe over Isabelle is repulsive. We're talking about the lives of two little girls, here. You seem to have forgotten that. Either you let me amend the application so that we seek custody of both girls, or I'm out. Take it, or leave it. I want your answer first thing in the morning."

Her stern tone left the men in no doubt she meant business. They glanced at each other and then, stony faced and muttering obscenities beneath their breath, almost as one they pushed away from her desk and stormed out of the room, slamming the door behind them.

Mallory let out a shaky breath and sighed in relief. She still trembled with anger. She couldn't believe the excuse they'd given her; their total lack of decency and morality. It was beyond comprehension. Good riddance, was all she could say. She couldn't believe the audacity and the absolute selfishness of Daniel Stone. He didn't deserve to be a father to either of those girls.

She stared down at the paperwork scattered across her desk. She hoped the Stone men would decide to end her representation and find another lawyer who would be a better fit. They'd already fired her once. She was sure they had it in them to do it again and this time, she welcomed it. She no longer cared what her managing partner would think of her losing such a lucrative client. She had to draw the line somewhere and draw it she had. She'd had enough.

A knot of tension sent burning pain across her shoulders. It had been a tough meeting and she still had one more client appointment before she could call it a day. The faint headache behind her eyes reminded her she hadn't had near enough caffeine and she was still taut with anger and disgust.

With another sigh, she pushed away from her desk. She needed some time out of the office to catch her breath, to clear her head and to try to forget she'd ever known anyone by the name of Stone. Grabbing her handbag and the gym clothes she stashed in her locker for just this kind of occasion, she tugged on her jacket. She stopped by her secretary's desk and pleaded a migraine and requested her last appointment be rescheduled. She needed to work off some of her anger and the best place to do that was the gym. With that, she headed for the elevator.

Relieved that she'd driven into work that day, she joined the steady stream of traffic heading south and took the exit to her gym. It was a swish place in the eastern suburbs, on the way to her house. Taking out some of her frustration and anger on the boxing bag was just the thing she needed.

CHAPTER 14

Rafe pulled on the regulation protective clothing required by the morgue and then stepped into the main chamber where most of the autopsies were conducted. Samantha Wolfe was bent over a corpse, her gloved hands covered in blood. She looked up when he entered and gestured him over.

"I won't be long, Detective Connelly. Take a seat in my office."

Rafe nodded, relieved to make his escape. He attended autopsies whenever the job required it, but he never volunteered. There was something unsettling and just plain sad about watching a human being dissected, with their organs weighed and measured and bits and pieces of them scrutinized, x-rayed and analyzed. He preferred to keep his distance.

Samantha's office was down the hall from the main workroom. Her name was embossed on a plaque and alerted anyone who didn't know that she was the Chief Forensic Pathologist. She'd earned that title through sheer dedication and exemplary hard work. She was the best pathologist in the country and Rafe was pleased to be working with her.

The door opened a short time later and Samantha walked in. She'd removed her protective clothing and now wore a custom-made suit. The jacket fit snugly around her enviable figure. The short skirt emphasized nice legs. She was probably close to forty, but she looked much younger than that.

"Sorry to keep you waiting, Detective."

He stood as she entered. "No problem and please, call me Rafe."

She inclined her head in acknowledgement. He cleared his throat.

"I understand you've managed to create an image of the woman we found in the cave?"

Sam nodded and made her way to her desk. She sat down and dragged the keyboard toward her. "Yes. Give me a minute and I'll pull it up for you."

She tapped on the keyboard. "That FaceFit technology is amazing, even to someone like me," she said conversationally. "You enter a few measurements and some DNA results and just like that, you have a face with identifying features. It's like magic."

She grinned like a kid in a candy store. Rafe couldn't help but grin back. "It sure beats the old ways of having a witness sit with an artist and pick out features, one by one."

"Yes, and this is far more accurate. Combined

with the thirteen points of measurement, the DNA tells us all we need to know—the distance between the eyes, the shape of the cheekbones, jawline, eye color, hair color, height. It truly is amazing. Of course, it can't tell if they've dyed their hair different to their natural color or how long they might wear it or in what style, but it pretty much knows everything else."

She tapped a few more keys and then smiled in satisfaction "Here you go. Here's your Jane Doe."

She turned the screen to face him and he gasped in shock.

It was Mallory.

No, that couldn't be right. It was Mallory's mother. His heart leaped out of his chest and blood rushed through his ears. He barely heard the rest of what Samantha said. He stared at the screen in mounting horror and disbelief.

They'd found Sofia Lopez.

His very next thought was that he needed to call Mallory and tell her everything.

"Are you all right, Rafe?"

Samantha's voice came as if from a great distance. He blinked hard and forced himself to respond.

"Yes, I'm fine. Could you... Could you email me a copy of this image?"

"Yes, of course. I'll do that now. It will be waiting for you when you get back to your office."

"Thank you," he managed weakly. "I have to go."

On the way out of the morgue, he reached for his phone and then hesitated. Something like this required a meeting face to face. Mallory would be devastated at the news. He wanted to be there to offer what comfort he could.

He checked his watch. It was a little past four. Court sessions were over for the day. With a bit of luck, he'd catch her in her office. Dropping his phone back in his pocket, he climbed into the unmarked police car and headed back downtown. He dreaded the thought of the pain he was about to cause. The responsibility of disclosing what he knew lay heavy in his heart.

For the next ninety minutes, Mallory lifted weights, jogged and kick-boxed her way around the gym. She was in a lather of sweat when she finally pulled up for a break.

"You're going at that pretty hard."

She turned to see a good-looking guy around her age dressed in fashionable workout gear. His muscles bulged and gleamed with sweat, illuminated by the overhead lights. He had a friendly smile and nice eyes and his quick once-over was filled with admiration. A few weeks earlier, she might have been tempted to encourage the frank interest she saw in his eyes, but since she'd met Rafe, no other man came close.

She offered him a polite smile and turned away. Exhausted now, she grabbed her bag and headed for the showers. On the way home, she found a parking space right outside her local café. She ordered a latté and then found an empty table in the back. She took a seat and sighed in relief. Now that she was away from the stress and drama of the office and had given herself a chance to work off her anger, she could relax and clear her thoughts and allow herself a few moments to think of Rafe.

Rafe.

Their night together had been magical. And, yes, he'd been right. It had *definitely* been worth the wait. He was a considerate and passionate lover and they were more than compatible in bed. It only further justified the way she felt about him. He was everything she wanted in a man, and he offered her more. Things she hadn't even contemplated.

Despite the fact he hadn't opened up entirely about his family, she could live with that. Everyone had baggage, like Sally-Ann had said and everyone had skeletons in the closet. Hell, Mallory's mother had run off when she was ten and she'd never heard from her again. Talk about skeletons. In time, she hoped Rafe would trust her enough to open up and let her know exactly what had gone on. She could tell it hadn't been good. Everyone dealt with trauma in their own way and she would leave it at that for now.

Her coffee arrived and she added sugar and then reached in her bag for her iPad. Most people surfed the Internet on their phone, but she much preferred the larger screen and usually only used her phone for calls and text messages. It meant lugging around another device, but when she was commuting on the bus, it was also easier to type memos and briefs using a keyboard and larger screen.

Idly, she flicked through news stories that had turned up during the day. She'd overslept after her night with Rafe and had skipped her usual breakfast routine. She enjoyed keeping on top of the news and current events and welcomed the opportunity to do so now.

A notification popped up on her screen from one of the local news channels. Police had a breakthrough on the Jane Doe case—the unidentified woman whose bones had been found in a cave.

Mallory's heart skipped a beat. That was Rafe's investigation. She scrolled lower. There was a picture of a woman—not a photograph or a drawing...something more like a composite that might have been put together by the police. She scanned the article. It was as she thought.

The picture had been put together by a forensic pathologist who'd worked with an embalmer and an artist to re-create an image of the woman who'd been found in the cave. It was amazing how far technology had come. From mere bones, the experts had been able to come up with an image of what the woman might have looked like.

Mallory glanced at the woman again. Something about the face and the hair looked familiar. In fact, if she didn't know any better, she might even think it looked a bit like her mom.

A shiver of foreboding feathered its way down her spine. And then she told herself not to be silly. There was no way the woman in the cave could be her mother. Perhaps it was just the red hair…

She stared again at the image and slowly shook her head. No, there might be some similarities, but it wasn't her mother. Her mother's hair was long and wavy and her lips were fuller than that. Mallory was imagining things that simply weren't there. It was just that her mother's disappearance had been on her mind lately. Yes, that's all it was.

In fact, the longer she studied the picture, the more certain she was that it wasn't her mother. After all, her father had driven her mother to the airport. He'd told her that. Her mother was homesick for her family in Argentina. She wanted to go back. It was a story Mallory knew by heart. She'd replayed it often enough in her mind. At least in the early years after her mother had left. Later, it got too painful and eventually it was better if Mallory didn't think of her mother at all.

It was just the discovery of the woman in the cave that had reignited old memories and brought all the unanswered questions rushing to the surface. She wondered if Rafe had made any progress locating her mother. *Perhaps he knew even now where she was?*

No, Rafe would have told her as soon as he came upon the information. He knew how important it was to her. If he knew anything about her mother's location, he wouldn't have kept it from her.

And that was another thing: the woman in the cave was Rafe's investigation. He must have already seen and approved the image for publication. If he'd had any suspicion the woman might be her mother, he'd have called her straight away. She was sure of it.

With that thought in mind, she rummaged through her handbag for her phone and then realized it wasn't there. She must have left it at the gym. It must have fallen out of her bag when she went to take a shower.

Damn!

The inconvenience was annoying. It was late and she was tired. The last thing she felt like doing was driving over to the gym so she could get her phone. It could wait until morning.

Rafe tried Mallory's number again. He'd lost count of the number of times he'd called and left messages. He'd tried to see her at her office, but her secretary had told him she'd left for the day. He wondered where she'd gone.

It was odd that she hadn't called him. *What was going on?* He thought their first night together had been wonderful. He'd had sex with other women, but with Mallory, it was the first time he felt like he was making love. Their night had been so special, so full of tenderness, passion and love. He was sure she felt it, too. *So why wasn't she returning his calls?*

Should he be worried? He wanted to go and tell her about what he'd found out about her mother, but she wasn't even speaking to him. Should he go over to her place? What if she wasn't there? What if their night together hadn't been so wonderful for her? What if she didn't *want* to talk to him?

He groaned aloud and scrubbed his hands through his hair. The endless questions were driving him crazy and he was getting nowhere. Besides, it wasn't like the story had already gone out. He'd contacted the newspapers on his way back to the station and they'd told him the earliest he could get it in was in the afternoon edition the next day.

It gave Rafe a measure of comfort that Mallory wouldn't find out about her mother that way. Besides, she didn't have the additional information that had set off alarm bells in Rafe's head. There was no reason for her to suspect the woman in the cave was her mother. Still, he needed to speak with her and come clean about everything he knew. He just hoped she understood his reasons for withholding the earlier evidence from her.

"Hey, good work on that FaceFit image. Samantha did a smashing job."

Rafe turned around as James came up beside him. "Yeah. Thanks. The papers have agreed to run it in tomorrow afternoon's edition."

James grimaced. "I hope you don't mind it hitting the Internet feeds earlier than that. It seems someone's already leaked it to the press."

Rafe sat up in alarm. "What the hell are you talking about?"

"This." James handed him his phone. Rafe stared down at a page on a popular local news site. The picture of Sofia Lopez stared back at him, along with an accompanying story about a police breakthrough.

"The hotline's been ringing off the hook since it was posted. Apparently she looks familiar to a lot of people. Who would have thought there were that many long-ago lost relatives out there?"

"Fuck."

James frowned. "What's the matter? We might get Jane Doe identified sooner than we think. Isn't that the idea?"

Rafe regarded him grimly. James' frown deepened and confusion filled his eyes. "What? I thought you'd be pleased," he said a little defensively. "Even a bunch of crazies is better than no leads at all."

Rafe fished the picture of Sofia Lopez Patterson out of his top drawer and handed it to his partner. "Remember this?"

James gave it a cursory look. "Yeah. It was on your desk the other week."

"Who does it remind you of?"

"Mallory Patterson."

"Exactly."

"Who is it?"

Rafe sighed heavily. "Her mother. Sofia Lopez Patterson. She left the family home twenty years earlier to board a plane to Argentina. Mallory hasn't seen or heard from her since."

James shrugged. "What does her father have to say?"

"According to Mallory, her father was the one who drove her mother to the airport. He says he hasn't had any contact with her since that day."

"Okay, but what does this have to do with our Jane Doe?"

Rafe picked up James' phone and handed it to him. "Take another look at that photo."

James peered down at the screen. He then looked at the picture still sitting on Rafe's desk. His eyes widened.

"Holy shit."

"Yeah." Rafe's gut swirled with dread. Even James had made the connection.

"What does Mallory think?"

James' question ricocheted through Rafe's brain. He clenched his jaw and then looked up at his partner. "I haven't spoken to her yet."

Once again, frown lines marked James' forehead. "Really? I thought you were growing close? Sally-Ann certainly gave me that impression."

Rafe blushed. He wished he'd been more discrete about his interest in Mallory.

"Hey, don't think too much of it," James added, "Sally-Ann has a vested interest. She had an inkling you and Mallory might hit things off. It's the reason she invited Mallory over."

Rafe was filled with surprise. "You mean, she was trying to set us up?"

James waved away Rafe's indignation. "Calm down, Detective. There was nothing deceitful about it. Sally-Ann and Mallory are friends. Mallory is single. *You're* single. She knows both of you. She just thought it might be nice if she introduced the two of you. It's not like you two were the only people at the barbeque." James shook his head and chuckled. "She wasn't *that* obvious."

Rafe reluctantly joined in; after all, he wasn't the least bit upset about being introduced to Mallory. If things worked out between them, he'd be praising Sally-Ann for her efforts. He decided to cut James some slack.

"Yeah, okay. Anyway, I tried to see Mallory at her work as soon as I saw the image, but she wasn't there. I called her then, but the call went through to her voicemail. I've tried several more times over the course of the afternoon, but she didn't answer and she hasn't called me back. I didn't stress too much over it because I thought I'd have time to catch up with her before the papers printed the story. I didn't count on it going live on the Internet within hours of its creation." He paused and then added in disgust, "I wonder who leaked it?"

James sighed in resignation. "Probably some overzealous constable hoping to curry favor with the press. They probably knew it was scheduled for release tomorrow and didn't see any harm in getting it out there early."

Rafe groaned. "That's the problem with these instant news services. They're constantly seeking fodder for their machine. They probably have contacts all over the city who can feed them tidbits."

"Well, there's always the possibility that Mallory hasn't seen it, yet. After all, she hasn't returned your call. That's got to be a good sign." And then James' gaze narrowed on him, as if a thought had just occurred to him. "Unless there's some other reason she's avoiding you."

Despite himself, Rafe flushed. "No, of course not. We had dinner last night. Everything seemed fine."

James gave him another searching look and then made a sound of dismissal in the back of his throat.

"Well, let's hope she hasn't seen it. If it *is* her mother we found in the cave, I sure as hell wouldn't like to find out that way."

Rafe's phone rang and his heart immediately skipped a beat. *Mallory.* Finally, she was returning his call. He checked the screen and frowned. It wasn't Mallory. It was his neighbor, Mrs Hubbard. All of a sudden, his heart beat faster for an entirely different reason.

"Mrs Hubbard? How are you?"

"I'm fine, Rafe, but I'm afraid Charli isn't."

Rafe froze. In less than a second, a barrage of awful scenarios ran through his mind. He could hardly bring himself to ask the next question.

"W-what happened?"

"Oh, nothing too serious, but she's not feeling well. She's burning up and feels sick. I think you should take her to the hospital."

Relief flooded through Rafe that Charli's illness wasn't fatal. He assured his neighbor he'd be there as soon as possible. He ended the call and looked at James.

"Charli's sick. I need to go home."

"Of course," James replied. "Is there anything I can do?"

"No, it's probably a virus. She was unwell the other night. I thought she'd gotten better. I might take her to the doctor and see what's going on."

"Sounds like a good idea. I'll see you tomorrow."

With that, Rafe shut down his computer, pulled on his jacket and left.

CHAPTER 15

Mallory slept through her alarm the next morning and woke feeling tired and disgruntled. She'd spent the night tossing and turning, thinking of Rafe and dreaming of her mother. The picture she'd seen on the Internet continued to haunt her. The woman looked enough like her mother that they could be related at least.

She climbed out of bed and padded to the shower. The house was silent. She'd waited up for her father, wanting to talk to him about the picture, but he hadn't come home last night. She thought after he'd broken things off with Alice she'd see a bit more of him, but apparently not.

Taking as little time as possible, she showered, dressed and applied her makeup. She had an appointment with the Stone men first thing. There was no time for breakfast or for detouring to the gym. She'd phoned them from the public phone outside the café yesterday afternoon and had confirmed they indeed had her phone. She'd left it in the change room. She was relieved to discover some honest person had handed it in. As much as she hated to leave it there any longer, she had no choice.

She thought of Rafe. She'd seen him only the night before last, but she missed him. It was possible he'd tried to call her. Without her phone, she couldn't tell. There was no other phone in her house. Both she and her father only used their cells.

And then another thought occurred to her. What if the woman in the story *was* her mother? What if Rafe had tried all afternoon to reach her, only her phone was at the gym? A sudden wave of foreboding washed over her. She wished her father was around to talk to. He'd reassure her, like he had before, that the woman in the cave couldn't possibly be her mother. He'd personally taken her to the airport. It's funny. Mallory had never before considered that her father hadn't seen his wife get on the plane. He only assumed she'd boarded one. All these years, Mallory had made the same assumption.

But what if they were wrong?

———————————

John Patterson stared down at the image of the woman that filled the screen on his phone and the world outside his office window disappeared. His gut was weighed down with dread. The resemblance to Sofia was uncanny. It was amazing how far technology had come. From a few bones that had lain dormant in a cave for twenty years, they were able to recreate something so eerily accurate. Of course, her hair was much longer than the woman's in the picture and she'd often curled it, and her eyes were more green than blue and her lips had been plumped out with fillers, but most of everything else was as it had been when Sofia was alive.

Dragging his gaze away, he stared out the window at the spectacular view of Sydney Harbour and Hyde Park. His suite of offices were on the top floor of Sydney Legal with all the other senior partners. It was a position he'd earned through plain old hard work and a determination to be the best.

He had an uncanny knack of reading people, of knowing when to push and when to ease up. He also sensed when his opposition was at its weakest and that's when he'd go in for the kill. He'd make an offer well below market value, but by then, they were too beaten down by the mind games to do anything other than accept. It had been the same for Sofia, only she hadn't capitulated like he thought she would.

Instead, his endless needling and mind manipulation seemed to instill in her an inner strength. It was like the harder he screwed with her, the tougher and more determined she got. She'd always known about his dalliances, of course. They'd started not long after his marriage. It seemed as though once he'd secured the prize that was Sofia Mary Lopez, he'd lost interest in the chase and even in Sofia herself. It was as if the thrill of the chase was the greater prize and once the chase was over, the prize no longer held any value.

Then Mallory came along and his world turned on its end. He could never have imagined how it would feel to hold his squirming, red-faced daughter in his arms. He fell in love immediately and vowed to do everything in his power to keep her safe. He doted on her from the moment she was born.

Despite the love and attention lavished on her which might have turned the child into a brat, Mallory grew up a happy, well-adjusted kid. She was smart and funny and beautiful. In John's eyes, she could do no wrong. They spent hours together, bike riding, swimming, talking about books and discussing current affairs. For a young child, she had an avid interest in everything that went on around her and he was happy to quench her thirst.

Unfortunately, relations between him and Mallory's mother weren't as convivial. Sofia became more and more angry over his affairs. They argued over it incessantly. He refused to give up his extracurricular activities. She said it wasn't fair. She was his wife. She had a right to demand his fidelity. She reminded him he'd vowed to remain true to her.

He'd merely laughed in the face of her objections. As to his vows, what did they matter? They were words he'd uttered because it was expected. He'd had no intention of keeping them then, or now.

The fights between him and Sofia became more virulent. It seemed they couldn't be in the same room with each other without arguing. It was tiresome, but he learned to tune it out. In the end, he barely listened.

But then Sofia came home one night and told him she was leaving. She was returning to her homeland. Her family would welcome her with open arms and they'd also welcome Mallory.

That got his attention. He'd looked up from the legal papers that were scattered across his desk and lowered his glasses.

"Mallory? What the hell are you talking about? You do what you want, but there's no way Mallory's going anywhere."

It was the beginning of the end. Sofia consulted a divorce lawyer. John knew the courts would look favorably on the mother of the child. Sofia had a respectable job. She was a doctor at the Sydney Harbour Hospital and though she worked long hours, so did he. She had a good chance of getting sole custody. And now she'd threatened to take his only child overseas.

The courts frowned on that kind of thing, but it wasn't impossible that they'd allow Sofia to take Mallory to visit her family in Argentina. After all, she was nearly ten years old and they'd never even met her. Once in Argentina, it could be a simple matter for Sofia to make a permanent home there and never bring Mallory back.

There was no way John could take the risk. Sofia would fight him for custody of their daughter with everything she had. It was only a matter of time before he lost his little girl forever. He couldn't bear the thought of that.

From that very night, he started plotting Sofia's demise. It had taken some clever planning, but it had all worked out perfectly, until now. Some stupid boys had found her bones where he'd hidden them in a cave. Now her face stared up at him from his screen. His long lost wife. The woman he never expected to see again.

Mallory thought all this time he'd been with his lady friends. The truth was, ever since he'd heard about the discovery of the woman's body in the Ku-ring-gai Chase National Park, he'd been hiding out in a hotel room, plotting his escape. It was only a matter of time before she got identified and then all hell would break loose. It pained him to leave his daughter, but he'd been left with no choice. Perhaps in time she'd forgive him and let him say his piece. Until then, he had to act cautiously and that meant protecting his ass.

Now that Sofia's image had become public, it was time to put his plan in motion, before it was too late.

Mallory made it into the office only a few minutes late. She waved hello to her secretary, Rhonda, and was about to hurry past when the woman called out.

"Oh, Mallory. I just had a call from Daniel Stone. He said he and his father were cancelling their appointment with you this morning and they were done with your representation, too."

Mallory came to a halt. "Oh. Okay. That's... fine."

"Mr Stone said if you'd bothered to answer some of the messages he sent you last night, he might have been willing to give you another chance."

She looked at Mallory pointedly. Mallory felt the urge to explain. "I'm sorry, Rhonda. I arranged to meet with Mr Stone this morning. I didn't think he'd contact me after hours. The thing is, I lost my phone yesterday afternoon. I've tracked it down, but I still don't have it. I didn't want to be late for this meeting."

"Well, it looks like you have at least an hour to spare, now. Perhaps you should go and collect it?"

Though Rhonda's tone remained non-judgmental, Mallory flushed in embarrassment just the same.

"Yes. You're right. I'll... I'll go and get it now." With that, she turned and left the way she'd come.

Rafe listened to Mallory's cell phone ring out and finally switch to voicemail. He cursed and left a message, asking her to call him. Then he found the number for Sydney Legal and dialed her office.

"I'm sorry, Detective Connelly," an older woman who identified herself as Mallory's secretary said. "She's just stepped out for a bit. Would you like to leave a message?"

He clenched his jaw against a surge of frustration and asked her to let Mallory know he'd called. He hung up the phone and cursed again. *What the hell was going on? Why was she out again?* The woman was proving impossible to find. He needed to give the newspapers the go ahead to run the story. They were expecting to print it that afternoon. It was important to keep up a good relationship with the media. Often he needed them as much as they needed him.

But there was still a chance Mallory hadn't seen the picture on the Internet and he wanted to speak with her about it before she did. Once it was splashed all over the papers, there was a much greater chance she'd see it.

But where was she and why hadn't she returned his call?

And then all his earlier insecurities rushed to the fore. The last time he'd seen her, she was flushed and tousled from their lovemaking. He'd told her he'd call her. And he had. Only, she hadn't called him back and now he couldn't help but wonder if his impressions of the evening were different from hers...

She hadn't given him any indication she was unhappy, but how would he know? As far as women were concerned, he was way out of practice. Maybe she'd been putting on a front and he hadn't known enough to see through it?

No, he refused to believe she hadn't been as into him as he was into her. What they'd shared together had been amazing. They'd explored each other's bodies with abandon and had given and received such pleasure. She'd assured him it had been worth the wait. And he'd believed her. Then and now.

No, there must be some other reason for her silence. He only wished he knew what it was.

James came over and set a Styrofoam cup of coffee on his desk.

"Thanks," he muttered.

"Any luck tracking down Mallory?" James asked.

"No. And I'm running out of time. I need to give the go ahead to the papers within the next hour or it won't make the afternoon edition."

"Have you tried to reach her at work? I could call Sally-Ann."

"Thanks, but I've already left a message with Mallory's secretary. Apparently she's out again."

"How's Charli?"

Rafe sighed. "She's fine. Well, not fine. She has chicken pox."

"Oh, poor thing! Travis had them last year, even though he was immunized. Not good."

"Yeah, Charli was immunized, too. The doctor said they can still catch them. The good news is they tend to get a much less severe case. At least it's nothing fatal. I can handle chicken pox."

"Have you had them before?"

"Yeah, when I was a kid."

"Where is she now?"

"At home with Mrs Hubbard. I'm lucky my neighbor has also had them when she was young. We should be fine."

"Doesn't she have a concert coming up?"

"Damn! Yes, I forgot about that. It's on in a couple of days. I'll have to let her teacher know she won't be able to make it." And then he remembered he'd have to tell Mallory, too. If she ever answered his calls, that is.

———

The morning rush hour traffic was heavy heading in both directions. It took Mallory more than thirty minutes to get to the gym. Once inside, the manager retrieved her phone from a locked cabinet and handed it to her.

"Thank you," she said gratefully.

"You're welcome. You might want to make sure it's secured properly next time." He smiled as he said it.

Mallory nodded distractedly, her attention already focused on her phone. "Damn it," she cursed.

"What is it?"

"My battery's gone flat."

"I have a charger if you want to use it."

She smiled. "Thanks. That would be great." Distractedly she noticed how good-looking the manager was and the frank interest that filled his gaze. It was just like the guy she'd spoken to the day before. She didn't feel a thing. Not even a tingle. It just went to show how into Rafe Connelly she was.

Taking the charger, she plugged it in at a

power socket against the wall of the reception area. She took a seat and waited for the phone to switch on. For almost a full minute, the phone beeped with incoming messages.

She grimaced. Perhaps she should have made the effort to come and collect her phone last night. She dreaded the messages from Daniel Stone. Still, he'd fired her for the second time, so she no longer needed to worry about what he might have said. Daniel Stone was no longer her client. She wished she could say she cared.

The first few missed calls were from Rafe. Her stomach took a nosedive. So he *had* tried to call. She hoped it was just about catching up after their night of lovemaking and not something more serious. There were also several text messages from Daniel Stone, each one increasingly terse. She gave them a cursory glance before she deleted them.

Good riddance, Mr Stone. Find someone else to assist you in your awful plan.

There was another text message from Sally-Ann inviting her to a girls' night out. She quickly responded by letting Sally-Ann know she'd love to attend. Then she listened to the messages Rafe had left on her voicemail.

There was an edge to his voice that immediately filled her with foreboding. Her mind strayed to the picture she'd seen. *No, it couldn't be...* Rafe hadn't left any details about the reason for his calls, but it couldn't be about the unidentified woman. The face had been reconstructed by a computer from bones found at a crime scene. A body that had been found in a cave her mother hadn't visited since Mallory was a child. There was no way it could be her mom.

Determined to put an end to the questions once and for all, she dialed Rafe's number. He answered right away.

"Mallory! Where have you been? I've been calling you since yesterday."

She bit her lip. "Yes, I'm sorry. I left my phone at the gym yesterday afternoon. I've only just gotten it back. In fact, I'm still at the gym. My phone was flat. I borrowed a charger so I could check my messages right away."

"Oh, okay. Well, I guess I'm relieved that's all it was."

Mallory frowned. "What else would it be?"

"Nothing, I mean... I left so many messages... When I didn't hear from you, I began to wonder if I'd done something wrong..."

His voice drifted off in embarrassment. She was quick to set his mind at ease. "Of course not. Our night together was perfect...in every way. I can't wait to see you again."

Rafe cleared his throat. "Well, that's a relief," he said. And then his tone changed. "There's something I need to tell you, but I'd rather not do it over the phone. It's about your mother."

Her heart sank and a thousand crawling insects filled her belly with cold, hard dread. "What about my mother?" she answered cautiously.

Rafe sighed. "I think you should come down to the station. We need to talk."

"Is this about that woman you found in the cave?" The stridency in her voice made her wince. She drew in a deep breath and made a conscious effort to remain calm.

Rafe sighed again and the sound of it sent terror hurtling through her veins.

"Please, Mallory. Just come down to the station. As soon as you can."

———————

Mallory drove to the station in a daze. Despite her best efforts, her mind kept returning to the picture and the possibility it was her mother. She still didn't want to believe it and clung to a tiny sliver of hope that Rafe was wrong. After all, the image had been computer generated. Sometimes computers got things wrong. It wouldn't be the first time.

She found a parking spot three blocks away and hurried to the station. Rafe met her in the reception area. His expression was grave.

"We have a recreated image of the woman found in the cave. Jane Doe."

She nodded. "I saw it on the Internet."

His lips tightened. "Let's go somewhere we can talk."

In silence, she followed him down a corridor. He came to a halt outside a vacant interview room. He switched on the light and they entered a small, sparsely furnished room. The industrial carpet muffled their footsteps. A table dominated the compact space. She took one of the three chairs.

Rafe sat beside her. Their knees touched. The contact reminded her of all they'd shared. Sudden tears burned behind her eyes. He pulled out a folded piece of paper from his pocket and smoothed it out on the table. She stared down at the face of the woman. Her body felt weighed down by lead.

"This is the original of the image we created using the FaceFit technology I told you about. Only one image was supplied to the news source, but the computer generated several others."

He pulled out three more sheets of paper that showed the same face, but with slight variations in hair color, hair length and eye color. Mallory looked at each one and became more and more convinced the image was of her mother. Her belly filled with dread.

"We were able to get all of these indicators from the DNA we extracted from the woman's hair and bones," Rafe continued softly. "When that information's entered into the computer program along with certain measurements, it generates the images." He paused and then added, "I compared the images to the photo you gave me of your mother. I think it might be her."

Even though she'd prepared herself for his announcement, Mallory still gasped in shock. Her mind spun out of control, barely able to process it. Her father had told her he'd driven her mother to the airport. *How could she have been discovered lying murdered in a cave?* It didn't make sense.

"I-I can't believe it. I don't *want* to believe it." She turned her teary gaze up to his. "But after seeing all these images, it's almost like looking into a mirror, especially this one with the long hair."

Rafe nodded, his expression filled with sympathy. "I'm so sorry, Mallory, but I think you're right."

The tears that threatened spilled over and slowly ran down her cheeks. She made no effort to wipe them away. She was still in shock about the discovery and she still didn't understand how it could have happened. She wondered if she ever would.

CHAPTER 16

Rafe stared at Mallory, helpless to stem her pain. The shock and devastation on her face was plain to see. He wished there was something he could do or say to make things better, but there was nothing. He hated to see her looking so lost, so vulnerable, so confused. The story she'd been told, the one she'd believed since she was a child, had now been torn apart. He couldn't imagine what she was feeling—like she'd been run over by a freight train. In an effort to offer her comfort, he reached over and took her hand.

"I'm so sorry. I wish I could take this all away. I wish it was someone else's mother. I wish she'd never been found."

"Don't say that," Mallory whispered, her voice ragged with pain.

Rafe nodded. "Okay."

"What happens now?"

He compressed his lips. "Although the woman in this image looks like your mother, there's only one way to know for sure. We need to take a DNA sample from a blood relative—from you—and compare it to the DNA we have. Are you…all right with that?"

She dragged in an unsteady breath and at last wiped away her tears. She looked up at him. "Yes."

He nodded and squeezed her hand again. "Okay. I'll make the arrangements."

"Can you do it now?"

He looked at her, his heart swelling with love and tenderness. "Of course. If that's what you want."

She shuddered. "I just want to get it over with."

"Of course. I'll be right back. Will you be okay?"

"Yes, but hurry. Please."

With that, he left her in the room and went up the stairs to the squad room two at a time. As quickly as he could, he collected the swabs and other paraphernalia he needed to obtain a DNA sample. He was back downstairs only a few minutes later. She remained seated where he'd left her, staring into space.

"Mallory, are you okay?"

She turned her head to look at him and gave him a wan smile. "I'm okay."

He set about obtaining a sample and instructed her about what to do. She opened her mouth wide and he swabbed it, taking care to get a sufficient sample of saliva.

"That ought to do it," he said and slid the swab stick into a sterile plastic bag. He wrote the time and date on it, along with Mallory's name and Jane Doe's case file number.

"How long will it take to get the results?"

Her tone was dull. Her face was pale. He wished he could take her in his arms. He wanted so badly to hold her, to comfort her, to bring her peace.

"Hopefully no more than a couple of days," he replied.

Her shoulders slumped. Fresh tears formed in her eyes. "What am I supposed to do until then? Continue on as normal? What about my father? What am I going to tell him?" she cried.

Rafe's heart clenched at the agony in her eyes. He'd never felt so helpless. He moved close and drew her to her feet and then hugged her close. She collapsed against him on a tortured sigh.

They stood there in silence for long moments until at last Rafe spoke again. "How did you get here?"

Her voice was muffled against his shirt when she replied. "I drove."

He nodded and pressed a comforting kiss against her hair. "I'm not sure you should get behind a wheel at the moment. Let me drive you home."

She looked up. Her eyes pleaded with his. "Will you stay with me? I don't want to be alone."

"What about your father?"

She shook her head. "He'll be at work, thank goodness. I don't know what I'm going to say to him. I don't know if I even want to talk to him just yet. At least, not before I know for sure. Do you understand?"

He stared down at her and his heart welled up with love. This was his woman. He wanted to take care of her. He wanted to keep her safe.

He nodded slowly. "Of course I understand." Once again, he pulled her close. He gently stroked her silky hair. "It's going to be okay, Mallory, I promise. It's going to be okay."

———————

It was the first time Rafe had seen Mallory's house in the daylight. The love and care that had gone into the restoration of the circa 1920s bungalow was even more evident in the light of day. Paint colors had been chosen with the era in mind, as well as complementing the lush greenery that filled the front yard. On his last visit he hadn't noticed the gardens that lined the concrete walkway that led to the front door. Thick bunches of agapanthus, with their glossy green foliage and delicate lilac-colored heads, nasturtiums, gerberas and even a rose garden filled the small yard. It was a plethora of texture and color and perfume and it made Rafe's senses spin. Being someone who enjoyed gardening, he appreciated the time and effort it took to have one looking so good.

"Who has the green thumb?" he asked as they made their way up the path.

She smiled slightly. "Me. It's my way of relaxing after a tough week."

He reached for her hand and squeezed it. "Me, too."

Her eyes widened in surprise. "Really? That's... amazing. We have so much in common."

He held her gaze, his look heavy with intent. "We do."

For a long moment, neither of them said anything and then Mallory turned away. "Come on. Let's go inside."

He followed her up the three concrete steps and strode across the porch. She pulled keys from her handbag and unlocked the front door. Pushing the door wide, she stepped into the entryway. He followed.

The first time he'd been there, Mallory had dragged him along the hallway and into her bedroom. He hadn't been given a chance to look around and he hadn't been of a mind to linger. Now he looked with interest at the framed photographs that lined the hallway.

There were plenty of Mallory at all stages of life, including several baby shots. Even then, she'd been beautiful. There were a few more pictures of her at her high school graduation and then her graduation from college. Her father appeared in some of these, looking proud as punch. *And why wouldn't he be?* She was everything a father could hope for in a daughter. The absence of pictures of her mother was noticeable.

"You don't have any pictures of your mother," he murmured.

She stopped and turned to face him. "No. Dad didn't want me to hang any, and I respected his wishes not to remind him every day of her betrayal. Now I'm not sure who was the one doing the betraying. It scares me to death that everything I thought was true is about to come crumbling down. At least, that's how it feels. I mean, it's possible my father's involved in my mother's murder. Who wants to contemplate for even a second something as dreadful as that?"

"Let's wait until we get the DNA results back. Then at least we'll know for sure if it's your mother."

He reached out and put his hand on her shoulder and squeezed it comfortingly. She patted his hand for a few moments and then moved off toward the kitchen. The hallway opened out into a large and airy space filled with high quality fixtures and fittings and an explosion of knickknacks—unique and expensive collectibles lined bookshelves, windowsills and cupboards. Once again, he noticed an array of framed photos of Mallory hanging on the wall.

"Who's the photographer?"

"My dad, mostly. He's always had an interest in photography. It's what *he* does to relax."

She smiled sadly and then moved almost on autopilot over to the kitchen counter. She filled the kettle and then set it to boil. "Can I get you a tea or coffee?"

"Tea would be great, thanks."

He wandered around the rest of the room which was half-kitchen and half-living room. An expensive leather sofa in a burnt orange color divided the space and looked out onto a wall of glass which framed another lush garden. Out the back, tropical plants grew in wild disarray. A large frangipani tree, laden with sweet blossoms, dominated the space. In addition there were tree ferns, bromeliads and other shrubs he couldn't name. Birds of paradise, exotic orchids and a proliferation of flowering added to the wonder of the space. He could imagine how peaceful it would be to sit on the couch and relax and look out on the garden.

"Do you take milk and sugar?"

Mallory's question snagged his attention. Rafe moved back to the kitchen counter. "Yes to both, thanks."

She fixed his tea as he liked it and then handed him the cup. "Thanks," he murmured.

She took her teacup and headed toward the couch. "Let's sit down."

He sat close beside her, their legs touching. In silence, they enjoyed their tea until finally, Mallory spoke.

"I just don't want to believe that woman is my mother, Rafe. I know everything points to that, but if so, it means my father lied to me about everything. How am I supposed to cope with that? What am I supposed to do? I love him. He's my father. He's everything to me. Perhaps my only family." Her voice hitched on a sob.

Rafe sat his half-empty teacup on the coffee table and then took hers and did the same. Turning to her, he pulled her into his arms and held her close.

"I wish I had the words to say to take all of this away," he murmured against the softness of her hair. "I wish you didn't have to go through this at all. Unfortunately, sometimes the people we love make decisions that hurt us and there's nothing we can do about that. Believe me, I know firsthand."

She looked at him. Tears spiked her lashes. "Are you talking about your father?"

He nodded. "Yes. My father and…Khloe."

"Tell me more about her," Mallory said softly.

Rafe drew in a deep breath and tightened his arm around Mallory. "Khloe was a beautiful girl, but we should never have gotten together. Our reasons for being together were all wrong. She was escaping a violent home, just like me. We were searching for answers, looking for love. *Needing* love. It was no reason for two people to come together, but it was the only reason that made sense. We were teenagers. She'd already left home. She slept rough under a bridge, most nights. I joined her there on the odd occasion, when things got too much at home."

"Was your father violent?"

"Yes."

"To you?"

"Yes. To me, to my mother, to my sister. None of us were spared. Mom copped it the worst, of course. When Dad was in the mood, he didn't care who he lashed out at or who ended up hurt. Of course, when he sobered up the next morning, he'd be all apologetic until the next time."

"How long did it go on for?"

"Too long. All of my memories of my father are of a violent and nasty drunk. I was fifteen when I finally got the courage to stand up to him."

"What did you do?"

Rafe fell silent and stared off into the distance. The memories of that awful night would stay with him forever.

"He was beating up my mother, like he had so many times before. I pulled a gun on him and told him to get the hell out of our house and never come back, or I'd shoot him."

"Did you mean it?"

He stared into her eyes unflinchingly. "I sure as hell did."

She held his gaze for a long moment and tears welled up in her eyes. Her lip trembled. "You poor boy. No child should be forced to go through such a thing. No adult, either. What did your mother do?"

"Mom was supportive. She hated the way Dad treated her, treated all of us. She just didn't have the courage to do anything about it."

"What about your sister?"

"Breanna was a few years younger than me, but not too young that she didn't understand. She was as relieved as I was that our father was finally gone from our lives. I still spent time with Khloe and eventually Charli was born, but life in my home after the departure of my father was better than it had ever been. Not for a minute did I regret my actions. It was the best decision I ever made."

She looked at him, her expression overcome with sadness. "Both of us had such tragic childhoods, childhoods we didn't deserve. I used to think I was hard done by, with my mother running off. But now I hear your story and realize you suffered even worse."

"I don't look at it in those terms," Rafe replied quietly. "Yes, I had a shitty childhood, but so did a lot of other kids. Look at Khloe. She never told me about her family, but no one chooses to live under a bridge without good reason, especially at her age."

He paused and then added, "I guess there was something in Khloe's background that prevented her from bonding with her child. I didn't blame her for rejecting Charli, but it was hurtful just the same. More than that, it hurt my baby. The mother she would never fully know. Of course, at the time, I didn't realize Khloe's life would end so soon and that Charli would never know her mother."

"How did she die?"

Rafe drew in a deep breath. "She committed suicide."

"Oh, no!" Mallory gasped.

Rafe dragged his gaze up to hers. "Yes. So I kind of understand what it was like for you to go through life without a mother. I've watched my baby girl do it since the day she was born. It's the reason I try so hard to be there for her, to love her, to support her and let her know she's never going to be alone."

Fresh tears welled up in Mallory's eyes and slowly ran down her cheeks. "You're such a wonderful father, a beautiful man, Rafe Connelly. I know we haven't known each other long, but... I'm falling in love with you."

His heart skipped a beat and a split second later, was flooded with joy. In this moment filled with the saddest of memories, he'd been blessed with the love of the woman he already cared deeply about.

"I love you too, Mallory. I can't believe you feel the same way. I feel like the luckiest man in the world to have found you."

"Me, too."

Unable to restrain himself, Rafe leaned across and cupped the back of her head in his hand. He pulled her close until their lips touched and he kissed her softly, tenderly, lovingly. She returned the pressure and in instant later, fire ignited in his belly.

The kiss deepened, tongues entwined, passion and desperation meshed together. They hadn't been together since the night they'd made love and their pent-up feelings came crashing in together. Blood pounded in Rafe's ears. It also rushed to his groin. His cock was rock-hard and throbbing. He wanted Mallory in a way he'd wanted no other woman before.

She tore her mouth away, her breath coming fast. Her nipples were pebbled beneath her shirttt.

"Bedroom," she rasped and then climbed off the couch. She kicked off her sandals and started on the buttons of her blouse. Blindly, he followed her through the house. By the time he got to her bedroom, she stood in nothing but her lingerie. This time it was white lace. It was just as erotic as the black.

Her breasts filled the cups to overflowing. His gaze followed a path down her flat stomach to the scrap of fabric that covered the most delicate part of her.

"Aren't you going to get undressed?"

Her pointed question zapped him out of his trance. He tore off his clothes in double time and was slightly embarrassed when she laughed. "I applaud your enthusiasm. It does wonders for a woman's self-esteem."

He might have felt even more embarrassed if it weren't for the teasing light in her eyes. It was so much better than the despair he'd witnessed in her gaze a few short moments ago. If this was what she needed to take her mind off things, he was more than willing to assist her. With a grin, he stepped forward and took her in his arms.

Their kiss this time was less fiery, but it was passionate just the same. Charli was at home with Mrs Hubbard and Mallory had taken the rest of the day off. She'd called her office on their way home and had told her secretary she was feeling unwell. It meant they had all the time in the world to get to know each other and though Rafe wouldn't be able to stay the night, he was determined to make the most of the time they had.

Slowly, he eased down the straps of her bra and then followed the movement with his lips. Her skin was soft and silky and smooth and smelled like peaches and cream. Every part of her tasted delicious as he nibbled his way across her chest. At last he came to her nipple and suckled her through the lace.

"Oh, Rafe!" she gasped and threw back her head to give him greater access.

Done with the lace, he reached around her back and unclasped her bra. It came loose and he pushed it away and then stepped back and looked his fill.

"You're so beautiful," he whispered, his voice hoarse with need.

Her hands slid down his chest and then lower. With one hand, she took his cock. With the other, she cupped his balls. The gentle feel of her soft fingers massaging him sent desire rocketing through him. He clenched his jaw against the erotic pain.

And then he drew her against him, unable to stand the torment anymore. With his arms around her, he held her tightly and kissed her all over again. Mouths opened, tongues tangled, they kissed until they were breathless. When they pulled away to come up for air, he was satisfied to see the depth of need that swirled in the emerald centers of her eyes.

She wanted him. More than that, she *loved* him. He could scarcely believe it was true. He'd found his woman, his soul mate and the best thing was, she felt that way, too.

Going down on his knees, he buried his face against her stomach. Her soft, cool skin was a balm to his heated cheeks. The fire of desire still coursed through him. His cock felt like it was going to explode, but he forced himself to count to ten. He wanted this to last as long as it could.

He reached up and pulled aside the scrap of white lace and then parted her soft folds with his fingers. He licked her in long, slow strokes. Her hands tangled in his hair, holding his head in place. He needed no further encouragement and stroked and suckled and tasted until little whimpers of need escaped her.

"Oh, Rafe."

Coming to his feet, he scooped her up in his arms and carried her to the bed. He lowered her to the mattress and followed her down, covering her body with his. His cock pressed against her entrance, still covered in the lace. She made an impatient sound and squirmed beneath him.

"You want to get naked, right?" he teased.

She muttered what he took for a yes. He slid off her and reached for the waistband of her panties. She lifted her hips to assist him as he pulled the scrap of fabric off. And then she was fully exposed to him in all her glistening glory. He licked his lips in anticipation of tasting her again. Unfortunately, Mallory had other ideas.

"I want to feel you inside me, Rafe. I want you to carry me away. Take me to some place far away, where I can forget, even for a little while."

She reached for him and he came back down on top of her, his cock now nudging at her entrance. And then he remembered protection.

She motioned toward her nightstand and he found what he needed. Within moments, he'd returned to his position between her legs. This time, he savored every moment, every second of her warmth. He stroked his cock up and down her slick entrance, enthralled with the feel of her.

"Please, Rafe."

The overwhelming need in her eyes almost did him in, but he gritted his teeth and once again counted to ten.

"All in good time," he soothed and prayed he could hang on to his self-control.

Once again, he swiped his cock up and down her slit. She was so wet, so willing. Her legs fell open, wide and inviting and all of a sudden, it was too much. With his jaw clenched, he slid inside her, slowly, inch by inch. When he was fully seated, he eased out his breath.

"You feel so good, Mallory." His words came out hoarse, sounding as strained as the muscles in his arms. All he wanted to do was to plunge inside her, over and over again.

But this time, he wanted it to last forever, or at least as long as he could maintain control. So he eased out and then slid back inside her, repeating the motion until he thought he would scream.

"Please, Rafe. Faster. Harder. Fuck me as hard as you can."

The coarse words, so foreign to her lips, did him in. He thrust hard, snatching their breaths and then did it all over again. The moment seemed to last forever, but it was over all too soon. They reached their climax together and collapsed against the mattress, spent. He gathered her up against him and with his face buried in her hair, fell asleep.

It felt like hours had passed when Rafe woke and glanced at his watch. To his relief, he noted he'd only been gone from work a couple of hours. He'd explained to James on his way out of the squad room that he was taking Mallory home. At least someone could account for his absence.

Moving slightly, he extricated his arm from beneath Mallory's head and slowly rolled off the bed. He picked up his scattered clothes and put them on. As much as he wanted to spend the rest of the day with her, and the night as well, he needed to get back to work. Besides, Charli was sick at home and even though his neighbor was taking care of her, she deserved to have her dad around in her time of need.

"Are you leaving already?"

Mallory's sleepy voice came from the direction of the bed. Rafe came to sit beside her.

"I'm afraid I have to go back to work and then I need to check on Charli." At the confusion on Mallory's face, he remembered she didn't know about the chicken pox. He quickly explained.

Mallory's expression filled with sympathy and then it changed to alarm. "Oh, no! What about Charli's concert? Poor, baby. She's going to be so disappointed. It's on next week."

Rafe's belly filled with warmth that she remembered and that she also knew what missing the concert would mean to his daughter.

"Yes. I'm afraid she's not going to be over the contagious period by then. She's under strict quarantine at home."

"Oh, poor Charli! We must do something special for her to make up for it."

Once again, Rafe's heart filled with tenderness. This woman had plenty to deal with and yet she was thinking of his little girl. He couldn't have asked for a kinder, sweeter woman.

"That sounds like a good plan," he said. "As long as you've already had chicken pox."

"Of course. When I was six. Didn't everybody?"

He chuckled and leaned down and kissed her. It was a soft kiss, a gentle kiss, a kiss that promised forever.

"I love you, Mallory Patterson."

Her eyes darkened. "I love you too, Rafe Connelly."

"I'll call you," he promised and quietly left the room.

CHAPTER 17

Mallory spent the afternoon contemplating what she'd say to her father. In between, in an effort to distract herself from the upcoming difficult conversation, her thoughts returned to Rafe. The sex between them had been so much more than she could have ever hoped. The first time had been wonderful, but the second time had blown her mind. It was so much more than sex—they'd truly made love.

It was the first time she'd felt that way with anyone. It was too bad their budding relationship was overshadowed by the question hanging over her mother and her disappearance. Despite the hours she spent that day replaying everything she knew and looking at it from all angles, she wanted to talk to her father about it, but she still didn't know what to say.

And then she heard his key in the lock and her time to refine her game plan suddenly came to an end. With her heart beating fast, she steeled herself for the confrontation. She heard the sound of her father dropping his keys on the hall table, like he always did. A moment later, his footsteps came down the hallway, toward the kitchen. Not wanting to take him by surprise, she called out.

"I'm in here, Dad."

His footsteps appeared to falter. But then his outline appeared in the open doorway. Hunched over and with his face drawn, he looked a hundred years older. In his hand he held a newspaper.

A fresh wave of dread filled her stomach. She stood and moved toward him, her fists clenched. He threw the paper on the kitchen counter where it landed face up. Her mother's face stared up at them. Mallory froze.

Her father glanced at her. "I take it you've seen this?" he asked, his voice brusque.

She bit her lip and then answered. "Yes."

"That woman looks so much like your mother." His tone remained terse.

"Yes."

Her heart beat fast. She could barely hear over the rush of blood in her ears. Her father peered at her intently.

"You know it can't be her, right?" he said.

Mallory stared back at him. "Right. Of course, you're right. You dropped her off at the airport. She got on a plane. There's no way she ended up with her hands and feet bound, hidden in a cave. It's ludicrous, isn't it, Dad?"

She held his gaze, though it took all her courage to do so. Inside, she prayed desperately for him to say something, to do something that would convince her he was telling the truth. Instead, he turned away and busied himself making coffee.

"Yes, of course it's ludicrous," he finally said, his tone dismissive.

All of a sudden, Mallory's courage deserted her. Her father was maintaining his story, a story he'd remained faithful to for twenty years. She had no choice at the moment but to accept what he said. Until she had the results from the DNA tests, there was nothing more to say. After all, there was always the slim possibility the woman in the cave *wasn't* her mother.

Mallory believed with every ounce of her being in the justice system. She'd devoted her whole life to it. She wasn't going to be her father's judge and jury and executioner until she had proof of his guilt beyond reasonable doubt. The presumption of innocence was firmly entrenched in article eleven of the Universal Declaration of Human Rights and it was a presumption she wholeheartedly believed in. The least she could do was afford her father the same respect. But he also had to realize she needed to know for sure this woman wasn't her mother before she could finally close that door.

"I-I've been speaking to Detective Connelly," she stammered, not quite sure how her father was going to react. "He's one of the investigators who've been looking into the identity of this woman. I met him at Sally-Ann's barbeque, remember?"

Not waiting for her father's reply, she pointed

toward the newspaper. "I went to him with my concerns that the woman in the story looked a lot like my mother. He said the only way to tell for sure, was to compare DNA samples." Mallory drew in a deep breath. "I just wanted to let you know I've given one," she said in a rush.

John Patterson was in a panic. Earlier that evening, his daughter had informed him she'd given a DNA sample to the police for comparison purposes with the woman whose body had been found in the cave. It was only a matter of time before the results came back. Then the whole world would know that instead of catching a plane for Argentina, Sofia Mary Lopez Patterson had been murdered and stashed away to rot in a cave...and that her husband was the man responsible.

The very thought filled him with fear. His anxiety ratcheted up another notch. Everything he'd worked for, lived for, loved would be gone. He'd be jailed for fifteen to twenty years, at least. He'd be an old man with one foot in the grave by the time he was released. That's if he survived the hellhole that was prison. He couldn't let that happen. He *wouldn't* let that happen. He needed to act. And fast.

He went to the cupboard that stood in the far corner of his study and opened the double doors. Bending low, he worked the combination to the safe that was stored in there. A satisfying click signaled the door was open. He reached in and pulled out a thick wad of cash. He'd been squirreling away money for years. Most of it was sitting in an offshore account. There were strict laws about how much cash a person could carry out of the country. He didn't want there to be any reason for the authorities to pull him aside and delve into his reasons for leaving.

He reached into the safe again and gathered together thousands of dollars' worth of jewelry and a small bag of diamonds. He'd been secreting away the stash for a long time, always cognizant of the fact that one day he might be found out. Though he hated the thought of disappearing and beginning a brand new life in a foreign country, at least he'd be doing it in style.

It had taken twenty years, but now that day had arrived...

After filling a duffel bag with his riches, he zipped it up and then stashed it beneath his desk. Then he picked up his phone and dialed his broker. It was well after eleven, but he paid Robert Brinkley enough money in brokerage fees that he was confident the man would answer his call at any time of night.

He was right. The call was answered on the fourth ring. Brinkley sounded groggy with sleep. John cut right to the chase.

"I want you to cash in all of my investments and deposit the proceeds into my Bahamas account," he said without preamble. "Do it first thing tomorrow morning."

His broker tried to argue, but John just cut him off. "I don't care if I lose money. Just do it! I want everything liquefied to cash."

He ended the call as abruptly as it had begun and tossed his phone down on his desk. It landed near a framed photograph of Mallory. She was about fourteen or fifteen in the picture. She wore a T-shirt and denim cut-offs that emphasized her long, slim legs. She smiled directly at the camera.

His heart turned over in his chest. Leaving her was going to be the hardest part of all of this, but he had to keep focused and remember what was at stake. When Mallory found out the truth about what he'd done, she'd never want to speak to him again, let alone visit him in a jail cell.

When she was a child and her mother was threatening to take her overseas forever, it was a risk he'd been willing to take. Now that the moment was upon him, he wasn't so sure he'd made the right decision.

It was because of Mallory that he'd been forced to murder her mother. He couldn't imagine not having his little girl in his life. When Sofia seemed hell-bent on putting into action her plan to leave him, there was no way he could take the risk that a court might allow her custody and that she'd slip out of the country with their child, never to be seen again.

It happened all the time. Parents offered the excuse they wanted their child to visit long-lost relatives overseas. The courts allowed it and when the parent and child failed to return, there was nothing much anyone could do. He refused to be put in that situation and there was no way he was giving up his little girl.

So he'd caught Sofia unawares one night and had strangled her from behind. There was no blood, no mess and almost no sound. He'd sneaked up behind her where she'd fallen asleep on the couch. He'd used a makeshift garrote out of a pair of her stockings. It hadn't taken long.

Now, because of his actions, he was never going to see his daughter again, unless she found it somewhere in her heart to forgive him. The hardest part was going to be acting completely normal around her, as if there was nothing wrong. Maintaining the façade that there was no way on earth the woman in the paper was her mother. The way he figured it, he had a couple of days at the most. He prayed he could pull it off.

———————

Rafe watched Mallory enter the café and stood as she approached his table. He'd called her earlier and had invited her to meet him for lunch. She was dressed for work in her customary tailored business suit. When she was close enough, he leaned over and kissed her gently on the mouth. He noticed the dark shadows under her eyes and his heart ached.

"Hey, you. How are you doing?" he asked softly.

She shrugged.

"You're back at work," he stated.

She nodded. "It was driving me crazy thinking about all the possibilities surrounding Mom. I needed to stay busy and I have plenty to do at work." She offered a half-smile, but it didn't reach her eyes.

"How's your dad taking it? I assume he knows?"

"Yes, but I'm not sure how he's taking it. He was gone when I got up this morning. I haven't seen him all day. We spoke about it last night. He came home with the paper. He's convinced the woman isn't Mom." She sighed. "I hope he's right."

Rafe reached across the table for her hand and squeezed it in a silent show of comfort and support. She gave him a grateful smile. He pressed a kiss against the back of her hand.

"I want you to know, Mallory, whatever happens, I'm here for you. I meant what I said yesterday. I love you, okay?" He waited a little nervously for her response.

Her shaky smile filled him with relief. She leaned over and kissed him softly on the mouth. "Thank you, Rafe. I love you, too. It means a lot to me to know that I have your support in this. Who knows how rough it's going to get before it's over."

A waiter arrived and took their orders and then disappeared into the crowd. Silence fell between them and then Mallory cleared her throat.

"Last night I spent a lot of time thinking about my mother and father and how different things might have been had she hung around." She looked up at him, her eyes steady on his. "I remember what you said about your father. I was just wondering, have you seen him at all since he left?"

Rafe tensed. His father was not a subject he enjoyed talking about. He shook his head. "No. And that's just fine with me," he said firmly.

She continued to regard solemnly. "Do you ever wonder where he is?"

Rafe was suddenly filled with irritation. He tried his best to control the anger that stirred in his gut. Through clenched teeth, he answered her.

"Look, Mallory. I get it. Your family is falling apart. You've never stopped wondering about your mother. Family's always been important to you. But my family—my father—isn't like that. I hated him. I still hate him."

Instead of his simmering tone discouraging her, her gaze remained intent on his. It was like she could see into his very soul. Right then, it wasn't a feeling he was comfortable with.

"*Do* you hate him?" she asked softly. "Do you *really?*"

Rafe stared at her for as long as he could bear it and then lowered his gaze with a curse. She made him feel things he didn't want to feel. She made him think of things he'd rather leave buried.

All of a sudden, he was filled with a sense of hopelessness and grief. The truth was, he still thought about his father and sometimes he wondered what things would have been like if Michael Connelly had straightened himself out, or had loved his family enough to even try.

Did he still hate him? No. Although he wished he did. It was easier to hate somebody and shut them out of your life than to be left forever wondering about what might have happened or whether they were doing all right.

———————

It was hours later, when Rafe was tucking Charli into bed that his thoughts returned to the conversation he'd had with Mallory about his father. It was true that he tried not to think of his father at all. The man was a no-good violent drunk who didn't deserve a family. But sometimes, like now, when he was talking quietly to Charli about his day and listening to her tell him stories about Mrs Hubbard's obsession with reality television shows, he was reminded of all he'd lost.

He couldn't remember ever sharing a tender moment with his dad, or talking with him about his day. It saddened Rafe beyond measure to know what they'd lost. Not only him, but his whole family. Even his dad. He wondered if Michael Connelly ever thought about his family and regretted his words and actions. He wondered if his father ever missed them.

"Did you see Mallory again today, Dad?"

Charli's quiet question broke the silence that had fallen between them. Though she was still unwell with the chicken pox, the worst of the rash had started to subside. She'd felt good enough to eat a proper dinner and had even finished two bowls of ice cream for dessert. He'd told her he'd been seeing Mallory and he'd been relieved when Charli had seemed pleased. It made things so much easier to know he had her approval and support.

"Yes, baby. I did. We had lunch."

"You really like her, don't you, Dad?"

He nodded. "I do."

"Would you ever get married again, Dad?"

The question took him by surprise. "Actually, honey, your mother and I weren't married. We were very young when we met and then... We didn't last. There really wasn't time for us to get married."

She nodded calmly. "Do you want to get married one day?"

He contemplated her question. Images of Mallory walking down the aisle toward him, resplendent in a beautiful white dress crowded his mind. He slowly smiled.

"Yes, honey, I think so. Would you be okay with that?"

She grinned and the resemblance to her mother took his breath away. "Yes! That would be so cool! Am I too old to be a flower girl?"

The earnestness on her face touched his heart. He laughed. "Surely, not!"

"Are you going to marry Mallory?" She looked at him with her face full of hope.

Rafe's heart clenched again. "You like Mallory, don't you?"

"Of course I do, Dad! She makes you happy and I want you to be happy." She paused and then added, "We haven't known her for very long, but you've changed since she's been around. You laugh a lot more and you smile all the time, even when you're going to work. It's nice, Dad. I like it and I hope it works out for the two of you. In fact, it would be really cool if you and Mallory got married."

Rafe blinked back tears and leaned over to hug her close. He kissed her on the forehead and then cleared the lump from his throat.

"Thank you, baby. You're so grown up. All wise and mature and wonderful. When did you get so clever? What happened to my little girl?"

"Oh, Dad!" Charli sighed. "We've been over this before. I'm thirteen. I'm never going to be your little girl again."

He shook his head and looked down at her and smiled. "That's where you're wrong, Charlotte Connelly. You'll *always* be my little girl."

A knock at the front door startled both of them. Charli frowned. "Who could that be?"

Rafe shrugged. He wasn't expecting anyone. He pressed another quick kiss on Charli's cheek and then reached over and switched off the light.

"I'll go and see who it is. In the meantime, honey, it's time for you to get some sleep. Have a good night. I love you."

"I love you too, Dad. Goodnight."

Rafe left the room and made his way down the hallway to the front door. He didn't bother to check the peephole. Pulling open the wooden panel, he stared in shock at the old man who stood on his porch.

"*Dad?*"

CHAPTER 18

"Hello, son. It's been a long time."

"What the hell are you doing here?" Rafe shouted, his voice intentionally harsh.

His father winced. "That's no way to greet your long lost father."

"How did you find me?" Rafe demanded.

"Do you mind if I come in? Perhaps this conversation is better had in the privacy of your home."

"No. You can't come in. I don't want you in my home."

"I'm sorry you feel that way, son. Can't say I blame you. I did the wrong thing by you, didn't I?"

Rafe glared at him. "You were a terrible man, Dad. You did some terrible things. Not just to me, but to Mom and Breanna. How can you expect me to forget and just invite you into my home?"

His father sighed and the heavy sound seemed to come from somewhere deep inside him. If it were possible, he seemed to age before Rafe's eyes.

"Of course you can't forget, but... I want you to know I've changed. I've been sober for the past four years. I... I'm sorry, son. I'm so sorry for the things I did. I wish I could take them back. But that's not possible. All I can do is look to the future and hope you can find it in your heart to forgive me. I... I want to reconnect with you, son. Get to know you again. Do you—?"

"Dad? Who is it?"

Rafe's jaw tightened. He forced breaths through his gritted teeth. Charli stood a few feet away, peering around him.

"Oh, you must Charlotte. Hello, there. I'm your grandfather."

Anger tore through Rafe like oil that had been tossed onto fire. He slammed the door shut in his father's face before he did something he'd later regret—or get arrested in the process. The last thing he needed was for the police to be called.

His breath came fast. His fists were clenched. He was so angry he wanted to punch something. *Hard.*

"Dad! What are you doing? That's your father, isn't it? You can't shut the door on him!"

Rafe managed to speak through his anger. "It's none of your business, Charlotte. Go back to bed."

"But, Dad—"

"Go!"

Rafe hated the hurt look that crossed her face, but was relieved when she turned and left. She murmured a goodnight to him halfway down the hall. The knock came a second time, but he ignored it. Still seething, he switched off the lights, leaving the hallway in darkness. He stumbled into the kitchen and collapsed on the nearest barstool. Leaning his elbows on the counter, he rested his head in his hands.

After all these years, his father had turned up again. He'd found him here in Newtown. He couldn't believe it. He was numb with shock. As far as he was concerned, it was too little too late. He didn't feel at all guilty for slamming the door in his father's face. Michael Connelly had forfeited his right to a family years ago. No sad story, no apology was going to change that.

Rafe's head throbbed. His face was hot. His body was tense. He got up and paced the kitchen and then sat down again. He needed to speak to Mallory. He needed to see her, touch her, hold her close. She'd know what to say, what to do to help him. He found his phone still in the pocket of his jacket. He tugged it out and dialed her number. He breathed a sigh of relief when she answered.

"I need you. Can you come over?"

"Of course. I'll be there as soon as I can."

Rafe ended the call and dropped down onto the couch. Anger still coursed through his veins, leaving him tense and on edge. He loved that Mallory hadn't even questioned the reason he called her. With all the drama going on in her life and she still dropped everything for him. At that moment, he'd never loved her more.

It seemed like a long time later before he heard a knock upon the front door. This time he checked the peephole and quickly opened the door when he saw it was her. She walked inside the entryway and stepped into his arms. He crushed her to him, burying his face in her hair. Hot tears burned behind his eyes. He was so glad she was there.

It was a long time later, when he found the strength to release her. She looked at him, concern etched across the smooth skin of her brow.

"Rafe? Talk to me. Is Charli okay? What happened?"

Her voice was soft and low, soothing. He took her hand and led her back to the couch with steps that felt like they were weighed down with concrete. She sat beside him and gave his hand a reassuring squeeze, silently encouraging him to speak.

He looked at her bleakly. "Charli's fine... My father's turned up."

She gasped in surprise. "Oh my goodness! After all these years? How did he find you?"

"I don't know," Rafe replied grimly. "I asked him the same thing. My address isn't listed in any of the directories. There's no way he could have known where I lived." He shook his head back and forth in confusion. "It doesn't make sense that he just turned up here, wanting to talk to me. I mean, what did he expect?"

"What did he look like?" Mallory asked.

Rafe took a moment to recall. He'd been so shocked to see his father standing on the other side of the door way, he hadn't taken all that much notice. What he did remember was that his father had looked old and weak and frail. So much older than Rafe remembered and not at all like the huge bear of a man he used to be. Of course, Rafe hadn't seen him for more than fifteen years. That was a long time in anyone's world, but especially the world of a heavy drinker who'd been living on the streets.

Mallory looked at him expectantly. Rafe shrugged. "I guess he looked like himself, only older. Much older."

"If he's been living rough all these years, I can understand that."

Once again, Rafe shrugged noncommittally. He couldn't care less where his father had been for the past fifteen years, or how rough he'd been doing it. The truth was, Michael Connelly had single-handedly destroyed Rafe's life, along with the lives of his mother and little sister. It was hard to feel any sympathy for such a man.

"I'm so mad at him, I can't think straight."

"What do you think he wanted?" Mallory asked quietly.

Rafe's lip curled up in disgust. "Somehow he found out about Charli. It's my guess he wants to try and worm his way into her life. Get back the family he never had, at least, part of it. What he doesn't realize is, it's too late. There's no way in hell I'd let him anywhere near my daughter. She knows nothing about him and that's the way it's going to stay."

"It sounds like you've made up your mind not to forgive him."

He stared at Mallory in disbelief. Anger reignited

in his gut. "How can you say that? After everything I've said? The reason I don't want to forgive him is because the people he hurt aren't here to speak anymore. If I forgive him, then there's no one left to be a witness to what he did to them, to us.

"I told you my sister, Breanna, died in a car accident. What I didn't tell you was that when she crashed, she was high on drugs. She'd turned to them as a way to escape the nightmare of her childhood. She was an addict from the time she was fourteen. So you see, Dad destroyed her, too. I hold him responsible for her death."

Rafe's breath came fast. Mallory continued to regard him solemnly. He tried again to get her to understand.

"Don't you see?" he cried. "It's my job to hold him accountable, to force him to remember. If I don't... Hell... He just gets away with it."

Mallory reached out and cupped his cheek in her hand. "I hate that you're hurting," she whispered. "It tears me up inside. I wish there was something I could do, something I could say to make it better."

He reached up and took her hand and held it tightly in his, his anger at her seeping away. "Just being here is all that matters," he rasped. "Please, will you stay the night?"

Her eyes widened in surprise. "Are you sure? What about Charli?"

Rafe drew her closer and kissed her gently on the lips. "Charli will be fine. In fact, I think when she wakes up in the morning and finds you here, she's going to be thrilled."

Mallory smiled. "Really?"

"Yes, really. She asked me if I was going to marry you."

This time, Mallory's mouth fell open in shock. "She said that?"

Rafe grinned, and it felt good to let go of the anger he'd felt over the arrival of his father.

"Yes, she did. Honest to God."

"Wow! I mean, most kids her age are protective of their relationship with their father. They're usually vehemently against him having any kind of relationship with another woman, let alone contemplating marriage."

Rafe shrugged. "Well, Charli's not like most kids and she wants her dad to be happy. That's what she said. She's noticed since we've been seeing each other that I've been happy." He paused and then added, "And she's right. I can't remember the last time I felt this happy and I have you to thank for it."

He leaned over and kissed her. What was meant to be a soft and tender kiss, a reaffirmation, quickly turned into something else. Mallory put her arms around his neck and tilted her face up to his. She opened her mouth, inviting him in and passionately kissed him back.

Rock-hard and aching, he stood and scooped her into his arms. With the aid of nothing more than memory and moonlight, he made his way down the hall and into his room.

They loved each other all night long and then held each other close. At some point, Rafe drifted to sleep only to wake again, searching for Mallory.

The love she'd shown him blew him away and he didn't feel worthy. She had so much turmoil in her life and yet, she'd put all that aside to help him in his darkest hour.

She was a special woman and one he loved with all his heart. He'd move heaven and earth to keep her. This was one woman he never intended to let go.

———————

Rafe tried to focus on the words on the screen in front of him, but his mind kept straying to Mallory and the night they'd spent together. When she'd woken with the sun coming through his bedroom windows, she'd been aghast.

"What if Charli finds me here? What will she think?"

Rafe had hurried to reassure her. "Hey, remember what we talked about last night? Charli's fine with it. In fact, she encouraged me to take the next step."

Mallory continued to regard him with uncertainty. "Are you sure?"

Rafe kissed her soundly on the lips. "I'm sure."

In the end, Mallory had showered in his bathroom and dressed in the clothes she'd worn the night before. Rafe had apologized to Charli for the way he'd spoken to her the night before. He explained in general terms that he and his father weren't on good terms but he was sorry he'd lost his temper with her.

She accepted his apology and even though he was sure Mallory could see the questions in Charli's eyes, he was grateful when she remained silent. His daughter appeared to take Mallory's presence at the breakfast table in her stride and he was relieved. He made pancakes and Charli showed Mallory how to spread them with Nutella. Mallory asked Charli how she was feeling and Charli assured her that a lot of the spots were gone. It was too bad she was going to miss her concert.

"But there'll be other ones," Mallory assured her and Charli had given her a wide smile. It warmed Rafe's heart that the two most important women in his life were getting along just fine.

He'd pondered what it all meant, as he drove Mallory to work and then headed for the police station.

The truth was, he wanted Mallory in his life permanently. He wanted to propose. They hadn't known each other long, but did that really matter? They'd both seen the back of thirty. If they didn't know their own mind by now, they never would. Besides, what were they waiting for? He was almost certain she'd say yes.

Feeling buoyed by the strength of Mallory's love, his thoughts turned to his father.

Somehow, the white-hot anger he'd felt the night before had eased. Instead, he felt a deep sadness for the things they'd lost and the things they'd never have. He wouldn't give up his relationship with his daughter for all the money in the world and yet his father had never known what such a precious thing like a relationship between a loving parent and their child could be like. He and his sister and his mother had gone without security, without their right to a safe and secure home, to a husband and father who loved them…but the more he thought about it, the more he realized it was Michael Connelly, the old man who'd stood on his doorstep the night before, who'd lost the most.

"Rafe. There's someone downstairs waiting to see you."

James' words slowly registered in Rafe's mind. He blinked. "Sorry? Who is it?"

"I don't know. Rebecca from downstairs just called me to tell you there's someone waiting for you down there."

Glad for the opportunity to leave his desk, Rafe headed down the stairs. He opened the door that led into the waiting room and came to a halt. His father sat on one of the hard plastic seats reserved for members of the public. Rafe's heart skipped a beat and then took off at a gallop. Upon seeing him, his father struggled to his feet. Rafe couldn't help but notice his frailty. The man, who once seemed as tall and broad and brawny as a bear, was now a dried-up husk.

Still, Rafe wasn't ready to do this. He spun on his heel and headed back the way he'd come.

"Rafe! Please! Can't we talk?"

Rafe tensed. There were other people in the waiting room, along with two constables and the receptionist behind the front desk. The last thing he wanted was to cause a scene. With gritted teeth and fists clenched, he turned back around to face his father.

"Follow me," he said curtly.

Not bothering to wait and see if his father did as he ordered, Rafe stalked down the hallway toward the interview rooms. It hardly seemed that long ago that he was in one of them with Mallory, talking about her mother. *What was it about parents that turned everyone's life upside down?* He wanted to hate his father for what he'd done, but as he drove to work he'd realized he couldn't and that was really pissing him off.

With his hands on his hips, Rafe started in on his father the moment the door was closed. "What are you doing here, Dad?"

His father shrugged. "I didn't think we got off on the right foot last night. I want to make amends."

"By turning up here? How the hell did you know where I worked?"

"There was an article in the newspaper a couple of weeks ago. You were quoted in the story as being the lead investigator. The story mentioned you worked here."

Rafe compressed his lips, still upset. "Well what about my house? You sure as hell didn't get my address from any newspaper story. How the hell do you know where I *live*?"

His father regarded him calmly. "I followed you home from work."

Rafe stared at him, aghast. "*What?*"

"Don't get your panties in a twist. I'm not a stalker. I just wanted to talk to you. I wasn't sure how to do it any other way."

Rafe sighed and scrubbed a hand through his hair. "What do you *want*, Dad? Do you have cancer? Is that it? You only have weeks to live? You've come to get my absolution before you depart this world and you're forced to take an accounting of your life before your maker? Is that it?"

His father stared at him with sad eyes, tears glistening in their depths. "When did you get so bitter, son?"

White-hot anger flashed through Rafe's veins. He glared at his father. "How *dare* you ask me something like that? As if nothing you did had anything to do with it! You beat me, Dad. You beat my mom. You beat my little sister, too. No one was spared. And it wasn't just a one-off. Night after night, week after week. It went on for years. We never knew what mood you'd be in when you stumbled through the door. Mean, mild or something in between. More often it was mean and look out for anyone who got in your path."

A look filled with agony passed over his father's face. He cried out, as if in pain. "Oh, Rafe! I'm so sorry. I had no idea. I'm not offering any excuses. I accept everything you say. But in my defense, I can't remember those years. It all passed in a blur. I viewed the world through an alcoholic haze. I was angry at life and all it had thrown at me. I was always spoiling for a fight and I didn't care who got in my way."

His voice had grown hoarse with emotion. Rafe continued to glare at him, refusing to feel sorry for the old man who sat slumped in the chair before him. It was all well and good for his father to make excuses for his behavior, but he hadn't been on the receiving end of someone else's fists.

All of a sudden he was beyond weary. It felt like he was wading through thigh-high water with the weight of a concrete pylon across his shoulders. He bowed his head and then collapsed into the chair opposite his father. With his head in his hands, he tried to regain some sense of control over himself. He was so tired of all this.

"What do you want, Dad?" he said. Weariness dodged his every word.

His father stared up at him with teary eyes. "It's like I said, son. I want to get to know you, reconnect. Maybe spend some time with my granddaughter."

Rafe stared back at him. "How do you even know I *have* a daughter? You even know her name! Just how long have you been watching us? Where did you come by your information?"

His father remained silent for so long that Rafe didn't think his father was going to answer. Then finally he said, "I'm not sure if you're going to believe me, but the person who told me about Charlotte was your mother."

Rafe's mouth gaped in disbelief. He stared at his father and then vehemently shook his head.

"No way. There's no *way* you've spoken to Mom in the past sixteen years. She wouldn't have given you the time of day. Do you even know she's dead? *Do you?*"

His father's calm stare almost did in his head. He pushed away from the table and began to pace. His father continued to regard him calmly.

"I accept that you don't want to believe me, Rafe, but it's the truth. I got into contact with your mother four years ago. She was still living in the same house."

Rafe squeezed his eyes shut in an effort to block out his father's voice. This couldn't be happening. There was no way his mother would have invited his father back into her life.

"You're lying," he rasped.

"No, son. I'm not." He sighed heavily. "It took some time, don't get me wrong, but your mother finally forgave me. It wasn't long after that, she was diagnosed with breast cancer. I went with her to a few of her appointments."

Rafe stared back in surprise and opened his mouth to protest, but his father cut him off.

"There were a few times when you couldn't make it. You were caught up at work. She called me those times and I went with her. I kept her company while she received her treatment. We talked about so many things and even though it was clear her condition was deteriorating, those times in that clinic were the happiest times of my life.

"She told me about you and Charlotte and how proud she was of you. She loved you both so much."

His expression sobered. "She also told me about Breanna." Fresh tears welled up in his eyes. "I was so sorry to hear about the accident. So sorry."

Rafe wanted to tell his father that Breanna's death was on his head, but all of a sudden he'd lost the stomach for it. *What good would it do blaming his father now?* It wouldn't bring Breanna back. All it would do was cause more animosity between them and right now, he'd had about enough of that. His father was no longer the tough and violent man who could inflict so much hurt and pain and as much as Rafe wanted to sustain his anger against him, he was exhausted.

"All right, Dad. You've come and said your piece. Now it's time to go. I need to get back to work. And you need to...do whatever it is you do."

His father peered up at him through red-rimmed eyes. "What about Charlotte? Would you let me speak to her for a bit? I'd like her to know me, at least a little bit."

Rafe's initial instinct was to refuse his father's request. Michael Connelly had no rights as far as Rafe's family went. But then his gaze took in the old, defeated man and he thought of the generosity of spirit his mother had found within herself in order to forgive her husband for all the dreadful things he'd done. If his mother could do it, so could he.

He sighed heavily. "Why don't you come over for dinner, Dad? That way you'll have a chance to talk to Charli. Would that be all right?"

A smile lit up the old wrinkled face and more tears glinted in his eyes. "That sounds wonderful, son. Thank you. You don't know how much that means to me."

A lump of emotion clogged Rafe's throat. He swallowed and then spoke. "Come back here at six. I'll pick you up and take you home."

With that, Rafe opened the door and guided his father back out to the reception area. With a muttered farewell, Rafe turned his back and headed back upstairs.

Chapter 19

Mallory pulled up outside Rafe's house and took a moment to check her appearance. Knowing Rafe's father had been invited to dinner, she'd dressed with care, nervous about the impression she might make. She knew about Rafe's strained relationship with his father, but still... This was his dad. He remained an important part of his family, despite the fact Rafe hadn't seen him for sixteen years.

She checked her reflection in the rearview mirror and was pleased with what she saw. She'd taken time with her hair and makeup. The wavy tresses hung long and glossy to her shoulders. Her burgundy lipstick was a few shades darker than her hair. She'd added smoky touches of light gray and charcoal to her eyes, emphasizing their green color. Eyeliner highlighted their almond shape and made her look a bit exotic. At least, she liked to think so.

The dress she'd chosen was a crepe silk in the most gorgeous navy-blue. Its halter neck style revealed her toned bare arms and the sensual fabric clung to her curves. Every time she wore it, she felt womanly, desirable, beautiful. She hoped Rafe felt the same.

She reached for her handbag and the bottle of red and then climbed out of the car. She tried to ignore the fresh rush of nerves that fluttered in her stomach. Not only was she on show for Rafe's father tonight, but she was also on show in a way for his daughter. Although Charli seemed to have amicably accepted her presence in their lives, it was still early days and Mallory needed to treat the budding relationship with care.

Charli's life had been tumultuous enough, with the death of her mother at such an early age, and then the deaths of her aunt and grandmother. It was a lot for a young girl to cope with. Mallory didn't know how many other women Rafe had brought home but she suspected it hadn't been many. Having another woman around was something Charli wasn't used to. Mallory had no intention of trying to replace Charli's mother but still, she wanted a good relationship with Rafe's daughter and wanted to be her friend. She hoped one day they might be even closer than that.

Rafe met her at the door. He looked cool, calm and sexy in his emerald-green button-up shirt that had the sleeves rolled up to his elbows. He'd teamed it up with a pair of Levi's that fit him like a glove. His feet were bare. She felt a little overdressed at the sight of him, but he quickly put her at ease.

"Mallory. Come in. You look gorgeous."

He leaned forward and kissed her cheek and then as if coming to the conclusion that wasn't enough, he drew her in close and kissed her properly. After a long moment, they drew apart. Mallory rushed to catch her breath.

"I brought some wine," she said and handed him the bottle.

He briefly glanced at the label and smiled his thanks. "This will go perfectly with the beef Wellington."

"Sounds delicious. What else is on the menu?"

Rafe laughed. "I know what you're fishing for. You want to know what's for dessert."

She laughed at his teasing. "Maybe."

He pulled her in close for a hug and then took her hand and led her down the hall. "I'm going to keep you in suspense, Mallory Patterson," he tossed over his shoulder. "Dessert will be a surprise."

She pulled a face behind his back. "Oh, Rafe! You're not playing fair! You know dessert is the only reason I came tonight. I want to make sure it's worth the effort."

He stopped and turned around, his gaze intent on hers. "Oh, it will be worth the effort, I promise you."

The heat in his gaze as he looked at her left her in no doubt as to what he meant. A shiver of desire ran down her spine and her nipples tightened involuntary. Before she could formulate a reply, Rafe tugged her into the kitchen. Charli was seated on a barstool at the counter. An elderly man who looked remarkably like Rafe sat beside her.

"Dad, I want you to meet Mallory. Mallory, this is my father, Michael Connelly."

The man turned to face her and slowly climbed off the stool. Once again, Mallory was taken aback at his likeness to his son. Although the once-blond hair had turned gray, the striking blue eyes and the chiseled features were the same. It wasn't hard to imagine what Rafe might look like in another thirty years.

Mallory held out her hand. "Hello, I'm Mallory Patterson. It's nice to meet you, Mr Connelly."

Rafe's father shook the proffered hand. "Hey, none of this Mr Connelly nonsense. Call me Michael."

Mallory nodded in acknowledgement. "It's nice to meet you, Michael."

"Oh, Mallory! I love your dress!"

Mallory smiled at Charli. "Thanks, Charli. I like it, too. See how it swirls when I move?"

Mallory did a little pirouette and the skirt obligingly flared out around her legs.

Charli giggled. "That would be an awesome dress to dance in, wouldn't it?"

"Oh, it sure would," Mallory replied. She glanced at Rafe and then back at Charli. "Does your dad like to dance?"

Charli frowned. "I'm not sure. I've never seen him dance." She looked at her father. "Do you like to dance, Dad?"

Rafe stepped forward and gave Mallory a hug. Ignoring the others, he planted his lips firmly on her mouth. "I *love* to dance."

Mallory's belly somersaulted. Her heart swelled with love. *Could this man get any more perfect?*

Setting her aside, Rafe took the bottle of wine and set it on the counter. "Can I get you a drink, Mallory?"

"Yes, thanks. I'd love a glass of wine."

Rafe busied himself collecting glasses from the cupboard. Mallory turned her attention to his father, curious about the man who'd caused Rafe so much pain.

"So, Michael. Do you live in Sydney?"

Michael nodded. "Yes. Although I've moved around a bit over the past sixteen years. Here and there, wherever I could get work. I moved from house to house, never staying in any one place for long. It was a lonely existence, but I had no one but myself to blame."

He sighed and then added quietly, "It wasn't until I reconciled with Rafe's mother that my life started to finally straighten out. It was like I suddenly had a reason to get clean, to work hard at being a better person. My only regret was that I hadn't done it years ago."

Mallory blinked in surprise. She glanced at Rafe who shrugged and looked away. She could tell he was uncomfortable with the direction of his father's conversation. She tactfully changed the subject.

"So, what are you doing with yourself now?" she asked him.

"Well, I've pretty much retired, now. I used to be a cabinet maker."

Rafe handed her a glass of wine and she

murmured her thanks. "Dad used to build beautiful furniture," he said quietly.

Michael started in surprise. He looked at Rafe and then a pleased expression filled his face. "Thank you, son. That's nice of you to say."

Rafe shrugged. "It's true. Other people thought so, too. I remember when I was a kid, you used to be overwhelmed with orders for custom-made furniture."

His father nodded sadly, a distant expression in his eyes. "I could have made a fortune," he said softly. "Instead, I stuffed it all up because I couldn't get off the grog. I lost everything. My business, my house, my family. That's what hurts most of all."

Tears glistened in his eyes. Mallory stared at him, her heart breaking. Rafe had told her about the violence he'd lived with as a kid, but it was hard for her to be angry at this frail old man who now felt overwhelmingly sorry for the mistakes he'd made. She wondered if Rafe would ever find it in his heart to forgive him.

And then she thought of her own father and a familiar feeling of dread settled in the pit of her stomach. She wasn't sure how she'd feel if she ended up discovering her father was involved in her mother's death. Right now, she was clinging to the hope that the woman in the cave wasn't her mother and that it was just someone who looked like her.

She didn't want to think about how she'd feel if the evidence proved it conclusively. That would involve too many questions about her father.

Questions for which she had no answers. At least, not the kind of answers she was prepared to accept. With a deliberate effort, she shied away from such thoughts and patted Rafe's father on his arm.

"We all make mistakes, Michael. As long as we learn from them, right? That's what's important."

She heard the words and hoped she could apply the same attitude toward her father if it turned out he'd done something unimaginably horrifying. It was one thing to offer platitudes to Rafe's father. It was another thing entirely to apply them to herself. In an effort to distract herself, she offered to help with dinner, but Rafe brushed off her offer.

"It's all good. I'm nearly ready. Why don't you all take a seat at the table? Charli very kindly set it for us."

Mallory moved to the small table and chairs. A white linen tablecloth covered the table. Sparkling silverware, red napkins and a vase of fresh flowers added a splash of color. There was a handwritten place card at each seat, written in swirly writing and decorated with a hand-drawn picture of a flower.

"Is this all your handiwork?" she asked, smiling at Charli.

The young girl nodded happily. "Yes. I was so excited when Dad said you were coming to dinner. And granddad, too." She lowered her voice to a conspiratorial whisper. "I've never even heard Dad speak about him and now he's sitting in our living room!"

Her eyes sparkled with excitement and Mallory's heart clenched. She glanced at Rafe who was busy in the kitchen and then looked back at his daughter. It was obvious Charli knew nothing of the pain and heartache her grandfather had caused and that was the way it should be. Her heart swelled with love and admiration for the man she was falling so deeply for. A good man, a kind man, a man who could be trusted with her heart.

"Well, you've done a great job, Charli. This looks lovely."

"Do you like the little name cards I made?"

"Yes. And I love the flowers. Did you draw them?"

"Of course."

"They're very good. You're a talented artist."

Charli blushed but Mallory could tell she was pleased. "Thanks for having me over for dinner, Charli," she added softly.

Charli's expression sobered. "I like you. And my dad likes you, too."

"How can you tell?" Mallory asked, intrigued.

She paused and then said quietly, "My dad isn't big on laughter. It's not that he's grumpy, but he just doesn't laugh a lot. Ever since you came into his life, he laughs all the time. Even watching television. It's like you've turned a switch inside him and he's learned how to relax. He's so different from the man he used to be, even from a few weeks ago."

She looked at Mallory, an earnest expression on her face. "I want to thank you for making him happy, Mallory." And then her expression turned fierce. "Just don't you go breaking his heart, okay?"

Mallory's heart turned over at the protectiveness in Charli's voice. She was a little warrior, looking out for her dad. Reaching out, Mallory put her arm around Charli's shoulders and drew her closer to her side.

"I promise I won't hurt your father, Charli. He means a great deal to me. I've fallen in love with him. He's a very special man and you're a very special girl. I would be honored if you'd let me be a part of your life."

Charli nodded, her bottom lip trembling. Tears glistened in her eyes. Mallory hugged her close. She pressed a kiss against Charli's dark hair.

"Of course, I also want a baby brother or sister," Charli added with a grin. "That's part of the deal."

Mallory laughed. "You never know, Charli. We might be able to accommodate you there. Who knows?"

"So, come and sit beside me, granddaughter and tell me all about yourself."

Michael's words drew them apart. Mallory let her arm drop and Charli moved away. She smiled at her grandfather and then showed him where to sit. She pulled out the chair beside him and the two of them started peppering each other with questions. They hardly drew breath for the rest of the night.

Mallory and Rafe sat close together, enjoying each other's company. They shared quiet conversation and occasionally answered a query from the other end of the table.

Mallory couldn't believe how comfortable she felt at Rafe's table, in the company of his family. She reached for his hand and squeezed it, hoping to convey the wealth of emotion that flooded her heart.

She was filled with joy when he returned the pressure and looked at her so tenderly, with eyes that spoke volumes of his love.

———————

Rafe spooned generous portions of ice cream into four bowls beside the tiramisu he'd purchased earlier that day. He wished he could claim he made the dessert, but he'd simply run out of time. Inviting his father to dinner had been a last-minute decision and one he wasn't entirely sure he wouldn't regret. But looking at his father and Charli with their heads together, getting to know each other, sharing stories of their past, he was glad he had.

For so long, whenever he'd thought of his father, his heart had been filled with bitterness. Too much had gone on that he didn't think he'd ever be able to forgive. The discovery that his parents had made their peace with each other had come as a shock. His mother had suffered at the hands of his father even more than he had. And yet, she'd found it within herself to forgive him. He wasn't sure he'd ever get to that stage. Until now, he wouldn't have even contemplated it.

But ever since he'd met Mallory, things had

changed. *He'd* changed. He couldn't deny it. He woke up each day looking forward to it, looking forward to seeing Mallory. She'd brought something into his life that had been missing and now he knew what it felt like to have the fog lifted, he didn't want to return to the way he'd been.

Even Charli noticed the difference in him. He laughed more. He watched TV. He'd learned how to relax. Life wasn't just something he had to tolerate. It was more than going to work and coming home again. It was now something he embraced. And he had Mallory to thank for it.

He picked up two bowls and carried them to the table, setting them in front of Charli and Mallory.

"Oh, tiramisu! My favorite!" Mallory squealed. Her face lit up with delight. Her eyes glowed with love. "You remembered."

"Of course. And I've also ice cream *and* whipped cream," he added, giving her a wink.

She laughed. "You can't have dessert without ice cream *and* whipped cream."

A moment later, he brought the other two bowls and after handing one to his father, he sat down once again beside the woman he loved.

"So, does it meet your expectations?" he asked with a teasing grin.

She lifted her spoon and took a bite, a look of pleasure filling her face. "Oh, yes. It's exceeded them, in fact."

He laughed. "Really? Wow, that's a lofty compliment, coming from Mallory Patterson, Sydney's very own dessert Queen."

"You betcha." She leaned over and kissed him on the mouth. Her lips were cold and tasted like ice cream. *Delicious.*

"I love you," he said, looking deep into her eyes.

Her emerald-green orbs darkened. The smile she gave him was so full of tenderness, it almost stole his breath. "I love you, too."

Much later, as they collapsed against the sheets, exhausted from a bout of long, slow lovemaking, he took her hand and held it tightly. It scared him a little how quickly and how deeply he'd fallen in love with her, but at the same time, he couldn't imagine things any other way. She'd come into his life and had filled every lonely corner of it. His heart was full to bursting and he couldn't wait to share every moment, every day with her for the rest of his life.

Beside him, Mallory's breathing slowed. He could tell she was on the verge of sleep when she murmured, "You were right. It was definitely worth the effort."

He fell asleep with a smile on his face.

Chapter 20

Rafe got ready for work the next morning with a smile on his face. Dinner the night before had gone so much better than he'd expected. Charli had embraced Mallory. Even his father had fit in.

At the breakfast table, Charli told him she was feeling so much better and she'd made plans to catch up with her granddad over the weekend, provided Rafe was free to accompany them. He was still angry at the pain and devastation caused by Michael Connelly, but Rafe's love for Mallory had helped him to reduce the anger to a slow burn. He wanted to think that one day he'd be able to bring himself to forgive the man for all he'd done. Right now, it was too soon.

"What are you up to today?" he asked Mallory as she drank coffee and read the morning paper. The scene of domesticity warmed his heart.

"I'll go home first and change and then go into work. I haven't seen Dad for a few days. I want to talk to him again. If I don't catch him at home, I might be able to see him at work."

Rafe nodded. "We might get those DNA results back today." He watched her closely for her reaction. To his relief, her lips merely tightened and she nodded.

"I guess it will be good to know for sure. Then we can put this all behind us and get on with our lives."

Rafe nodded again. Inwardly, he wasn't so sure this would be the end of the matter for Mallory—or her father. Still, there was always a chance this Jane Doe wasn't Sofia Lopez Patterson. He clung to the thought.

Pushing away from the table, he rinsed out his coffee cup and left it to dry on the sink. "Do you need a ride to school, Charli?"

"No, thanks Dad. I already asked Mallory."

Rafe's heart turned over. She said it so casually, as if there was nothing unusual about having Mallory take her to school. Just like that, it seemed Mallory had become part of their lives. He couldn't be happier.

He came back to where the two women in his life sat at the table. He kissed Charli on the forehead and then took time to kiss Mallory properly on the mouth.

"You two have a good day, now," he said.

"You, too, Dad."

"I'll call you," Mallory said. "We might be able to do lunch."

He smiled. "Sounds like a great plan."

Rafe took the stairs to the squad room two at a time, whistling. He couldn't remember the last time he'd been in such a good mood. The moment he strode into the squad room, he knew that something was wrong. James sat at his desk, a grave expression on his face. An envelope and a sheet of paper lay on his keyboard.

The smile faded from Rafe's face. His heart hammered with sudden nerves and he was filled with a sense of foreboding.

"What is it?" he asked by way of greeting.

"Mallory Patterson's DNA comparison to Jane Doe."

The concrete in Rafe's belly shifted. "What about it?"

"We got the results back."

Rafe's gaze shifted to the piece of paper on James' desk. He hardly dared to ask the question, but he had no choice. Besides, nothing he said or didn't say was going to change the results.

"What do they say?" he eventually asked in a choked voice.

James drew in a deep breath. He looked at Rafe. The bleakness in his partner's eyes told Rafe all he needed to know.

"The two parties are related by blood," James confirmed. He compressed his lips, his expression grim. "It's official. Jane Doe is Mallory's mother."

Though Rafe had already guessed as much from his partner's demeanor, to hear him state the bald truth was like a dagger to Rafe's heart. He immediately thought of Mallory. She'd be devastated. The odds that her father was responsible for the murder were high. Apart from Sofia's killer, by his own admission he was the last person to see his wife alive.

The coroner had estimated the time of death to be around twenty years earlier. They knew from both Mallory and her father that neither of them had seen Sofia since the day after Mallory's tenth birthday. Mallory was now thirty. The math added up.

So did the DNA results and DNA didn't lie. The chances that Sofia Lopez had been murdered shortly after the last time Mallory had seen her was high. Still, there was always the slight possibility Sofia hadn't caught the plane as Mallory's father had said and had disappeared instead, only to run into trouble a short time later, trouble that eventually led to her death.

It was possible, but Rafe wasn't buying it. He'd been a detective long enough to learn to trust his gut. What were the odds a woman like Sofia Lopez Patterson, a medical doctor, a wife, a mother got in with the wrong crowd within weeks of leaving her husband and child and was murdered as a result? Mallory hadn't given any indication her mother was in trouble, apart from the trouble at home. Any other scenario didn't make sense. It gave Rafe no pleasure to know everything pointed to John Patterson being his wife's killer and he was going to have to break that news to John Patterson's daughter.

With a heavy heart, he turned and made it to his desk. Pulling out his phone, he called her. She answered on the third ring with a smile in her voice, but within moments, he could tell she knew something was wrong.

"What is it, Rafe? What's wrong?"

"Are you at work?"

"Yes. I just arrived. What's the matter?"

"We got the DNA results back. I need to see you."

Her voice held a note of panic. "Tell me now."

"I'd rather do it in person."

"Rafe." He heard the warning in her tone. "Tell me."

He swallowed to ease the tension in his throat.

"I can tell from your silence the news isn't what we wanted," she rasped.

He clenched his jaw tight against the pain in her voice. "No. It isn't."

"So the murdered woman you found hidden in the cave is my mother?"

The words sounded harsh in his ear. He winced, but there was nothing for it. Nothing he said would change the truth or ease Mallory's pain.

"Yes." He bit the word out and braced himself for her reaction. She was silent for a few long seconds and then he heard her howl.

"*Nooooo!*" The cry of pain sounded like it had been ripped from the depths of her soul. Sitting there, helpless to comfort her, hearing her pain was the most difficult thing Rafe had ever had to do.

"H-how? How could it be?" she cried. "He told me he'd taken her to the airport. He told me she wanted to return home. Everything I thought was true all these years was a lie! How could he?"

Rafe heard the distress in her voice, the sobs that thickened her words and wished there was something he could do to ease the pain. He clenched his fists, he clenched his jaw, he agonized over the feeling of helplessness that overwhelmed him. He wanted to hold her, whisper words of comfort. He wanted to make the pain go away. He wanted her father to be a better man, a man who didn't murder his wife and get away with it. Almost.

"There's a chance your father might not have killed her, Mallory." Even though in his gut he didn't believe it, Rafe forced himself to speak the words.

Her sobbing stopped. "Really?"

"Yes. It's a long shot, but it's possible."

"How?"

Rafe explained how her mother might have led her father to believe she was flying to Argentina, when all along she'd planned simply to disappear. She might have met with foul play shortly afterwards at the hands of a stranger. It was possible.

"But what about her bank accounts? They haven't been touched. Not even in the early days. What you're suggesting is that someone else stumbled across her and murdered her within days, maybe a few weeks of meeting her. That doesn't sound too convincing."

Rafe agreed, but what was he to say? The woman he loved was hurting. He'd say anything to make it go away, even for a little while.

"I guess it *could* have happened that way," she added slowly, almost as if to convince herself.

"Where's your father now?" he asked.

"I'm not sure. He wasn't at home when I dropped in there this morning to get changed. I assume he's at work. I'll call him," she said, sounding stronger.

"Let me know if you reach him. We need to have a chat."

———

Mallory tossed her phone down on her desk, alarmed to see her hand was trembling. Though she'd half-expected Rafe's news, it still shook her to the core. To have confirmation that instead of flying off to Argentina to begin a better life, her mother had ended up dead and buried in a cave was shocking. She could hardly process what had happened. All these years she'd been angry at her mother for leaving her, preferring a life in her home country to the one she had with her husband and child. Many a night Mallory had cried bitter tears. There had been times when she hated Sofia Lopez Patterson.

Only to discover that all this time she'd been dead, murdered not long after she'd left. Her mother had lain there, hidden in a secret grave, alone with no one to mourn her, or to hunt down her killer. A killer who could very well be Mallory's dad.

The thought was almost too much to bear. She thought of the alternative Rafe had suggested—that someone else was responsible for her mother's murder—but as much as she wanted to cling to that possibility, in her heart she didn't believe it. No, it was time she confronted her father with the truth and demand answers. She wouldn't be satisfied until he told her everything.

———————

John Patterson glanced at his watch and cursed. He didn't have much time. It was lucky he'd been planning for this day already or he'd be in a mess. Late last night, a cop friend of his had given him the tip-off that the police had identified the woman who'd been found in the cave. Sofia Lopez Patterson.

Surprise, surprise…

He'd gone into work early that morning and cleared out his office of anything personal, leaving the unfinished files and statements scattered across his desk. He was careful to make things look to the casual observer that he'd merely gone out for an appointment or even an early lunch. No sense in letting anyone know, too soon, that he was gone and wasn't coming back.

Throwing the last of his things into the suitcase, he zipped it up and hauled it to the front door. The cab he'd ordered should arrive any minute. He grabbed the duffel bag from under the desk of his study and took one last look around.

The hallway was lined with pictures of Mallory. His heart clenched at the thought of leaving her. He hadn't even been able to say good-bye. She hadn't been at the breakfast table that morning. He assumed she'd spent the night with the detective. He frowned. He still wished she'd chosen a lawyer...

Still, what did it matter now? Where he was going, he'd be lucky to see her once a year and that was only if she found it in her heart to forgive him. He'd lie low for the next few months and wait for her anger to blow over. Then he'd send her an email from an undisclosed location and see if she responded. He'd explain everything, tell her he had no choice. He'd done what he had because he loved her too much to let her go.

Surely she'd understand? He hoped so.

The sound of a car horn outside his door snapped him out of his reverie. He patted his shirt pocket to make sure he had his passport and plane ticket and was reassured that they were there. With his suitcase in one hand and the duffel bag in the other, he glanced one last time around the house he'd shared with his daughter, and left.

He didn't look back.

Rafe hung up the phone, feeling grim.

"What did you find out?" James asked.

"John Patterson hasn't been to his office today. His secretary was expecting him by now. He has appointments scheduled all day. She's tried to call him, but his cell goes straight to voicemail. She's wondering if he's okay."

"What does Mallory say?"

"She spent the night at my house," Rafe said and was relieved when James didn't offer a comment.

"She stopped by her home this morning—the one she shares with her dad. He wasn't there. She assumed he'd already left for work."

"So he's not at home and he's not at work. It's ten o'clock in the morning. Where else could he be?"

"You tell me," Rafe replied.

Though he didn't want to voice his concerns, both of them knew what the other was thinking. It came as no surprise when James said, "We need to get an APB out on John Patterson."

Rafe nodded grimly. "I'll call the airports and put out an alert. Let's hope we're not too late."

The phone on Rafe's desk pealed. He leaned over and answered it. "Detective Connelly."

"Rafe. It's Clayton. I finally have those Interpol results back."

Rafe's heart skipped a beat. He'd forgotten to phone Clayton and let him know they'd found the woman they were searching for and she wasn't overseas.

"What did you find out?" he asked.

"There's nothing to say your lady isn't traveling on a fake passport, but Interpol assures me she isn't traveling on the one she was issued. There hasn't been any movement on that passport anywhere in the world for the past thirty-five years."

It was information Rafe already had. Knowing

where Sofia Lopez had been all these years was no longer a surprise. After thanking Clayton for his efforts and once again promising the two of them would catch up soon, Rafe ended the call.

And that was that.

———

Mallory listened to her father's cell phone ring out and waited for it to go to voicemail. It was the third message she'd left for him after checking with his secretary and being told that he was out. Her nerves were frayed. Her stomach churned with dread.

Where could he be? Why wasn't he answering his phone?

She needed to find him and confront him with what she'd learned. Now that there was no doubt it was her mother who'd been buried in the cave, she needed to hear him say he had nothing to do with her mother's murder. Even then, she wasn't sure if she'd believe him.

Unable to sit there without doing something, she pushed away from her desk. "I'm going upstairs," she told Rhonda and headed for the elevator.

She'd sit in her father's office all day if she had to. According to his secretary, he had clients scheduled to see him throughout the day. He had to turn up sooner or later. If there was one thing her father didn't do it was shirk his work responsibilities.

The elevator opened on her father's floor and she strode toward his office. She wasn't surprised to see it was empty, just like his secretary had said. Still, he couldn't hide out forever. He had clients waiting. He'd be back. She was sure of it.

She took a seat on the expensive leather couch she used to love to lounge on when she was a girl. Sometimes her father would take her to his office on the weekends when he had to work. She'd sit on the couch and read a book and dream of the day when she'd have an office of her own, just like his.

Now the couch didn't feel quite as comfortable and she certainly wasn't in a dreaming mood. A few minutes after she'd taken a seat, she was on her feet again. She paced around the office. She stared out the window at the day. The beauty of the morning went mostly unnoticed. Her mind was on other things.

She sat down again and jiggled her foot impatiently. She tried his cell phone again. Still no answer. She stood and moved behind his desk, hoping for something that might distract her and make the wait a little more tolerable.

At first glance, his desk looked like it usually did—cluttered with files and papers and letters. It routinely looked a mess. And though it still looked a mess, she noticed things were missing. Gone was the framed photograph of her on her graduation from law school that had taken pride of place on his desk. The expensive crystal paperweight she'd given him for a recent birthday gift was also missing, along with another framed picture of the two of them taken a decade earlier. In fact, the closer she looked, the more she realized there was nothing personal left in his office at all.

A heavy sense of foreboding filled her veins and weighed down her feet. She couldn't move if she wanted to. It was like she was frozen to the spot. She looked around her in disbelief, tears blinding her.

He was gone.

She knew it. Somehow he'd found out about the DNA and he'd made a run for it. Everything inside her rebelled against the idea because surely he'd only run if he were guilty, but the proof was there before her, in his office that was cluttered with everything but the things that really mattered.

In a panic, she ran out of the room and caught an elevator to the ground floor. She dashed out of the building and hailed a cab. She gave the driver her home address and spent an anxious thirty minutes praying she was wrong. The moment she unlocked the front door, her worst fears were realized.

She heard his absence in the silence. In a daze, she went from room to room, noticing things that were missing. Mostly photographs and sentimental items. Gaps in the bottom of his wardrobe where shoes used to be and empty coat hangers were more revealing signs.

A couple of small, expensive paintings in his bedroom were gone. The telltale places where they'd hung on the wall now glared back at her accusingly. She turned away and jammed her fist in her mouth in an effort to hold back her devastation.

With a sob she could hold back no longer, she sunk to the bedroom floor. The smell of his cologne was still heavy in the air. He must have left only a short time ago and he hadn't said a word. She'd been calling him all morning and he hadn't said a word.

Hadn't answered her call. Hadn't said goodbye. He'd simply disappeared. Just like her mother. Only this time, she was under no illusion what had happened. He'd murdered her mother all those years ago and pretended she'd abandoned them. Now when the police were putting it altogether, he'd made a run for it. He'd left without a backward glance and she could tell he had no intention of coming back.

The knowledge broke her. Bending over her knees, she cried and cried until she had nothing left. And then she cried some more.

The phone at Rafe's elbow rang and he snatched it up. "Detective Connelly."

"Detective, this is Lincoln Maxwell. I'm part of the security team at the airport. We've just received an alert that John Allan Patterson has checked in. He's on a Virgin Airlines flight to the Bahamas. Would you like us to detain him?"

Rafe's gut clenched with anticipation. "Yes."

He thanked the caller and hung up the phone. Pushing away from his desk, he grabbed his jacket and keys.

"Let's go," he said to James.

"Where to?"

"The airport. We've found him."

John Patterson was being held in an interview room inside the airport security offices. He bluffed and blustered about his legal rights and the fact that he was innocent, to anyone who cared to listen.

Rafe took no joy in arresting Mallory's father and he knew the days and weeks to come would prove just as arduous. He sighed at the thought of what lay ahead of him, least of all bringing Mallory the news of her father's arrest for the murder of her mother.

It was a long time later, after John Patterson had been interviewed for more than four hours and despite the evidence against him, continued to protest his innocence that Rafe formally charged Mallory's father and watched as the corrections officer led him off to a jail cell. They'd taken a DNA sample and soon they'd know if it matched the sample left on the rug that had been wrapped around Mallory's mother. Tired beyond all belief, Rafe completed the final paperwork and headed for home. His cell phone rang and he glanced at the screen.

Mallory.

His heart turned over with pain. If he could take the next few moments away from her, he would. But it was not to be.

"Hi, baby."

"Where are you? My father's gone."

The heartbreak in her voice almost killed him. Anger at her father and what he'd done ignited in his gut, spurring him on.

"I've just left work," he said. "It's been a big day. I'm beat."

"Will you...come over? I need you."

"Sure," he said without hesitation and changed lanes so he could do a U-turn. A horn blasted behind him, the driver upset at his sudden maneuver, but he was past caring.

He refrained from saying anything about what had happened. There would be time enough when he and Mallory were face to face to tell her about her father. In the meantime, all he wanted to do was hold her and promise her that one day, everything would be all right. He hoped he managed to convince her.

CHAPTER 21

Mallory felt sick to her stomach. For hours, she'd called her father's phone in the hope he would answer. She'd lost count of the number of messages she'd left, each one filled with disbelief, hurt and anger. And still, she hadn't heard from him.

A knock at the front door gave her hope and sent her heart into overdrive and then she realized it was Rafe. Of course it wasn't her father. He wouldn't knock anyway.

Rafe had said he'd come over. She needed him, and so he was there. The knock came again and she stumbled down the hallway to answer it.

She opened the door and there he was: the man she loved with all her heart. He stepped forward and she fell into his arms, sobbing. After all the tears she'd already cried, she'd thought she was just about done, but apparently not.

Rafe gently led her back down the hall and into the combined kitchen and living room. He made it over to the couch and pulled her down beside him. Once again, he took her in his arms and comforted her. Tenderly, he kissed her hair, her cheeks, her eyelids.

"I can't believe it!" she sobbed. "All these years! He knew how much I missed her! He knew what it did to me to believe she'd left. And yet he kept the truth from me. Over and over again. No wonder he pretended not to remember when I reminded him how he used to take me to the caves in the Ku-ring-gai Chase National Park. He didn't *want* to remember, and he didn't want me to associate us with the park, either."

She sat up and stared at him, tears pouring down her cheeks. "Do you have any idea what it feels like to be lied to all your life? Not only that, but to know he murdered the mother of his child! I was ten! How *could* he?"

Rafe gazed at her and she could see the helplessness in his eyes. "I wish I could help you, take away your pain," he whispered.

She framed his beloved face between her hands and kissed him on the lips. "I know you do and knowing that is enough. I just don't know how I'm ever going to forgive my father. Right now, I can't even think like that. I don't even know where he is!"

Gently, Rafe told her about the arrest at the airport and the subsequent police interrogation which resulted in her father being charged with murder.

He stroked the hair back from her forehead. "You might think now that you can never forgive him, and I know better than most how that feels.

I've spent a lifetime holding a grudge against my father, and where has it gotten me? So many wasted years of hate and anger. It almost ate me alive. If it weren't for Charli and my mother, I probably wouldn't have survived."

He paused and drew in a deep breath before continuing. "It's only since last night, with my father sitting across the table and the two most important women in the world by my side, that I realized the hating was getting me nowhere. I have a choice: I can keep on hating my father and let the anger eventually destroy me and everyone I love, or I can forgive him and let the pain go. You see, because if I don't, then *I'm* the one who's broken."

Tears formed in his eyes and she was crying, too. He cleared his throat and began again.

"Your father did a terrible thing, Mallory. An unforgivable thing. There's no denying that. And he'll be punished for it."

"No punishment is going to give me back all that he stole from me," she cried, her voice hoarse.

Rafe stroked her cheek with the pad of his thumb. The tenderness in his eyes took her breath away.

"I understand, baby. I truly do. My father was a selfish man who stole so much from me, too. He stole my right to a happy and safe childhood, the security of a family who loved each other, a beloved sister who threw away her life and who died much too young... But if I let the hate consume me, *he's* the one who wins."

He cupped her cheek in his hand, his eyes imploring her. "Your mother's gone forever. Nothing is ever going to bring her back. Accept that. Let it go. Look to the future, a future we can share together. A future filled with love."

She stared at him, loving him so much it hurt. Pressing her lips to his, she kissed him. Thank you," she said.

"You're stronger than you could ever know, Mallory Patterson. You can do this. Let the hate go and never think of it again. Mourn your mother. Celebrate her life. Remember her with love. Don't ever let your father steal anything more from you."

This time, she threw herself against him and kissed him with all the love she had in her heart. The kiss went on forever and she was glad. What lay before them wasn't going to be easy, but she was up for the challenge. With the man she loved beside her, anything was possible. She was exactly where she wanted to be.

EPILOGUE

The late summer day was resplendent, as only late summer days in Sydney can be. The sky was so clear and blue it was breathtaking. Almost as breathtaking as the bride. With Sally-Ann as Mallory's matron of honor and Charli as her bridesmaid, the three of them walked down the aisle toward the man who looked at her with such love and tenderness it stole her breath away.

Her body trembled as she reached him, filled with nerves, anticipation and hope. As if sensing her turmoil, he smiled and drew her in close beside him. Taking her hand in his, he squeezed it and the simple loving motion immediately set her at ease.

This was the man she loved with all her heart, the man she was committed to for life. The fairytale wasn't over. In fact, it was just beginning. She glanced at Sally-Ann who looked beautiful in dark red satin. The color contrasted nicely with the brilliant white of Mallory's dress. Charli looked far too grown up and sophisticated in the cream and lace concoction that she'd chosen. She smiled at Mallory and winked at her father. He teared up.

Sally-Ann smiled encouragingly and gave her a thumbs up. Mallory giggled nervously, still overwhelmed by the knowledge she was about to become Rafe's wife. She looked over her shoulder at the crowd of people who'd turned out to support them and wish them well.

So many of her friends and colleagues from Sydney Legal—Ben and Abby Fitzgerald, Blake and Natalie Harton, Colby and Monica Shearer, Daisy and Christian Grayson and Trey and his wife, Kyeisha Walker, who was now a judge of the District Court. Jessie Wolfe, along with her husband Mack Callaway were seated a few rows back, along with Zane and Meghan Sullivan.

All of her friends and none of her family, but that's the way it was. Her father had been refused day release to attend his daughter's wedding. She didn't think she wanted him there, anyway. The betrayal was still so hurtful, the wounds still too fresh. He'd sent her a letter from his jail cell, explaining his actions, begging her to understand. Maybe someday in the future she'd find it in her heart to forgive him, but not right now.

"You look beautiful," Rafe whispered, squeezing her hand again.

"So do you," Mallory told him.

He blushed in his disarming way and her heart swelled with love. She looked at Charli again and smiled at the wide grin that flooded the young girl's face. Michael Connelly sat tall and proud at the front of the row of pews. Every time he glanced at his son, tears ran down his cheeks.

It was perfect in almost every way. Mallory couldn't ask for more. She tilted her head heavenwards and said a silent prayer.

"I know you're up there, Mom, and I know you loved me so much. Be happy for me. I've found a man who loves me even more. I wish you could be down here with me. I wish you could meet him. But I know you're watching over us. Every step of the way."

"Are you ready?" Rafe asked, his eye shining with love.

She smiled at him. "I've been ready for you all my life."

NOTE TO READERS

I do hope you have enjoyed reading Rafe and Mallory's story. If you've enjoyed this book, I would appreciate it if you could leave a review for Malicious Love at your favorite digital retailer. Every review increases visibility and helps other readers to find books they enjoy.

Looking for another series to get your teeth into? You might like to check out Book One of the Munro Family Series. The Profiler is Clayton and Ellie's story. Here is an excerpt:

Excerpt from

THE

PROFILER

Book **One** of the
Munro Family Series

CHRIS TAYLOR

A psychopathic killer is stalking the women of Sydney...

Federal Agent Clayton Munro, a criminal profiler with the Australian Federal Police (AFP), has been called upon to assist in hunting down a vicious murderer who is intent upon carving up his victims while they're still alive. Guilt-stricken over his wife's suicide, Clayton's forced to leave behind his personal issues in order to focus on the case.

Detective Ellie Cooper is also no stranger to heartache. Pregnant and abandoned at the altar by a fiancé intent on pursuing a career with the AFP, her opinion of the elite body of officers is anything but favorable. Angered when her boss orders her to partner with the Fed, she's determined not to cut him any slack.

But women are dying on the streets of western Sydney and the pressure is mounting to find the person responsible.

Will Clayton and Ellie be able to set aside their animosity and work together to catch a killer before it's too late? And what about the special fascination the killer seems to have with Ellie...

Prologue

Bradley Cole smoothed the doll's silky, blond hair with a hand that wasn't quite steady. He loved the fair ones. They were his favorites. They were the ones he tucked in beside him in bed at night. The ones that kept him safe.

Sometimes.

He leaned over and pressed a kiss to the hard, plastic forehead.

The door to his bedroom flew open and slammed against the wall. He cringed at the look on his mother's face. With surreptitious movements, he pushed the doll further under the bedclothes and prayed she wouldn't notice.

"What have you got there, you disgusting little boy? Don't tell me you have one of those filthy dolls in your bed. How many times have I told you boys don't play with dolls? Bradley Cole, you are a naughty, naughty boy."

She stumbled closer, close enough so that he could see the redness that rimmed her eyes.

He almost gagged on the stench of alcohol and stale body odor.

Her cheap cotton nightdress flapped around her large frame. She collapsed onto the side of his bed and the steel frame groaned in protest. She reached out and tore off the bedclothes, exposing him to her sharp-eyed gaze.

"What have we here?" she crooned. Her gaze landed on the collection of dolls beside him. Her eyes went wild with excitement.

Terror liquefied his limbs. His stomach clenched.

"Well, well, well. You *have* been a naughty boy." Her fist caught him plumb on the cheek. He gasped from the pain. Tears burned his eyes.

"And now we have tears from the sissy boy. A ten-year-old who plays with dolls and cries like a girl. What am I going to do with you?"

She tut-tutted and then hauled herself to her feet. When she turned back to face him, her expression was as icy as her voice.

"Down to the basement. Now."

Bradley froze. He thought fleetingly of making a dash for the phone that sat amidst the clutter on the hall table and then remembered the other times—lots of other times—when he'd dialed the police only to be told not to waste their time and if he made a nuisance of himself again, there'd be consequences.

"I *said*, get up."

She loomed over him. Her fetid breath turned his stomach. Her fist poised for another strike and his fear ratcheted up another notch. Moments later, his bladder gave way.

"You stinking little boy. You're going to pay for that. Do you think I have nothing better to do than to wash your stinking sheets?"

With vicious fingers, she dug into his shoulder and hauled him from the bed. He blinked away the pain, knowing it was nothing to what he'd be forced to endure in the basement.

"Now, get down there like I told you and make it quick. Real quick."

CHAPTER 1

Detective Ellie Cooper climbed out of the unmarked police car and waited for her partner, Luke Baxter, to come around from the passenger side. Drawing her jacket tighter around her slight frame, she tucked an errant strand of chestnut hair behind her ear. The afternoon was cold and dreary, just as it had been the day she'd buried her son. Three years today. It felt like yesterday.

Memories she'd tried hard to hold at bay all day threatened to bring her undone. Familiar pain and anger, combined with deep loss and a yearning for answers surged through her. She compressed her lips against the sudden rush of emotions and made an effort to push the thoughts aside. She was at work. Now wasn't the time to fall apart.

As usual, she took refuge in her job. She flashed her badge at the huddle of fresh-faced, uniformed policemen who stood inside the blue and white, checked crime scene tape that cordoned off part of the scrubby bank of western Sydney's Nepean River. Not far away, photographers and TV crews haggled over positions.

"We're Detectives Cooper and Baxter. Penrith Local Area Command," Ellie said to one of the young officers. "We're here about a head."

The officer nodded and offered his hand. "I'm Constable Jacobs, Richmond Police Station. I took the call from Griffin."

"Griffin?" Ellie asked.

"Yeah, the bloke who found it." His gaze flicked toward the crowd and his voice turned dry. "And presumably the one who called the media."

"Where is he?"

"I put him in the back of the squad car. I thought he'd gotten enough camera exposure for today."

Luke and Ellie looked toward the police cruiser. The profile of a man seated in the back seat could be seen in the late afternoon light.

"What's his story?" Luke asked.

Jacobs consulted his notebook. "He came down after lunch for a spot of fishing. Apparently, the fish were biting, so he didn't notice the bag right away."

"The bag?" Ellie asked.

"Yeah, the head's wrapped in a trash bag." He glanced at his notebook again. "Anyway, he was here about an hour when he had to take a leak. Walked over there a bit."

Jacobs pointed in the direction of a stand of bottlebrush trees nearby. Their scrubby branches provided effective cover from the road twenty metres away. "That's where he says he found it."

Ellie was relieved the area had been included within the taped barrier and nodded toward the young constable. "Good work on securing the scene, Jacobs."

He flushed. "Thanks, Detective."

She looked at Luke. "Let's go and talk to our fisherman."

"I'll get the camera from the car," he responded. "We need to get a few pictures before we lose the light." He glanced back at Jacobs. "Anyone call the morgue?"

"Yes. I got onto them straight after I called it into the station."

"Good thinking, Constable. Shows initiative," Ellie said. "Why don't you join me while I talk to our witness?"

Eagerness lit up the young constable's eyes. "That would be awesome. I can't wait to apply for the detective's course. I know I've only just come out of the Academy, but it's all I've ever wanted to do and—"

"Jacobs," she interrupted gently, "let's just get on with it, okay?" Ellie hid her amusement. She wasn't *that* old that she couldn't remember feeling exactly the same way.

Even in the fading light, Elle saw the mortification that flooded his expression and felt a twinge of guilt, but they were wasting time, and in homicides, every second counted.

Turning abruptly, she made her way through the tall grass toward the squad car that was parked a short distance away. Jacobs stumbled behind her.

Ducking under the police tape, she came up to the vehicle and rapped her knuckles on the glass.

The man she presumed was Bill Griffin unwound the window and stared up at her with wary blue eyes. His wild gray hair was windblown and in desperate need of a shampoo. Grizzled cheeks covered in a rough beard emphasized the belligerent thrust of his chin. He smelled like fish, river mud and body odor. A damp hessian bag lay on the ground near the car, along with a fishing rod and tackle box.

"Mr Griffin? I'm Detective Cooper." Ellie indicated Jacobs behind her. "I think you've already met Constable Jacobs?"

"Yeah. I already told 'im everythin'."

"Okay, but we've got a head lying in a trash bag over there and so far, you're the only witness."

He shot a furtive glance at the hessian bag and suddenly his reticence made sense.

"I'm not from fisheries," she added. "I couldn't care less whether you have a license, how many fish you have in there or how big they are. That's between you and them. All I'm interested in is how a woman's head came to be lying in a bag under a tree near the river." She gave him a hard look. "You got that?"

Griffin gave a reluctant nod and his gaze slid away. "It's just like I told 'im." He gestured with a dirty finger to where Jacobs stood beside Ellie. "I was doin' a spot of fishin', like I always do. Right 'ere, every Friday. Fish were bitin' good. I'd gone through 'alf me bait already and I'd only been 'ere an hour."

He paused to scratch a scab on his arm. "I 'ad to take a piss, just like I told the constable. I pulled in me line and left it on the bank with me tackle box. Then I wandered over to them trees over there. That's when I found it." He gave a shudder. "Frightened the shit outta me."

"What made you open the bag?" Ellie asked, pulling out her notebook.

Griffin shrugged and looked away. "I dunno. Just thought I'd take a look."

Ellie knew the area was renowned for break and enters and petty thefts. More than likely, he'd hoped to find something he could sell.

She gave him another hard look. "What did you do then?"

"I picked it up. It was bloody 'eavy. Carried it a ways over there, toward me gear."

"Then you opened it."

The man bristled. "Got curious, that's all. Nothin' wrong with that." He shuddered again. "Wish to Christ I 'adn't. That thing's gonna give me nightmares for months."

"Can you show me exactly where you found it?"

Not giving him time to refuse, she opened the door and waited for him to step out. She followed closely behind as he walked over to the stand of bottlebrush trees. The night was closing in. Light would soon become an issue.

Luke jogged up beside them. Ellie turned to face him.

"We need to get forensics out here with some

lights," she said. "It's my guess it's just been dumped here, but you never know what you might find. On more than one occasion, a cigarette butt at the scene's been enough to nail a killer."

Luke issued a brief smile. "Yeah, on *CSI*, at least." His expression turned serious. "I'll give the boss a call. See what he's organized."

Luke pulled out his cell phone. Ellie caught up to the fisherman.

"Just 'ere, it was. Right near the trunk of that one." He pointed to an area at the base of one of the bottlebrushes. There was a faint indentation where the grass had been flattened.

Ellie waited for Luke to finish on the phone before calling out to him.

"Bring your camera over here." She indicated the flattened area. "This is where our fisherman says he found it."

Luke closed the short distance between them and came to a standstill beside the witness. He leveled the man with a hard look.

"When did you call the media?"

Griffin's gaze skittered away and he ducked his head. "It wasn't me that called 'em."

Luke snorted. "Right, they just happened to magically appear." He gave the fisherman a hard look. "You want to hope you don't have anything in that fishing bag of yours that you shouldn't. We might not be from fisheries, but it doesn't mean we don't know where to find them."

The man opened his mouth to protest again and Luke cut him off. "Whether you did or whether you didn't, I don't give a damn. This is our show now. It's a murder investigation and we won't stand for any interference—from you or the media. Got that?"

The man's gaze fell to his feet. He nodded with reluctance.

"Good." Luke handed her the camera and she fired off several shots, taking care to photograph the entire area.

She turned to the fisherman. "We need you to come down to the station so we can take a full statement. Constable Jacobs will bring you in." She turned to the constable who'd come up behind her. "Is that all right with you, Jacobs?"

He nodded emphatically. "Of course, Detective. We'll leave right away."

Ellie nodded her thanks. "We'll be there shortly. Just as soon as forensics arrives and we give them a quick rundown."

Moments later, headlights swept the riverbank. "Looks like them now," she murmured.

Ellie pushed away from the bench and moved closer to the stainless steel gurney where Dr Samantha Wolfe, the head of Forensic Pathology in the Westmead Morgue, examined the head of the unknown woman. The doctor's glossy black hair was tucked up in its usual position under a blue surgical hat and although Ellie knew the woman wasn't much older than Ellie, the years spent working with the dead were etched into the lines of fatigue on her face, making her appear older than she was. Even so, Ellie was pleased Samantha had caught the case. The doctor was the best forensic pathologist in Sydney.

"So, what do you think?" Ellie asked, trying hard not to breathe in too deeply of the smell that was unique to the morgue. It was well after nine, and Ellie was feeling the effects of the long day. And it wasn't over yet. She'd told Luke to go home. No sense in both of them hanging around. At least one of them ought to get some sleep.

Samantha peered at her from behind clear plastic safety glasses.

"There's no trauma to the head, as such." The doctor sent her a wry look. "If you don't count the fact that it's been severed from its body."

Ellie smiled reluctantly. There was something very weird about trading jokes while a woman's head lay on a gurney between them.

With gloved hands, Samantha examined the girl's face. "She's definitely Caucasian. I'd hazard a guess she's of European or Mediterranean descent. From the broadness of her features and the olive tones of her skin, even taking into account its deterioration, she's not an English rose."

"How long do you think she's been dead?"

She shrugged. "Hard to put an exact time of death. This time of year, tissue breakdown is slowed down by the cold. We've had some fairly severe frosts over the past few weeks. A bit like being kept in a freezer. If I had to guess, I'd say two, maybe three weeks. She's still in pretty good shape, but as I said, the cold weather would have something to do with that."

With a clank, the doctor dropped a small metal object into an empty kidney dish lined up beside several others on a trolley next to the gurney.

Ellie leaned in closer. "What's that?"

"An earring. There's one in the other ear, too." A few seconds later, another object clattered into the dish. Ellie hunted around for a plastic evidence bag.

"Over near the door." Samantha indicated the rack of shelves on the far side of the room beside the door through which Ellie had entered.

"I'll take these with me," she said scooping them up with gloved fingers and dropping the jewelry carefully into the evidence bag. "They might help us identify her."

"No sign of the rest of her?"

Ellie shook her head. "Not yet." She sighed wearily. "I guess we'll see what tomorrow brings."

"Come and look at this."

The doctor's tone had sharpened. Ellie's heart accelerated. "What is it?"

Samantha was working her way through the woman's honey-blond, matted hair with a pair of tweezers. Bending closer, she extracted a small particle and dropped it into a clean kidney dish.

"I don't know, but her hair's full of it." She continued to part sections of hair, retrieving more and more slivers.

Ellie moved closer and peered into the dish. It was difficult to say what they were. Pinkish-brown in color, the particles were irregular in shape and size, the biggest about half the size of her smallest fingernail.

"I'll send them to the lab." Samantha indicated with her chin toward the other dishes lined up beside the gurney. "Along with those. Hair and tissue samples, blood samples, mouth swabs. Until someone comes forward with an identification, it's the best I can do."

Ellie suppressed a sigh. Someone out there was missing a daughter, a sister—maybe even a mother. "I appreciate your help, Samantha. Any clues on how it was removed?"

The doctor turned the head until it rested on its side. Ellie tried not to look at the single, milky-brown eye as it stared sightlessly up at her. Pointing with her tweezers, Samantha indicated the area where the woman's neck should have been.

"Have a look here. See the striations in the vertebrae? It looks to me like it's been sawn off."

Ellie swallowed and shook her head. "What sort of a monster does something like that?"

"I'm afraid it gets worse." Samantha poked at the ragged, exposed flesh. "There's still blood in this tissue." She raised her head and stared at Ellie. "Have you ever seen a dead heart pump?"

The Profiler is available now in digital format and paperback from your favorite digital retailer.

About the Author

Chris Taylor grew up on a farm in north-west New South Wales, Australia. She always had a thirst for stories and recalls writing her first book at the ripe old age of eight. Always a lover of romance and happily-ever-afters, a career in criminal law sparked her interest in intrigue and suspense. For Chris to be able to combine romance with suspense in her books is a dream come true.

Chris is married to Linden and is the mother of five children. If not behind her computer, you can find her doing the school run, taxiing children to swimming lessons, football, ballet and cricket. In her spare time, Chris loves to read her favorite authors who include Richard North Patterson, Sandra Brown, Kathleen E Woodiwiss and Jude Devereaux.

You can find out more about Chris and sign up for her newsletter at her website:

http://www.christaylorauthor.com.au

www.ingramcontent.com/pod-product-compliance
Lightning Source LLC
Chambersburg PA
CBHW061054190726
48286CB00006B/1740